THE
WXITE
COUNTRY

ALSO BY BOSTON TERAN

God Is a Bullet
Never Count Out the Dead
The Prince of Deadly Weapons
Trois Femmes
Giv — The Story of a Dog and America
The Creed of Violence
Gardens of Grief
The World Eve Left Us
The Country I Lived In
The Cloud and the Fire
By Your Deeds
A Child Went Forth
How Beautiful They Were
Big Island L.A.

THE

W✗ITE

COUNTRY

BOSTON TERAN

ISBN: 978-1-56703-102-7

Published in the United States by High Top Publications LLC, Los Angeles, CA and simultaneously in Canada by High Top Publications LLC.

Special Thanks to MY COUNTRY, 'TIS OF THEE by Samuel Francis Smith…OLD BLUE-Traditional…LORD'S PRAYER…AROUND THE WORLD IN EIGHTY DAYS by Jules Verne.

Interior Design by Alan Barnett

Printed in the United States of America

To the past...which is always one step ahead.

ACKNOWLEDGMENTS

To Deirdre Stephanie and the late, great Brutarian…to G.G. and L.S.…. Mz. El and Roxomania…the kids…Natasha Kern…Janice Hussein, for her fine work…Charlene Crandall, for her brains and loyalty…the Drakes at Wildbound, all talent and hard work…And finally, to my steadfast friend and ally, and a master at navigating the madness, Donald V. Allen.

PROLOGUE

SUMMER 1911

WORD CAME TO WADSWORTH BURR by Western Union in the dead of night. He turned on the light beside his bed and there in the shadows holding a telegram stood the young Chinese girl who cared for his needs. He took the envelope and with the slightest movement of the eyes excused her. She touched his hand, and he sat up along the edge of the bed and waited until the door had closed. He stared at the envelope and tried to breathe away the worst that he suspected. He tore off the edge of the envelope, blew into it, and slid out the wire. He read:

A warrant has been issued for John Lourdes for the disappearance and murder of five Texas Rangers and two employees of the Big Medicine Corporation. He is being hunted with impunity across Webb County. And there are rumors he is badly wounded.

Burr walked out onto the balcony of his mission style mansion at the corner of Yandell and Corto Way. He lived in the Satterwhite Addition, an enclave of the city's well-to-do that looked down upon the world of El Paso. The perfect home, it turned out, for a disbarred member of the privileged class.

He followed the lights of the downtown trolleys as they made their way through the warm distance toward the Rio Grande, slowly jostling along, their lights flickering as they went. He was trying to escape the dreadful reality he held in his hand.

My boy, he thought…as if he could call to John Lourdes across a clear and star pierced night. The youth was as close to a son as the fifty year old reprobate attorney could ever imagine for himself. The boy had climbed out of the squalor of the Segundo Barrio, survived a tortuous and troubling past to become an agent for the Bureau of Investigation, the first of his kind. And now this, Burr thought.

The moon was huge and white and full upon the river. How many nights like these had he and the youth sat on this balcony, with this very backdrop to their talks.

He went and sat now, and he looked down at the telegram. "Even an unjust world," he whispered, "could not be that unjust."

DOS DIABLOS

— SPRING, 1911 —

CHAPTER 1

BY 1911 THERE WAS AN UPRISING in the wind. Mexico was ravaged by famine and internal warfare. The culture and government of that country was crumbling into chaos, creating a bloody political and social upheaval that would lead to the overthrow of the despot Porfirio Diaz and drive the country into the hands of bureaucratic uncertainty. To escape the poverty and violence thousands of desperate refugees illegally crossed the Rio Grande into Texas only to fuel long existing racial hatreds that America would live and relive for a hundred years.

The Rio Grande Valley became a lawless sweep of frontier. The coming of the railroads had populated it, had created a middle class of townships and agribusiness, but the misery to the south was poisoning it. Murder and rape were not uncommon. The rise in the selling and procuring of illegal contraband, including narcotics, became a feeding ground for bandits. Along the Mexican side of the river, children hunted the roadways, weighted down with bandoleers and rifles as tall as they were. On the American side bodies could be come upon in the sweltering daylight, swollen and rotting.

Outside Del Rio, Texas, south of the San Felipe Bridge, a pair of bandits known as Los Diablos worked the river and the creek that fed into it. They had eluded or escaped capture so many times the newspapers took to writing about them, turning their Texas Ranger hunters into futile incompetents. In their brazen folly, the two youths would leave at the scene of their crimes articles written about them and the Rangers' failure to exact their will.

Their most infamous night came at the San Felipe Springs below the river. There was a campfire by a grove of persimmons and anacahuita, where a Mexican woman sat with her newborn in swaddling. She had a shawl pulled tightly around her head and shoulders against the night cold. Along the banks, the brush was thick with cast iron and nandina. The bracken chitting with the breeze, the springs' water tumbling over bone white rock. This is from where the two bandits surveyed the little encampment.

She looked to be a poor woman with nothing more than a rickety cart and slat ribbed burro. A man lay sleeping under a blanket, his face covered from the firelight by a roadcap.

It would be easy to fall upon them, these paupers. But what did they have for the taking? A little food, coffee, from the smell of it, heating on the fire, that burro in its barely held together hide, a few blankets, maybe some hidden silver or a family crucifix of gold. Something for these peons to bank their dreams upon. And there was always the woman.

They came out of the brush with the swiftness of wolves. Lean, raggedy men. One with a cap and ball musket and the other a machete. The creek water spilling over the rocks hid their footsteps. The shadow of the woman rocking the baby in her arms cast up from the campfire upon the night moved with a suddenness as the men were upon them.

The musket fired and there was a puff of burning smoke from the blanket that covered the sleeping man. The other raised his machete and screamed.

He saw that was no woman sitting by the fire and covered in a shawl, but a youth not much older than themselves. Dark eyed and with a fixed stare. And in all that swaddling was no precious child but a sawed down shotgun.

The blast from the weapon set the swaddling to flame, and the bandit with the machete was thrown back into the campfire sending up a spray of red hot ash.

John Lourdes stood now and swung the shotgun loose of the swaddling and turned the barrel on the second bandit and fired. The shot caught the one with the musket in the side of the face and he grabbed at a blinded eye.

He was on his knees, wracked and crying out when John Lourdes stepped over the body that lay charring in the flames. He pulled off the shawl and cast it away and reached for a pistol in his shoulder holster.

The bandit was terror stricken and rambling in Spanish, enraged and defeated, blood running through his fingers and down his face, and John Lourdes kicked at the blanket that covered the sleeping man, but it was no man there, just patched together brush.

In Spanish, John Lourdes said, "You are mine to arrest."

And that was the last John Lourdes said until the next morning when he came riding up Main Street, Del Rio, leading a horse with one dead bandit draped over it and the other on that poor excuse of a burro, the bandit's head bound up in rags like some Hindu and the blinded eye covered. The Mexican youth was still rambling on like a madman in Spanish—loud enough for all in the street to hear—that he was one of the infamous Dos Diablos outlaws.

They were quite the spectacle in the glory of all that dusty Texas sunlight, making their way past wagons and automobiles and the site of the almost completed Del Rio Bank and Trust on Losoya. John Lourdes could have gotten to the jail more quickly and quietly side stepping that staring traffic along the main thoroughfare but decided against it.

CHAPTER 2

THREE RIDERS CROSSED a raining desert at night toward the mining town of Santo Tomas, thirty miles north of Laredo. Their slickers soaked, the rain dripping mercilessly from the brim of their hats. The men leaned into the slanting downpour and pressed on urgently, forcing their mounts along the slopping gruel of the roadway.

What began to appear out of the blackness was the iron machinery of a mining operation and a long line of coal cars on a railroad siding. The riders slowed and crossed over the tracks, the hooves of the animals clanging against the rails like shackling chains, and on the lakebed flats beyond were the lights from a few blocks of crudely constructed workman's shacks.

Santo Tomas was about three quarters of a mile from the Rio Grande. Most of the miners, the water peddlers, and mule drivers were from Coahuila and Nuevo Leon. So there was a lot of allegiance in Santo Tomas for Mexican nationals of influence on the run.

It was a well-known crossing point for revolutionaries and activists who wrote about the mistreatment, racism, and murder of non-whites by Americans, both known and unknown.

The riders made their way toward a rundown residence on a small rise away from the workmen's shacks where the mining company doctor lived and tended to the ill. On that night he had in his care a young Mexican woman who had just gone into labor. Her hair matted across the pillow, her face beaded with sweat, the muscles about her belly trying to press out a new life. Her husband in the next room, sitting at a plain desk, his sleeves rolled up, writing an editorial by a kerosene lamp about the "Gringo" corruption he had witnessed firsthand along the Nueces Strip against his kind, an editorial written with the pent up rage of youth and coming fatherhood. To be delivered from hiding, most probably, to Senor Barros and his daughter who ran the newspaper, *La Cronica*.

The doctor entered the room, wiping at his face and hands with a rag. He was a tired out old character with a poor white shirt and threadbare trousers. A relic of endless decades nursing the poor and needy. "It's going to be a long night," said the doctor.

The young man set his pen down. "I feel guilty sitting here," he said. "…Even though…Is there anything I can do or should—"

"Would you rather I do the writing and you have the baby?" said the wife, her voice enough to carry through the pitiful slatbed wall. The young man made a gesture with his hand as if to say—I have been so ordered.

That is when the front door was kicked open and three men stormed in upon them with revolvers drawn and their heads covered by sacks with cutouts for eyes. The one who stood the most forward, his sack had a coating of white paint on it.

The woman in the bedroom had heard the commotion and called out, and the one most forward ordered, "Get in there and quiet her."

"She's in labor," the doctor said. "You wouldn't—"

The husband looked toward his holster and jacket draped over a chair. The leader of the three said, "It will be a pointless footrace, Mister Puerta."

The woman's cries were swiftly muffled.

Puerta stood.

"How it satisfies me to see the look of desperation on your face," said the leader.

He motioned with his revolver for Puerta to stand back. As he did, the leader walked toward the desk and picked up the sheaf of paper that had been written on. "You know who I am," he said to the youth.

"I know who you are…and who you are not."

He began to read, his eyes moving between the youth and the editorial. He read aloud. "The Mexican in America, be he immigrant, Tejano or pure blooded citizen, has become the new Jew, the new Negro. To be segregated and ostracized. And his greatest enemies are the state, the government, the Texas Rangers, heads of industry and business, and the owners of the great ranches."

When he finished reading, he rolled up the paper with the fingers of one hand and then slipped the paper into the flame of that kerosene lamp. The paper turned to red ash burning up through the belly of that glass.

"You can't burn up the truth," said Puerta.

"No? People do it all the time. History…all the time. History is nothing more than hearsay. The truth…burned up. Dispensed with. Tossed to the ash heap. Just like this. What's left is a tale told by the victors."

The leader leaned back and whispered something to the man who stood guard silently behind him. As the man started for the bedroom,

Puerta followed him with his eyes. Out and out fear for his wife had hold of him now, but he contained himself. "A man forgets the *first* amendment," he said, "he could end up looking down the barrel of the second."

A quiet laugh came from inside the hood of the man staring at Puerta. "The beauty of the second amendment is in the eye of the beholder."

There was a commotion now coming from the bedroom. The two men were dragging the woman out into the hall. One by the hair, the other by the arm. Her mouth was bound up, her screams muffled. She was naked. Her huge belly glistened with sweat. She tried to protect her child with her one loose arm.

"At least let her deliver the baby," said Puerta. "Please."

"She's going to deliver the baby. Just not in the United States."

Puerta did not understand. The doctor did not understand. Puerta looked to the chair and the pistol.

They had dragged the woman out into the rain. Through the open doorway, the light stretched far enough to see one of the hooded men had taken a rope from his saddle and was looping it under the woman's arms as she tried to writhe and kick her way free.

"Drag her? You mean to drag her," said the doctor.

"It's only three quarters of a mile to the river."

Rather than try to make a rush for the weapon on the chair that he knew he could not reach, he charged toward the desk which was closer instead. He grabbed the first thing that he could get a hand on which was the heavy bottle of ink, and he flung it at the hooded man. It hit him square in the face as he fired, affecting his aim just enough so the shot, even at that close range, did not instantly kill Puerta, though better it had.

He lay on the floor on his back, his legs widely spread out. He was gasping violently, his mouth moved like a fish taken from its rightful place in the water.

"Can I go to him?" said the doctor.

The hooded man waved him to go if he wished. They could hear the clopping hooves of the mounts outside as they took off for the river. They could see the woman just for a moment there in the rain framed by the doorway, her body lurched by the rope till there was nothing left but the darkness.

Puerta suffered until finally his body just buckled. A terrible gasp at the last. The hooded man stood over him all the while, a reckoning judge, silent and ghastly. The doctor looked up. Long streams of ink that had run down the hood looked almost like tears.

"I guess you're going to kill me now," said the doctor.

"If I had planned to kill you, I would never have covered my face."

CHURCH OF THE
GUARDIAN ANGEL

CHAPTER 3

JOHN LOURDES WOKE from a night of hard drinking well worse for the wear. The sunlight burned in along the edges of his bedroom shade till his eyes hurt. The woman he'd slept with was nowhere to be found. He tried to stand but he was like a defeated prize fighter. The bathroom seemed about a hundred miles away as he tottered toward it. He stood naked over the toilet and tried his best to aim. He needed to brace a hand against the wall to keep from tipping over when a scream almost launched him off his feet.

The woman, whose name he did not remember, came running down the hallway waving a letter. John Lourdes did not recall her being so overtly dressed...or so damn demonstrative.

"A letter," she said. "A priest just handed it to me at the door. He brought it for you."

John Lourdes was totally fixed on his piss.

"It's from the church," she said.

"What...church?"

"Look at the envelope." She was holding it near his face. He would have liked to knock it out of her hand.

"You're not some kind of defrocked priest, are you?"

He was defrocked all right. He finished pissing. He had to lean against the door jamb to keep his legs right.

"You should have seen the way that priest stared at me!" she said.

John Lourdes quietly laughed, as the answer was obvious. The woman seemed offended. He took the damn letter and looked at the envelope. It was embossed with the stamp of the Jesuit Society and the Catholic Church. He had no idea what this was about. He had not graced the inside of a church since his mother's funeral a near decade ago, The woman, meanwhile, was practically breathing into his ear. "Don't open it," she kept saying. "Just throw it away."

He paid her no mind. He opened the envelope and took out a hand-written note from within. It was on stationery from the Church of the Guardian Angel. She read aloud, "The Church of the Guardian Angel." She had been pointing at the embossed lettering, and he slapped her hand away.

"I can read," he told her.

And he did. The note was in a rough and choppy script.

> Dear Mister Lourdes,
>   I would very much like to speak with you on
> an urgent matter, at your earliest convenience.
>
> Yours in Christ,
> Father Carlos Pinto

She had been reading aloud, and again she pointed a finger at Father Pinto's signature. "The Apostle of El Paso. My goodness." She was somewhat awed, and in no small measure disturbed. "It's bad luck," she said. "A bad omen to get anything like this from the church." He walked to the bedroom and slumped down on the edge of the bed. She followed him all the way, prattling on how he should burn the letter. "It's a bad omen."

He just sat there looking at the note, exhausted, naked, and hungover, and wondering...where did she get the fuckin' energy?

"You're not going, are you?"

He didn't offer her an answer.

"There's only two things the church wants from you or any of us. You know what they are?"

"No," he said.

"Do you want to know?"

"No," he said.

"Why not?"

He did not offer her an answer.

"Well, I'll tell you anyway...The church wants two things. They want money...and they want martyrs. And you don't have any money."

• • •

John Lourdes shaved and showered. He put on a neat white shirt and vest. He managed to look almost human. He breakfasted on eggs, aspirin, and two shots of tequila, then boarded a trolley at San Antonio Avenue. The Church of the Guardian Angel was on the north side of town, at the barren edge of the foothills. It was a simple but comely brick structure with a righteous steeple that stood out against the brown, burned country beyond it.

He was not a religious person. The church had no day to day meaning in his life. He only attended Mass at Christmas, and that was as much about memories of his mother as it was the candles and the choirs that come with the season. Yet he felt a discomfort somewhere inside him as if he were being now called to task for what he did not know.

Why he should feel this way weighed on him. It was a long, hot, dry ride in that trolley, so he had lots of time to tend to this question.

He was no wiser when he reached the church. A novitiate guided him to the weathered Craftsman bungalow in the spare and sandy lot next door that now served as a rectory.

Father Pinto was almost seventy when John Lourdes and he met. He had the handshake of a man who'd lived a hard and sobering life. And he carried this atmosphere about him of a man who had bled for others in the service of humankind for over forty years as a missionary on the frontiers of the West. He spoke with an Italian accent, having escaped the revolution there as a youth.

Father Pinto invited the young man into a private office where the curtains were drawn, and the air cooled by a kerosene fan in an out of the way corner on the floor. A novitiate brought coffee, set the serving tray down on a table, then left. As Father Pinto poured John Lourdes coffee, he said, "I heard that my letter was brought to your living quarters at a most inconvenient moment."

The muscles in the youth's face tweaked a bit. "Well…it certainly made for an interesting conversation."

John Lourdes was pointed toward a worn leather couch. The priest sat at his desk. The room was very still, and the priest looked the young man over as one who made a life of looking people over. "You're probably thinking," said the father, "I hope the old priest quickly gets to why he asked me here."

"Well…" John Lourdes seemed somewhat embarrassed "…not in so many words, but pretty nearly." He then took a drink of coffee.

"I learned you're twenty-four," said the priest.

"Yes."

"I also learned that you are not a religious man. You're not a practicing Catholic anymore."

"No, padre."

"I would assume having to be the legal hand that brings one's own father to justice would be the cause of great personal conflict."

John Lourdes came to a place of private disquiet and anger. "If you mean did bringing my father to his death affect my view of the world? Who can answer?"

Father Pinto politely studied the youth while he sipped his coffee. He then calmly went on.

"I enjoy the company of non-religious men," said the priest. "And I have come, over time, to put a great deal of faith in them. You see…men who are not religious have this uncanny flexibility to keep alive under the most dubious and dire of circumstances. This earth, being all they believe they have."

The priest then drank his coffee. His eyes over the rim of the cup looking at and into John Lourdes. "And that," he said, "is why I asked you here."

John Lourdes did not understand, but it only heightened the gravity of what he felt was coming.

"Why am I here?" said John Lourdes.

"I'm going to ask you, son, to put your earthly life at risk."

CHAPTER 4

JOHN LOURDES WALKED OUT OF THE RECTORY at dusk and what does he see, but the Rolls Royce that belonged to Wadsworth Burr parked in front of the church. The Chinese concubine behind the wheel of the yellow Silver Ghost. She nodded to John Lourdes as he approached, and he nodded back, then he leaned down under the canvas top and there was Burr in the back seat all gentlemanly and with a glass of whisky, or was it bourbon?

"Why am I not surprised to see you here?"

Burr noted the intense look on the boy's face, which he expected. "Get in," he said.

John Lourdes swung the back door open and slipped in beside the former attorney. The Chinese girl pulled into the street, shifting gears with swift precision.

"Did you volunteer yourself?"

"You told him everything about me, didn't you?"

Burr saw he was angry. And it was true. Burr had confided to the priest the truth about John Lourdes. How his mother was an illiterate Mexican immigrant and his father a gringo gunman and assassin known as Rawbone. A killer who had been taken down by his own son. How the youth had changed his name to Lourdes to bury his heritage. A name he took from the shrine in France, it being the one place his mother dreamed of making a pilgrimage. Even the Bureau of Investigation didn't know the truth of him. Or the reason Wadsworth Burr had become a sort of godfather to the youth…that his only true friend ever had been the boy's late father.

"I thought it best under the circumstances," said Burr, "to be honest with the Jesuit."

"I wish you hadn't."

"It wasn't for him that I was doing it."

John Lourdes' face darkened, he glared at Burr.

Evening had set in about the city. Lights came on in the street, in shop windows, and apartments along the downtown boulevards. People moved through the pools of lights, soft images on the way to the rest of their lives.

The girl driving made smooth time, and she was not hesitant about working the horn or cursing out some wagoneer or carriage driver that got in the path of the Rolls Royce. This petite flower was deft at stringing together vulgarities in two languages. And she could spit the length of a car.

"How was it left with the Jesuit?"

"I'm to sleep on it. Call him tomorrow. If I agree, he'll go to the bureau and sign off on it."

Burr refilled his glass from a silver flask. He handed the glass to the youth beside him, elbowing him to take it. John Lourdes stared out upon the city, but he saw nothing. He was looking inward, at the severe trials he felt that constituted his own life.

"You knew for days, didn't you?"

"Father Pinto and I had talks. He sent me the article from the Laredo newspaper."

"They dragged the woman all the way across the river. Found her and the baby's body. Still attached to the cord. She must have lived long enough to—" He shook his head in dismay.

• • •

The three ate dinner at the mansion. The Chinese girl sat quietly as Burr elucidated about a world that was on a collision course with its living hatreds. How poverty and a collapsed government were driving thousands of illegal Mexican immigrants across the Rio Grande. How the American citizen of mixed heritage had become a target for racism and hatred. How they bore violence against them, how their businesses were ransacked and robbed, destroyed, sometimes forcibly taken. A long festering toxic animosity was seeping out of the American social armor under the banner of injustice. Vigilante committees disguised as political organizations came more into being. The most feared, or beloved, depending on one's point of view, was The Social Committee for an American Republic, known formally as SCAR, but throughout the length and breadth of Texas as 'The Society.' The doctor at Santo Tomas declared the murder of the pregnant woman and her journalist husband the work of 'The Society.' An accusation the organization neither admitted nor denied.

In the silence that ensued, the Chinese girl looked up from her listening and stated quietly, "Same everywhere. China, no different. Han,

Manchu, Muslim, foreigner…all treat like beasts. In China…" She made a sudden swipe bringing the side of her hand down on the table with such force the glasses shook, and the plates rattled. The men were caught off guard. "…Head chopped off. Head left to roll around in basket. Head later put on stick then fed to dogs." She stood, and politely said, "Want dessert? Brandy?"

"And that," said Burr, "comes from the lips of one of the world's oldest and most refined cultures."

While they sat there, John Lourdes heard a motorcycle go past the mansion and then another quickly followed. He remarked on this, it being unusual, and Burr explained that one of the Mexican dictator's generals had decided to retire—which was code for getting out of the country with the gold while the getting' was still good—and that he'd bought himself a luxurious estate farther up the hill. "Which proved," said Burr, "that our white privileged world was being encroached upon by Mexican privilege."

He then did not change the subject, as much as alter it slightly. "Have you considered the task the priest discussed with you?"

The task was simple enough on paper—*the agent was to clandestinely proceed to Laredo to seek out and discover the identity of the murderer known as "The Whiteman" and to create and execute a plan to capture and-or kill such person, or persons, as yet unknown.*

"When the priest approached you with the plan," said Burr, "that had been discussed with your commander why do you think they finally decided to ask you? Because you are Tejano? That you can pass for white or Mexican?"

"I know where you're going with this line of attack. They picked me because the commander could not be entirely sure about the other agents. Who are all Gringo. And may have private sympathies that would be in conflict with the task at hand."

"The priest approached the Bureau of Investigation because of what he was seeing and hearing all along Rio Grande Valley," said Burr. "The Texas Rangers have proven hostile, even dangerous. Many of the local sheriffs are impotent if not outright afraid. Why do you think the doctor in Santo Tomas was spared?"

"So he'd tell the newspapers. So a political war could be waged in the press. He was being used. He's as good as dead now anyway. And I may be put in the same position as the doctor."

John Lourdes heard something that caught his attention. Or felt he did, anyway. It was a faint popping sound far back up in the quietude of the estates.

"When you brought the two brothers in," said Burr, "you should have done so without the fanfare. You acted more like your father would have."

John Lourdes angered at just the mention of this. "The attorney in you is forever busy, isn't he?"

"And that is because life is not mistake proof."

"I wanted people to know. To see I had proved myself."

"You proved yourself with their capture. The rest was—"

There...again he heard it. This time the sounds were more defined. John got up quickly and went to the window. He looked out toward the street. The girl came running in from the kitchen. She was frightened. She'd heard it, too.

"What?" said Burr.

"Gunshots," said John Lourdes.

Burr rushed to the front door. The girl pressed up behind him on the porch, her fingers digging into his arm. The gunfire was a few blocks farther up in the Addition.

"Where's John...?" said Burr, looking about him.

He had immediately gone to the den where Burr had an extensive collection of weapons. The gentleman's hobby. When John Lourdes came out of the house, he was chambering a magazine into a Winchester rifle. The gunfire had grown more frenetic. "You better go inside and keep the lights down," he said.

He made his way down to the street then trotted up through the darkness toward the sound of all the shooting.

There was moonlight and deep shadows. He held the rifle at the ready as he ran. There were people at lit windows or framed in open doorways. Some called out. To them, John Lourdes must have looked like some silent, ominous spirit.

He reached the first corner, but there was nothing. The homes this far up were bathed in a blue light. It was at the next corner, he came upon the scene.

A handful of men in the street—maybe three, he couldn't be sure— were firing into a huge adobe mansion from the edge of the property. There was return fire from the house. Voices in the street yelling in Spanish.

"Traitorous pig…murderer…" From what he could gather, it was the former General's house, and these were countrymen come to seek retribution.

There was an explosion and a car parked in the driveway was blown straight into the air and came crashing down in a burning heap on its side. He knew it must have been to be a gunpowder bomb or dynamite for that kind of blast.

For a moment he just stood staring at this otherworldly scene. In the middle of all these monied homes, with their automobiles and carriages, their decorative fountains and fine furnishings, a pitched battle was taking place. Black shadows with guns moving in and out of the profoundest dark, playing out a tale of pursuit, revenge and death. In this patch of night the world had become unmoored. The revolution to come was being prologued on an El Paso street.

John Lourdes unloaded a magazine into the air to try and drive the men off, but when they gathered up, they trained their weapons on this new threat. John Lourdes had chambered another magazine. He had more firepower than they did. One of the men was backlit by the flames from that burning wreck, and John Lourdes unloaded enough rounds to shred the man's coat. He slanted in one direction from being hit and then another and was finally spun around. He was dead there in the road before he ever realized.

The two other men scattered. John Lourdes could hear the motorcycle engines rev. He caught a brief look at them. They had swung up the front expanse of the mansion across from the vehicle burning in the driveway then veered toward the back of the property.

John Lourdes sprinted back down the street from where he'd come. He meant to cut them off if he could. He saw them for brief moments, then they were lost in deep strips of darkness, only to reappear again in long blocks of light cast from living room windows and rows of French doors.

He could follow the sound of the engines, and when one of them came flying out of a black wall of trees, John Lourdes fired until the magazine was empty. He'd hit the rider or the motorcycle because it went out of control swerving crazily toward the side of a house. It hit the wall full throttle and blew apart. Like burning stars, bits of shorn metal were thrown everywhere.

With the sweat burning his eyes and out of breath, he was chambering another magazine when the other motorcycle swept right past him. It was pure shadow with a trail of grim and choking exhaust. He could feel the heat of the engine and the rider was crimped down low against the handlebars.

The motorcycle was making its escape down a roadway of streetlights when John Lourdes emptied a full magazine into it. The night air crackled. He must have hit the gas tank because the motorcycle ignited, and machine and man were fueled into the air to come crashing down with the machine hissing violently. The burning motorcycle bounced and caromed, like some massive out of control holiday fireworks. He assumed the rider was dead, but he assumed wrong.

Something rose up out of the smoking hell of that street. The wrecked black outline of a man, flames fanning out from the back of his clothes like huge deformed wings. Screaming out his anguish in Spanish, cursing the world of America. Calling it the devil's whore. Swearing that one day it would be taken down like the beast it was. Promising that it would be choked to death on Mexican blood. And that all that was stolen from Mexico would be returned in Gringo coffins.

The man had slumped to his knees. He was burning to death, his body twisting in the night wind. John Lourdes chambered another magazine. He walked toward the man and when he could see his face, or what was left of his face, staring at him, eyes widened and white with hatred even in death, he fired a pity shot.

CHAPTER 5

WADSWORTH BURR WAS A MORPHINE ADDICT and had been one for twenty years. His need for drugs was in part what precipitated his private fall from grace. That, and the fact he had made political enemies in Texas for his work as an attorney fighting the anti-Chinese restriction laws. And yet, when there was need for him to be pressed into action, he was without fault among his peers. And this night demanded such.

By the time the authorities arrived at the Addition, John Lourdes had been driven home. After dropping him off, the Chinese girl was to pass the night at a relative's, and to remain there until Burr sent her word. With the task ahead, notoriety would not play to the young BOI agent's advantage.

Throughout the Addition, the authorities were gathering evidence. Yet no one seemed to be able to identify the person, or persons, who shot down the attackers. Burr had had the foresight to make his young friend sign a short and quickly sketched letter saying he had hired Burr as his attorney. Though he could no longer practice in Texas, he was still a member of the bar in California, thanks to a certain legislator that Burr had compromising information about.

He could now nimbly avoid the truth as he stood in the doorway and was confronted with questions. Later, he was sitting alone in his den in the dark having shot himself up with the drug, when his telephone rang.

When he heard it was her, he said wearily, "Hello, my love."

"How you?" she said back.

"I'm scared in my heart for the boy."

"I write prayer on paper, burn in bowl."

"Sorcery," he told her. "Good intentions aside."

• • •

The next day John Lourdes boarded a train for his journey to Laredo. He was carrying a letter of introduction from Father Pinto to Senor Barros and his daughter Marisita who together ran *La Cronica* newspaper there. They would serve as confidants, passing any information the agent acquired onto the Jesuit, who in turn would relay it to the commander at the Bureau of Investigation in El Paso. This chain of secrecy was to minimize the number of people knowing John Lourdes' intent and who might prove untrustworthy.

On the station platform he said goodbye to Burr. The unfazed lawyer masking the man who agonized over the boy's survival. The youth saw through that reprobate's facade but played the innocent and only held his friend for a few moments and whispered, "When I get back, we'll drink up a night and get ironical with each other."

The young woman who cared for Wadsworth held John Lourdes' face and kissed him, then forced into his hand a necklace chain that held a Chinese coin with a square hole in the middle.

"Taoist sorcery," said Burr.

She did not know what the word 'sorcery' meant but she understood the insinuation, and she cursed vehemently. And there in the Texas sunlight, on the hot station platform, John Lourdes realized this was all the family he had in the world.

As he walked away, looking back at them there, he felt the very earth was sending him a message.

John Lourdes assumed the seven hundred mile journey, first to San Antonio where he'd change trains for Laredo, would be at most, inconsequential. But this proved to be injudicious, as shortly before departure, a convoy of four cars pulled into the dusty lot.

From the front and rear cars came a squad of policemen who fanned out and formed a barricade guarding the platform. From the second vehicle stepped four Mexicans in suits, and they were heavily armed. They cornered the third car, guarding it, and from where the General, whose house had been attacked the night before, exited. With him were his wife and two teenage children.

The family filed up the platform with the four bodyguards flanking them. John Lourdes watched them pass by his window. The General had a manicured grey goatee and a fancy suit. There was an air of unconcerned dignity about him. Whether it was a pose—his wife and children looked terrified.

It turned out the lead passenger car had been emptied and was at the disposal of the former General. By the time the Southern Pacific reached Sierra Blanca and the steep and rocky crags of the Quitman Mountains, every passenger was aware of the attack on the General's life. The country that lay ahead was raw and barren, a parched flat landscape where a train was defenseless. As night fell, a growing sense of anxiety spread among the travelers.

Who put the General on this train? Who allocated him his own car? The government? The railroad? The Southern Pacific had vast economic interests in Mexico. Was the General an informant of some kind? A traitor? Was he knowingly being brought to his own slaughter?

Most of the people on the train were Anglo, a handful were Mexican. There was a palpable tension among the people. The Mexicans knew if something went bad, the Anglos on board would hold them accountable, at least partly, if for no other reason "or crime" other than their race. John Lourdes watched from his own private silence, could feel the conflict. After all, it was a conflict he lived out every day of his life.

Burr had talked to him of this endless times, because he, too, understood a life of emotional conflict.

"War," he said, "is our personality acting out its tragedy. So beware."

CHAPTER 6

WHEN HE HAD A FURTIVE MOMENT, John Lourdes opened his beat up leather suitcase and from it took a semi-automatic Colt and a few extra clips and slipped them into his coat pocket. He sat back and looked out into the night. The tracks were following the banks of the Rio Grande. He could see the train there, reflected upon the glisteny surface of dark waters. He watched himself passing swiftly by. How small and finite he looked and yet, this feeling came over him that his very soul was being marked upon the border itself. And that some future John Lourdes would come to this very same moment.

At Marfa, a trio of rough boys boarded the train. Sidearms, rifle scabbards. A little filthy, a little older than John Lourdes. The tips of whiskey bottles peeking out the rim of a saddlebag. They looked the type that would turn on you over a gesture. They drank and talked among themselves. They were loud.

They were heading for Big Medicine, which everyone knew was the largest ranch in Texas. Surveyors claimed it vaster than the state of Rhode Island. It was also where 'The Society' was born. There was to be a rally there, and Doctor English would be speaking. He was a strange and infamous character who had been in the service at leper colonies in Louisiana and Texas.

That trio of hardcases was swilling it down. They had learned about the General and his entourage, and they were none too happy about paying for a seat on what was a moving target. They even started in with snide comments for the Mexicans in the car with them. Asking if they were the General's maids or bathroom attendants. The insults started from the crass to the flat out racist and threatening. The Mexicans spread about the car took it as John Lourdes remembered his own mother had, and a little bit of the grave that his past was buried in opened up.

He suddenly spoke out so damn loud, everyone in the passenger car heard, "Why don't we just throw them the hell off the train?"

This got everyone's attention. The conductor, who was in the car, walked up to him. "What do you mean by that?"

"You know damn well…those greasers." He jerked a thumb toward the next car. "This is our country…or am I missing something?"

His notion had worked and a few minutes later he was sitting with those hardcases feasting on whiskey and filthy racist slurs. A brother of the white soul now. He had given them a fictitious background he'd developed with Burr about being in the Army and working security for companies that shipped goods across the border. He was laying out a foundation for his purpose and attending that rally at Big Medicine was one of them.

• • •

At about three in the morning, the train had to stop at Ulvalde for the engine to take on water.

"We'll be here for a while," John Lourdes said to his newfound compatriots. "I'm going to stretch my legs."

But that was not the reason. John Lourdes knew the track well from his time working as a railroad detective before he joined the Bureau. And if there ever was a stop where the train was vulnerable to attack, this was it.

Unlike most towns along the route, the depot was outside of Ulvalde by a good half mile. Travelers got to and from the station by a horse drawn trolley. The depot and water tower were lonely cutouts on a dark stretch of prairie with a deep grove of live oaks across the tracks, their vast spreading branches stretching for a hundred yards in either direction, and where the night could easily hide the shapes and shadows of men lurking there.

John Lourdes stepped out into the night, and while the fireman watered the engine, he took in the scene about him. It was still as a graveyard, the air as dead. Only the steady huff of that waiting engine could be felt in the ground beneath your boots.

Two of the General's guards had exited their traincar and taken up positions on both sides of the track. They were mere silhouettes and motionless as statuary as they watched the country about them, their rifles poised. John Lourdes assumed the other two guards were holding positions in each doorway.

Something caught John Lourdes' eye. The trolley—it was just sitting there. The two horses that pulled it grazing at a few bits of turf within their reach. But where was the trolleyman?

"I got to take a piss."

John Lourdes turned. He had been joined by the lead dog of that trio, who undid his trousers and started to drunkenly piss away right there onto a crusty patch of dirt. His name was Micajah Adams, but his friends called him Cager. He had no sense of decorum, to be sure, and while he urinated, he shouted boldly at the guards. "You ought to get your greaser asses back across the border. We don't want any of you here."

He got back a look of cold displeasure, but not a word. "Yeah…I'm talkin' to you, greaser," said Cager.

John Lourdes started toward the trolley.

Cager called out to him, "Where you going?"

"Park your cock and get out your revolver."

The horses pricked their ears and their heads rose and sniffed the air, and John Lourdes whispered, "Easy, now."

And Cager, a few paces back and suddenly more sober, said, "Something wrong there, fella?"

He need not answer for he stopped short of the trolley and rose an open hand in caution and then he pointed. Cager pressed in alongside him. The driver lay on the iron stairs, his skull blasted away, his blood dripping to puddle blackly in the dirt.

"Wake everyone in our car."

John Lourdes raced back to the depot to warn them of impending trouble. He was running along the tracks towards the locomotive. The fireman was atop the tender, feeding it with water from the tower spout. The engineer stood beside that black monster lighting his pipe. John Lourdes was trying to get his attention, calling out, waving his arms. "We've got to get clear of here…Now!"

The engineer could see a silhouette down the track, hear the voice, but the huffs from that huge engine and the hissing steam had him cup a hand to his ear. It made little difference. A streak of blood and smoke exploded off the back of the fireman's overalls and he was driven from the tender. He grabbed onto the spout for a moment and it swung wildly, water spilling everywhere, and then he fell.

CHAPTER 7

A HANDFUL OF RIDERS came howling up out of the trees. Men afoot swarmed from a sandy wash. The prairie night filled with gunshots. Puffs of smoke all up and down the trackline. The riders swept past the train-car, firing into the windows. Shattered glass and wood shards everywhere. Banshee sounds coming out of the riders' mouths. The engineer tried to escape, stumbling along, making for town. John Lourdes had to chase him down and drag him back to the locomotive. He shoved that pathetic pleading excuse up the engine steps at gunpoint.

"Get this train moving," he said, "or I'll kill you where you stand…Do you want to die here?"

One of the General's guards was trampled under. The hooves of the animals leaving the man's face unrecognizable. And the screaming, the panicked helplessness from all quarters of the train. The wounded lay on car seats, or on the aisle floor. The depot was a calamitous scene with the dust of the riders obscuring everything.

An attacker on foot slid under the General's car. He jammed a cluster of dynamite sticks up into the wheel well. He went to light the fuse when the train suddenly lurched forward. The huge iron wheels ground over his legs. John Lourdes leaned out from the tender and fired back into the riders.

The engineer tried to jump from the train. John Lourdes caught him and flung him toward the throttle. He grabbed the man by the hair. He put his face right against the engineer's and brought a sound up from his chest like some unholy beast.

A rider came out of the darkness carrying a gunpowder bomb. He drove his mount until it was right alongside the General's car. He threw the bomb through a shattered window. Before he could veer his mount away, there was an explosion that turned the window frames into black-ened shells. Stalks of flame drove out into the night with the agonized cries of those being burned to death. The horse buckled then reeled toward the traincar. The rider tried to jump but it was too late, and man and beast were pulled under.

The train was gaining speed. The riders began to pale, and their cursed firing faded off into the opaque night and there was then only the sound of that locomotive upon a vast prairie. They were leaving the horror behind, except for that which they carried.

"I'm going to see how it is back there." He held up his handgun as a warning. The engineer kept to the throttle silently. John Lourdes climbed upon the tender, braced his legs, and stood.

The train was a vision of carnage. The General's car a ruined hull—long strips of roof missing or caved in, the shell, fireburned. The other cars, windowless and bulletridden. He just stood atop there in the wind, lost in questions of existence and the notion of fate.

He lowered himself from the tender onto the platform of the passenger car. The door had been blown away, and there he entered. The smell of torched flesh in the air. A rubble of seating and roofbeams. The General lay dead, his wife dead there beside him, their clothes and flesh poxed where the gunpowder had scored them. He looked down the length of the car and there in a runner of moonlight from the open roof was Cager, a pistol in hand.

"You're alive," said Cager.

John Lourdes started down the length of that car stepping over debris, dipping to get past a collapsed section of roof. When close enough, he pointed at Cager's blood stained shirt.

"Not my blood. My partners'…lost both of them. But look here."

He pointed his revolver toward a dark corner of the passenger car. The General's teenage son lay among the wreckage. His eyes were open but seemed empty. He was still breathing though. John Lourdes leaned down over the boy. He saw a piece of metal railing had speared the boy beneath the ribs.

Here's just another youth, thought John Lourdes, done in by the wrongs of the world, and dyin' for no good reason. And all in the wink of an eye. 'God…what am I doing here?'

"Step back," said Cager.

John Lourdes looked up. He saw Cager meant to shoot the boy. "What do you think you're doing?"

"Doing? I'm going to give him a taste of the Whiteman. Because if it wasn't for these Mexicans…" He waved his arm with the weapon across the whole scene.

"Let him die peacefully. You don't want it on your conscience, do you? He's just a boy."

"Sure," said Cager. "Why not?"

John Lourdes looked at this dying teenager. For a moment there was enough life in the face, in the eyes, to see the boy knew he was coming to his end. He gripped the boy's hand.

There was a shot from behind John Lourdes' head. The boy's body jerked violently and then sagged back.

"Why?" said John Lourdes, standing. "He was going to die."

"He was taking too long."

EL NIGRITO
EN AL ARROZ

CHAPTER 8

By the afternoon of the following day, the train made its somber entry into San Antonio. Wires had been sent ahead about the catastrophe, and the depot swarmed with police and Texas Rangers, military personnel, doctors, nurses, reporters with cameras, and a fiercely curious and politically enraged public.

John Lourdes had it in mind to slip from the train as inconspicuously as possible as it snaked through the railyard. Cager had calmed down by then and had his wits about him and with suffering trepidation questioned John Lourdes. "You wouldn't tell, would you...what I done back there? I'm a good Christian Protestant, you know."

He slapped Cager on the shoulder in a show of rough camaraderie. "What's one more, more or less?"

Cager felt easier now. "You want to get in touch with me in Laredo, send a letter to General Delivery."

"Maybe you'll take me with you out to Big Medicine...for the rally."

• • •

He looked like just another castoff in need of a bath and a shave and some unbloody clothes walking through rows of box cars and freighters, the battered suitcase he carried banging against the outside of his leg. The train to Laredo did not leave until nightfall, so he took the ten minute walk to the Alamo to spend what little time he had there remembering.

He sat on a bench in the shade of the plaza facing the Alamo mission, alone with thoughts of his mother and father, watching the tourists, the sellers of candy, of ice cream and soda. "A national shrine reduced down to pleasantries. It's always the way!" his father had said. "Nothing more, nothing less."

It was one of the few places on earth he had gone with both of his parents. He was near eight years old at the time. That was before his father, the notorious Rawbone, was wanted for murder and hunted by Rangers. His old man had replayed the battle in detail probably making up most of that bloody conflict from the wicked pastime that was his mind. "I'll give you something to think about," his father had said. His eyes gleaming, he made this huge wink. "Your mother would have been on one side of the battle and me on the other. She'd be out there with Santa Ana. And me holed up with Crockett and Bowie. Though it ain't my desire to go dyin' for glory. Ain't it so, woman—"

She'd loved him but cursed him for the thoughts that he put into the head of a child. She'd ordered they follow her so a picture could be taken in front of the mission. An American family in relative sunshine. Where was it now, that faded reminder? It had been wrapped up in cloth after her death, then put in a tin for safe keeping, only to end up lost to the world. He couldn't say when and he didn't know how. Gone like the dust across Alamo Plaza, gone like the light on the trees with the dusk.

Our unfinished business will never be finished when the dead are no longer with us, or those that are missing are forever denied us. He covered his eyes. Why do I hurt so? He heard himself ask. Why am I crying? I don't understand why I cannot take down the conflicts that seem to possess me.

• • •

He arrived in Laredo in the rain. The Hamilton Hotel was well up on Salinas and too far to walk in that weather. He had no way to get there until he paid a Mexican freighter to drive him.

"How is it here?" he said to the driver in Spanish.

The old man looked John Lourdes over, unsure. "You mean…about the funeral?"

He had no idea what the driver referred to but saw that the old man was reticent. He just nodded, that yes, he meant the funeral.

"It will be a bad day," said the driver hunched over the reins. He called out to his mules then sat there looking away.

"It is safe to talk to me," said John Lourdes.

"There will be 'whitemen' or so is the rumor."

This far downriver, the Mexicans had a name for members of 'The Society' that was not a term of endearment.

The hotel was newly built and three stories. The rain dripped from the scrollwork of an iron veranda that ran the length of the building on each floor. He waved the old man a goodbye then shook the rain from his coat and his hat before entering.

The lobby was brass and mahogany with electric lights and runners of carpet. The desk clerk wore glasses and was too thin for his suit. Burr had made all the arrangements, and the clerk rang for a porter as he said, "You here for the funeral?"

"I'm here for a funeral, all right."

The porter came along quietly and from his looks could have been a teacher at sixty with a gentleman's moustache. The clerk handed him the key. "Two eleven," he said.

The porter had a heavy Spanish accent. "This way, sir, if you please." He took John Lourdes' luggage.

"Your room's second floor front," said the clerk, "And if the sun's out tomorrow, from your veranda you'll have a grand view of the funeral."

The door opened to a suite that was comfortable and neat—and with a bathroom. The porter set the suitcase on a stand by the closet as John Lourdes opened the veranda door.

"Might I ask," said John Lourdes, "what is your name?"

"Manuel Aguirre," said the porter.

"Well, Mister Aguirre," he said while taking a packet of bills from his pocket and peeling off a few that he handed to the porter. "Might you see your way to getting me a bottle of good whiskey and copies of *La Cronica*? I'm sure there's some about."

The porter took the request most curiously then pocketed the money. "It will be my pleasure, sir."

When he returned, John Lourdes was on the veranda smoking. He looked out upon a city tempered by mist and a soft, shiny drizzle.

The porter set the bottle and a couple of glasses on the table by the bed. "This is gentleman's whiskey." He laid copies of *La Cronica* on the bed.

"Tomorrow," said John Lourdes, "what is that about?"

The porter singled out a copy of the newspaper and set it beside the bottle. "It's all there."

"Thank you very much, Mister Aguirre."

"You're welcome, sir. And if there's anything else that you need, do not hesitate to ask for me." He stopped at the door before leaving. "I pray that tomorrow…there will not be bloodshed."

CHAPTER 9

HE DRAGGED A LOUNGING CHAIR onto the veranda and drank. It was, as the porter said, good whiskey, and he read the editions of *La Cronica* from front to back. He learned the funeral was for the journalist and his wife who had been murdered in Santo Tomas. It would be a lot more than the poignant laying to rest of a couple and their unborn infant. It would be a full pitched political protest. The editors of the paper, Eduardo Barros and his daughter Marisita, who were to be his contacts there, had made it clear in their writings about the dangers and how the people must comport themselves for their safety and their cause.

He sat in the dark watching the lights of the city through the rain that stretched across the river border to Nuevo Leon. Lights that looked like wild vapors of fire. Since the coming of the railroads, Laredo had grown from a settlement of a few thousand to a city seven times that large. The main Mexican train line extended all the way from Monterrey to the border. An American paid for and owned line. There came with it an endless, growing body of traffic in business and people crossing the border, along with the nefarious and outright violent. The future of mortal man was playing out right there in the brooding silhouettes of a border city on that hard desert plat. And if the newspaper was anywhere near right, the future was going to have a very difficult birth.

His eyes lit with the sun. He'd slept away the night in that chair covered by a blanket. He could feel the day would be hot, the air being so still and dry this early. He shaved and bathed then opened a package Burr had waiting for him in his suite. He tore away the brown paper packaging to discover a new white shirt, black vest and matching trousers—and a note:

John—
　　Some people dress for the occasion, a few people make the occasion, a very few do both—

Wadsworth

42

He went out early to walk the funeral route as it had been laid out in *La Cronica*. The Barros' had been instrumental in creating this "event" which is how he would describe it, along with a number of other Mexican and Tejano organizations. He was hoping to get a sense of the father and daughter, if not see them and watch them from a distance, as his success and survival were inextricably tethered to these strangers actions and attitudes.

The services were to be held at Saint Augustin Church, which was the heart of the city. It was also where the well-to-do lived, Anglo and Mexican alike. And where the banks, the trading markets, corporate entities and railroads had established their corporate headquarters.

Winging out from there were the barrios. El Ranchero to the east and El Cuatro, the Fourth Ward, to the west. Blacks lived among the Mexicans there. Children of the Negro infantry that had been stationed at Fort McIntosh.

John Lourdes had learned from Burr years back, that his father had spent time in Laredo after going on the dodge, when Burr was his only living contact to the old life in El Paso.

After the service, the cortege would proceed up Flores. John Lourdes walked the length of it. The sun was bleaching the street dry but there would still be deep pools of filthy rainwater along that wide boulevard when the funeral train came through. Flores was the city's main artery and using that route to the camposanto for burial was a public statement of defiance confronting the racism and violence exacted against the innocent.

Every telltale sign told him things were going to go bad. People were gathering outside bars, restaurants, retail shops. Men with drinks in hand spreading their states of mind fueled by liquor. Women in small clusters with their frayed attitudes and social outrage about the public spectacle meant to defame their city's good name. From the windows of apartments and offices above the street shops were hung our flag and a striking number of banners of the Social Committee for an American Republic.

There should have been more police on the street, more deputies tempering a crowd that could easily become an unsavory mob. And the Texas Rangers, where were they? There was conflict about the organization, in many quarters they were not considered honest brokers of justice when it came to racist violence along the Rio Grande, but a prophylactic against a growing Mexican insurgency.

On the other side of the street was a two story hacienda that turned out to be the business headquarters of the Big Medicine Ranch. There were cars parked out front and trucks with the Big Medicine logo painted across the slatted sides. There were men in suits and cowboys milling about.

Big Medicine was more than a ranch, it was a corporation with book-keepers and salesmen, a chief financial officer and a member of the Pacific Stock Exchange, the Texas Cattleman's Association, the Cotton Grower's Organization. And Big Medicine thrived on one thing—Mexican labor. And labor is only as good as it can be lorded over.

John Lourdes crossed the street, and as he walked among the men there, he eavesdropped. He bummed a light for his cigarette, even engaged in small talk. He heard one of the men behind him say, "He's coming."

"Who?" said a second man.

A third said, "He's gonna make a show of it?"

"He's not coming alone either, I heard," said the first.

"Rumor," said the third.

"He don't deal in rumors."

"Who?" the second repeated.

"The Whiteman," said the first.

CHAPTER 10

Two coffins were carried to a glass sided hearse drawn by four white horses. The "unborn" body of the child was wrapped in gold swaddling donated by the church to be laid to rest with its mother. It was a vast cloud rich sky that awaited the funeral train. There were maybe two hundred mourners in the procession, a number of them Anglos. Directly behind the hearse were two dozen women, mostly young, that wore the same long black skirts and white blouses, and they had silk mantillas to cover their heads and shoulders. These women carried placards that read: COMPASSION…HUMANITY…JUSTICE…

John Lourdes followed the procession moving along the crowded sidewalk and wondering if one of those young ladies was the daughter of the editor he was to meet.

He was following along with the hearse, moving among the onlookers when he heard a man yell out, "Marisita…Marisita… Hey…I have a story to show you."

A young woman among the others turned toward the sound of her name. The man on the sidewalk had undone his trousers and was exposing his genitals. He was burly and uncouth, and he had to hold down his hat as he took off into the crowd as a sheriff's deputy gave chase. The deputy was Mexican.

Could this Marisita be her? He watched and studied this young woman in the purple mantilla. How she cloaked her rage and disgust at the insult with a stare of utter disregard. A look that bordered on serenity, but not genuine serenity, a serenity that was as much hard discipline. He knew this look. He had seen it on the woman in the barrio of his childhood. A look that spoke to the day to day religion of surviving unfounded hostilities.

She turned back to the gravity at hand, and all he had left was her mantilla covered profile, the sun through the lace upon her copper skin rendering it with some diaphanous beauty.

And then a pack of kids, teenagers mostly, broke through the crowd with lit firecrackers. Real Texas busters they flung at the procession. There came the explosive pop, pop, pop, pop, pop which scared hell out of the mourners thinking it gunfire. And did they scatter until they came to realize. The horses pulling the hearse reared back and the coffins within rattled. The police gave chase as the youths flung another round of busters then scattered themselves, screaming like wild Indians. And this was only the beginning.

Attitudes along Flores stiffened after that, greetings grew decidedly more hostile. People were shouting—"America, America, America, America." Men were taking off their hats and striking them toward the sky with outstretched arms—"America, America, America, America." John Lourdes walked past the Big Medicine offices where their employees stood on the hoods of cars and upon the flatbeds of their corporate trucks shouting at the mourners—"We don't want your kind here!" "Go back where you came from!" "This is our country!" "It was born white, and it will die white."

It was a phrase he'd never heard before—the country was born white and would die white—but it was something that seemed alive within him, something unspoken but articulated in the dark realms of everything he'd ever felt or had known, that he'd ever experienced. And that had the power of a Bible. All up along the boulevard, people in open windows were waving American flags, Texas State flags. It was an awesome vision—the furling colors, the endless sky—that spoke of determination and destiny. A vision that he was fighting against.

What he could not see was what the people in the windows above the street could, and that drove their passion. One street over, horsemen were approaching the procession from both ends of Houston. They were coming on slowly, Indian file, and would converge at the corner. The riders had donned hoods painted white.

As the priest, followed by the hearse and the young women with placards, passed through the intersection, the horsemen snaked in alongside them. One group to the left of the funeral train, the other to the right. And they continued on at the same pace as the hearse, as if they were its knightly guard. It was a silent maneuver, and all the more threatening for its orchestrated simplicity.

Marisita saw fear and uncertainty spread across the ranks of the mourners. A fear she herself could not overcome. And that it aroused the passions of the people even more. This was their spit in the face to the funeral train, and no one need be enlightened to understand the monstrous face of it all.

The words were already alive in her head—the Whiteman was everyman, and the everyman who was everywhere.

John Lourdes shouldered through the crowd that was pressing out into the street to see better the terrible thing that might take place. One of the riders lifted an arm and shouted something he could not understand, and down through their ranks revolvers were drawn and there came this horrifying volley of gunfire that tore into the hearse.

The women behind the hearse were cut and scored by spears of lacquered wood and stars of glass. The undertaker leapt to the street as the riders made hell out of that death wagon. The priest had been trying to quell the riders, but he now saw the hearse horses wheel and turn back on each other, their eyes wild and teeth bared, and he tried for the leads to keep the hearse from charging forward recklessly.

All along Flores, people were scattering. There was a blind indifference to reality playing out. Half a dozen mourners rushed toward the hearse, John Lourdes among them. But they were too late. The riders had turned their mounts and fired one last volley at the ravaged wagon then went thundering up that long boulevard leaving behind long tails of smoke.

The horses lunged just as the men got there. The priest clung to the reins and was dragged from his feet. John Lourdes leapt up to the boxseat and got hold of the footbrake, but it was too late and too little. The horses were already racing through a sump right there in the roadway. The wheels spewing out grime. The priest went down and the horses stumbled over him. They skittered and tried to turn, and they clambered over each other, their necks stretching, their muscles bowed and the hearse railed right into them and lifted. The sheer weight of that wagon and caskets caused it to topple over. It came crashing down in that filthy rainwater and a casket came skidding out through broken glass and listing to one side, the top just damn opened. Right there in the middle of Flores Street. Water spilling in over the bodies. As disgraceful a baptism as ever there was one.

CHAPTER 11

MARISITA ROSE FROM THE FRENZY in the street all around her. Dazed and unsteady where she had been knocked over. She saw the priest had been unloosed from a tangle of horses and carried away alive. Her rage matched the fear she had been through. A fear for her life that made her feel ashamed that such fear could be alive within her. That it might somewhere compromise what was necessary and best.

Your voice must be able to withstand fatal choices—she'd told herself this over and over. But the body can't always live up to expectations of the deep mortal wish to do more.

She was trying to see and hear through the chaos. Where was her father?

Swimmy headed, a man's voice behind her. "Miss," he said. His hand touched her shoulder. She came about quickly, her senses still raw and on edge. She was staring. Angry, not knowing what to expect. "You're bleeding," he said. And the hand that he pointed with held a bandana.

She dabbed at the flesh just under her eye, where an arrow of glass had cut her, leaving teardrops of blood on her fingers. She took the bandana, and then there was her father pushing through mourners and she walked away from this kindness without even a thank you.

John Lourdes retreated from the street to the crowded sidewalk where he lit a cigarette and like everyone else along Flores, watched as they righted the hearse and got those muddied white horses in position to pull the casket, getting it closed and lifted with as much delicacy as was possible and carrying it to that ravaged death wagon, the casket dripping water from its damaged shell. It was a sight to make one ashamed at the depths humanity will sink to make a point.

From what he saw, Marisita Barros had gathered herself. She had finished talking with her father and was now in a more animated dialogue with the women she had walked with behind the hearse. And as they gathered up their placards, Marisita lifted the hem of her skirt and slogged through the water and touched the side of the caskets in passing and upon reaching the intersection she stopped and called out. But it was not to the mourners she was talking.

"Is this your idea of America? Did those flags you wave from your windows and on these street corners propagate this?"

She pointed with a bandana in hand given to her by a stranger toward that picture of a shot to hell hearse and four stained, filthy white horses being led out of the muck.

"Are the words compassion…equality…justice foreign to your aims and will? Is the good that is within you limited to your aims and will? Are we not Americans, too?"

At first, the people along the street were silent. John Lourdes thought she must have caught them off guard, unprepared for this verbal insurgency. Then he wondered—was it shame and not shock that kept them still?

"Have you forgotten this country was once in our hands and we did not treat you this way…Have you forgotten that before the railroads came we ushered you into our homes and our lives…Have you forgotten that it was us who helped you clear this brutal country of brush and creosote so you could farm…Have you forgotten that we picked your cotton and worked in your mines and herded your cattle and helped make you rich… Have you forgotten we helped you make your churches…Have you forgotten that we worship the same god—that we partake of the same host and wine—the same prayers and confession…Have you forgotten God's Ten Commandments…Thou shalt not kill…Have you forgotten?"

There was scattered applause and supportive cheering, but this only incited their antagonists and the caterwauls began in earnest, and the slurs, rising until a man finally yelled out, "Hey, Cinderella…Get the hell out of there and take your carriage with you." The floodgates of resentment poured forth after that.

But the girl was not done with her say. She was riding a wave of unstudied boldness wherever it would take her. "Have you forgotten," she said, "something known as the First Amendment…The freedom to speak your piece?"

"What do you think *we're* doing here, girl?"

Flags waved as howls went up. The Texas Rangers finally appeared on horseback. A half dozen armed Anglos. They rode among the mourners ordering the funeral train to move.

"You can't kill us away," she said, keeping on. "God will not allow it, even if it is your aim. You cannot humble us into submission, even if it is your intention. We have too much pride."

"What about the second amendment?" someone squealed out. "Don't forget that one."

A Ranger rode up to her and told her to move on. Her father had pressed through the crowd and made it to her side. John Lourdes watched as the peace officer edged his mount ever closer to father and daughter in a not so subtle statement of fact. And yet being forced back foot by foot, there was unfinished resolve to get off her chest.

"You cannot turn us into novelties," she said, "like we read about in your books and your magazine stories and your plays…the smarmy greaser desperado."

"If you don't move," said the Ranger, "you will be arrested."

Her father forced her now by physically pulling at her. And the girls she had walked with—they too circled around her, forcing her to move. But she still had ghosts inside her pressing their say.

"Look where we are," she said, pointing at the very intersection where they gathered, the bandana hanging from her outstretched fingers, blood trickling down her wounded cheek. "Flores Street goes in one direction, Houston the other. One is Mexican named, the other Anglo. You might say they are going in different directions today, but I prefer to see them coming together at this very place. But it's up to you what this place is."

The Rangers had gotten the cortege moving now. The horses pulling, water dripping from the hearse as it wheeled free of that sump.

John Lourdes saw, no one was listening to her now. Events were carrying the day. She was talking to the wind as she was herded along with the others like so many sheep.

CHAPTER 12

THE BARROS LIVED OFF OF ITURBIDE STREET in the Ranchero barrio. The offices and print shop of *La Cronica* fronted the street. The building was flat roofed and of quarried sandstone. Their front, too, was a flat wall, and there was but a door and a small handpainted sign that read *La Cronica*. The Barros' home was at the rear of the building where there was an adobe wall and a gate that opened to a small garden of olive trees and a Manzanita.

They were dropped off by car late that evening of the funeral. Once alone, and upon reaching the gate, Marisita said to her father, "You've been sullen toward me since this afternoon."

He did not answer.

She followed quietly through the darkened garden. The obedient daughter. He was a stocky shouldered gentleman in a fine suit with coarse grey hair, who refused to wear a moustache because he thought them classless and unfit for the modern world.

"You are still being sullen," she said, upon entering the house behind him. "Father?"

"Put up the lights," he said. "I'm going to the kitchen to make some coffee."

She did as she was requested.

Before going to the kitchen she stopped at a small mirror on the wall at the entry. The glow of the light alongside her face causing one side to be left in shadow. The light though on the cheek with the small cut, which she looked over and studied, moving her face slightly. A moment of pure vanity. It would leave no scar, she thought. It had stopped bleeding, but she licked the bandana and daubed at the spot with its dried blood. She then looked toward the kitchen. She knew why her father was sullen.

She joined her father in the kitchen.

"Father."

He had taken the coffee mill and a small pouch of beans and set them on the counter.

"I am not sullen," he said.

"No?"

He stood there hands fisted, knuckles pressing into the wooden countertop. "Sullen means bad tempered…gloomy…morose… sour."

"I was a teacher, Father, remember? I know what sullen means. I also know what it looks like and feels like."

"With all of that in your favor, maybe you should go back to being a teacher, because you are no journalist."

"You didn't think that this morning. Or yesterday. Or the day before yesterday for that matter."

"Yes, but this isn't this morning, is it? Or yesterday? Or the day before yesterday for that matter."

He stood there staring at the coffee mill and the beans, as if he had no idea what to do with them.

"Why don't you let me make the coffee?" she said, coming toward him. "It will free you up to be sullen."

"I don't want the coffee anymore. And your humor is just as unwelcome."

"Was I being humorous, Father?"

He got that dark and starchy expression that she knew so well. The one that said—silence is golden. He walked over to the cabinet where the whiskey was kept. He got out a bottle and a glass. He blew into the glass to get rid of any dust. He uncorked the bottle and he poured a little whiskey, then the hell with it, he thought, and he poured more. His daughter watched him fill the glass.

"You must be very sullen," she said.

"I am not sullen. I am angry."

"I see."

He took a small drink.

"What is the first responsibility of a journalist?" he said.

"The truth, Father."

"And what must a journalist be?"

"Honest, Father."

"What else?"

"Objective."

He repeated, "Objective."

This was dialogue that they had had many times.

"You failed that today," he said.

"Yes, Father. I know."

"You should."

"It doesn't please me to say it," she admitted. "But there it is."

"We were in that funeral procession to report on it. On what we saw, on what happened. The facts, the details. That was our job. You became the story. And that was not yours to become."

"I know that," she said, walking up beside him. To be close to him.

He cocked his head to one side. "How is your face? Where you were cut."

"It's nothing," she said, leaning in so he might have a better look.

"Nothing," he said. "Talk about shoddy, inaccurate journalism. It is everything."

He took a drink of whiskey. The tide of his anger was going out, but the tide that was coming in brought an all the more anxious state.

"I lost my way today, Father. Anger. Such anger took hold of me. I felt possessed. I was someone I did not seem to know. I wonder if, in this world, at this time, I am unfit to be a journalist. Or if not unfit, ill suited."

He took another drink. To hear this from one's own daughter. "Journalism is more than a profession. It is a discipline. It is a discipline built on traditions of discipline. It is like being a priest. But more demanding. For a priest can excuse himself from the world and still be a priest. There are no such excuses from a journalist."

He looked his daughter over now, as a father with the loves and terrors of any parent. She reached out toward the glass. "May I, Father?"

He let her take it from him. She sipped a little. She then handed back the glass.

"I'm not prepared to see you hurt," he said. "I am not prepared to see you killed."

"I am not preparing to be killed. And I want to apologize to you about today."

"Apology accepted...Reluctantly." He took another drink and stared into the near empty glass. "A parent expects their sons to have an experience like you did today. One expects their sons to do what you did today. Even bearing the consequences. But not a daughter. One is prepared with a son going forth, even when there is violence. But not a daughter."

"You sound suddenly so old fashioned, Father."

"It comes as a shock, let me tell you. Especially to a man who considers himself modern, if not postmodern. But...I'm sure I'll get over it. I'll evolve from the intricate dependencies of the past, as there is no such thing as settled law when it comes to the interpersonal lives of people."

"You know, Father," she said. "Where we are today is a lot of your own making."

He set the glass down and started for the door. A slow, deeply settled walk. "As we enter upon a new world order, let us not forget to pack the old clichés."

"It's true," she said. "You shouldn't have allowed me to be taught about anything more than the catechism and cooking."

"What is the old saying… 'How sweet the fruits of candor.' I'm going to bed."

Alone there, she looked at the glass of whiskey on the counter. A draught's worth left, which she finished.

"I'm sorry," she whispered. "I did not mean to fail you." What she'd said was not meant for him to hear. She went and turned off the light. She passed the small kitchen window on her way to the door. The moon upon the trees and the garden wall caught her eye.

"Father," she said with some urgency.

"What?"

"There is a man in the garden."

CHAPTER 13

SHE LEANED BACK AGAINST THE WALL where she could see out, but not be seen, her long boned hands pressed flat against her chest. Her father stood in the doorway and shut the light so the room behind him went dark. He came up beside his daughter and peered out. The garden was a blue landscape. And if you looked just right, she told her father, by the Manzanita there in the corner, was the figure of a man. A man watching.

His eyes were not as good as hers, so he could not be sure, but she was sure. That black cutout did not move, was still as the shadows it was part of, and this only frightened her all the more.

"Stay here," said her father, "and keep watching."

He left as stealthily as his blocky frame could manage, and when he returned, he was carrying a pistol. He opened the chamber to make sure it was loaded and the first cylinder clear.

She clasped the gun, "I don't think you should go out there."

"Neither do I," he whispered. "See where he is? That way I know which door to go out." He cocked the hammer.

She looked. The garden was like a piece of dark silk finery. She squinted. She moved just a bit to see if that might shift the shadows. He was gone. Like something that had been drawn in black smoke.

"He's gone," she whispered.

"Can it be?" said her father. "Look again."

She looked again. She scanned the garden. She tried to make out the man amidst the moonlit blackish shades.

Her voice shivered. "He's gone I tell you."

"No, he's not," came a voice from behind them.

A rush of fear from the girl's throat. Her father trained the gun on the doorway to the room from which he had just come.

"Don't fire that gun...for your own safety."

"If you come through that doorway, I will shoot."

"Listen...I am the man sent here by Father Pinto. My name is Lourdes...John Lourdes. There were men here before. That's why I was watching from the garden. I think you are in danger."

Marisita looked to her father. He was unsure.

"If I had meant to hurt you…I certainly had the chance."

"What do you want?" said Eduardo.

"Is there somewhere in the house we cannot be seen so we can talk in safety?"

After some consideration, Eduardo dropped the gun to his side and walked through the doorway, followed by his daughter.

John Lourdes had backed away. He was just a darkened outline, face-less. He was not holding a gun. He stood with hat in hand.

"Follow me," said Eduardo.

John Lourdes was led down a hallway in silence. Eduardo took an oil lamp from a table. He opened a door and John Lourdes followed him through. Once in the room, Eduardo held up the lamp.

"Do you have a light?"

John Lourdes got out a match which he lit with the flick of a thumb. The light bloomed from the lamp, and John Lourdes saw that he was in the *La Cronica* print shop. The windows were all shuttered.

"I have to keep the place locked up," said Senor Barros, "…political vandalism."

As he set the lamp on a worktable, Marisita said, "It's you."

John Lourdes turned to her. Once the light had fallen across his face, she had recognized him right away.

"The cut doesn't look too bad," he said, moving a finger across his own cheek.

"You know this man?"

"Yes, Father. He's the stranger who gave me the bandana."

"You were there today?" said Eduardo.

"I was, sir."

"He helped raise the hearse," said Marisita. "I did not thank you today…I'm sorry."

"Under the circumstances, you have no need to be."

"When did you arrive in Laredo?" said Eduardo.

"Yesterday."

"Why didn't you come to us then?"

John Lourdes felt the question carried with it more than a matter of pure curiosity.

"I needed to get my bearings, sir."

"You said you saw men outside," said Marisita.

"I was waiting for you both to get home and it was dark. I was across the street when I saw two men come in through the gate. They looked about for a while, then left. They didn't seem right."

"Were they Mexican?" said Eduardo.

"Anglo."

Marisita looked to her father. The three stood together over the lamp like conspirators plotting out the future.

"How do we proceed?" said Eduardo.

"There's a man I want to take me to the rally at Big Medicine."

"Doctor English," said Eduardo, "who prefers the Reign of Terror to the Age of Reason."

"This man," said Marisita. "Can he be trusted?"

"Trusted? He's not to be trusted...He's to be used."

"How old are you?" said Eduardo.

Marisita was privately displeased with this question and what it meant. Especially from what she had seen of this John Lourdes today.

"I'm twenty three, sir."

"You're awfully young."

"Father..."

"It's not meant as an insult. He understands."

"I did everything I could to make myself older, sir. But I just didn't have the time."

"We have to put our faith in you," said Eduardo. "Our faith and... our lives."

"It is the same for me...with you. May I smoke?"

She observed him with almost downcast eyes, so he would not notice her watching him. He took a pack of cigarettes from his vest pocket and struck a match on the side of the printing press. Through that long trail of smoke, he glanced at her for what was a moment. He was a year older than she. His dark straight hair hung down one side of his forehead, and he was clean shaven. He did look young. But there was an angularity to his face, a sharp geometry to the features that affected his expression and gave what he said an effortless authenticity.

"Mister Barros," he said "I'm the only person the Bureau felt they could send. The few agents in El Paso were all Anglo. And my commander wasn't sure if any were...racially or politically biased."

He took a moment and smoked. His features tightened. "When I say it out loud like that, it doesn't exactly inspire confidence, does it?"

"No, son, it doesn't," said Eduardo.

He inhaled again. He watched the smoke as he exhaled. He watched as it changed color through the light, then drifted away. "I'll try to lie better next time," he said.

Eduardo could not quite believe what he'd heard. For a moment there was what looked like to Marisita a sharp smile around the young man's mouth.

"You said you came down here yesterday?" said Marisita.

"Yes."

"You came by train?"

"Yes."

"Did you see the train that was attacked?"

"I was on that train."

This certainly got the attention of father and daughter.

"You saw what happened?" said Eduardo.

"More than saw, Senor Barros."

There were sounds suddenly outside. They quieted, they waited. Their attention on the heavily framed and bolted front door. Men's boots scraped along the stones that made up the walkway in front of the shop. Voices on the night, slight as the air itself. Then a bottle smashed, there was laughter.

"Civilization at work," whispered Eduardo as the voices faded away.

"In order to hunt out this…Whiteman…as they call him," said John Lourdes, in a hushed voice. "I'll want you to get a list together. Ranchers, businessmen, anyone who's been threatened, intimidated, asked to sell out. And if there's someone who's had a confrontation with this gent, who can inform me. So I can try to piece together who he is, discover his identity."

"What about the funeral?" said Marisita. "He must have been among the riders today."

"Maybe."

"What makes you suggest that?"

He studied the tip of his burning cigarette. "I overheard my father once talking about men like this. 'The best,' he said, 'walk alone, wherever they can.'"

"I'll put the list together," said Eduardo. "But what if it gets you nothing? What then?"

John Lourdes blew ash from the tip of his cigarette. He stood there thoughtfully. "I go about the business of trying to draw him out."

"How do you do that?" said Eduardo.

"Well, sir…I start killing folks."

• • •

She could not sleep. She kept thinking of him as she lay there in bed, seeing his face where the soft glimmer of lamplight fell away into shadow. He seemed in possession of some dark presence born of the stony fastness of the world. You might not suspect it from his demeanor, or boyish good will. And it gave her pause even as it reached down inside her.

She sat up and looked out the window where the moon resided above the tips of the trees. She could feel the blood running through her body, and it frightened her. She was tense and alive as she listened to her own breathing, because she knew without recourse that today had changed the path of her life.

She rose and put on a robe. She was going down to the kitchen when she noted the burning light around the edges of the door to the print shop.

There her father was sitting at his rolltop by the press, sleeves up, hunched over, and writing with his usual blind determination. When he finally looked up, he was surprised to see his daughter there. How long had she been watching him he had no idea, nor did he care to ask. "I'm putting together the list…and my thoughts."

"I'd like to write an editorial, Father. It will be about how I failed today at the funeral as a reporter, but succeeded, I believe, as a social and political human being."

He sat back. He rubbed at his tired and somewhat surly looking face. "As your father, I am against it. For reasons which I am sure you can appreciate. But as senior editor of this paper, I encourage you to write it."

She crossed her arms and leaned against the doorframe. "Father… what do you think of this John Lourdes?"

He raised a hand demonstratively. "El nigrita en al arroz."

She understood…The black in the rice…the person who is a discomfort and hindrance, who is bothersome, who finds the bad in things, the unpleasant, the serious.

"Do you think that unfair? If not inaccurate, father?"

"It is fair and accurate if he is the black in the rice to whom he has brought about their downfall. If he fails, he will be the black in the rice at our death."

DEAD RATTLESNAKES

CHAPTER 14

EMMANUEL VARGAS WAS CONSIDERED A SUCCESSFUL MAN and one, he believed, to be envied. After all, he had three of the Riddle Company's finest glass and leather hearses, though one was in dire need of repair.

Vargas had started out as many funeral entrepreneurs of the time did—he was a carpenter. He saw this was a limited profession except in the case of Jesus Christ, as he sometimes joked, so he learned embalming and the burial business, and with the money he saved over the years—he was well known as a penurious bastard—he opened the Heaven's Door Funeral Home.

He'd established this business in the Ranchero barrio, being Mexican himself, and offered quality funerals that were sensitive to the social and religious needs of his people. The truth being unknown at the time, Emmanuel Vargas was not Mexican at all, and had only donned this ruse to take advantage of the people of the barrio. This would only come to light after his untimely death. But funerals were not where he made most of his profit, for he had another talent.

He was a photographer and a rather fine one when it came to the art of postmortem imagery. This is where he charged premiums to the Mexicans for whom he provided funeral services. After all, the postmortem photograph was quite often the only commemorative the family had of a deceased loved one. And the walls of his studio were lined with these remembered dead, courtesy of a virtuoso craftsman.

But this night, there would be a different kind of a picture taken altogether. Vargas lived alone in a well-appointed house within sight of the river. The house also served as his photographic studio. He disliked children most vehemently, and not liking them he certainly did not need a wife, since wives always want children. So he was content in his selfishness to live alone. And as dreadful and costly as the day had been, besides the fear he'd lived through for his own survival, he'd managed a much deserved sleep.

But sometime in the middle of the night, he awoke to an invasive light bearing down upon his eyes. Something behind the light approximated an apparition and a voice coming from it said, "Call out…Shout…Make a sound…And you will face a well-documented wrath."

Vargas covered his eyes. "What do you want here? Money? I don't keep money—"

"Your presence is requested downstairs in your studio."

"What?"

He was grabbed by his shirt front and forcibly lifted.

"Get up."

"Who are you?"

Vargas saw there were three lights, handheld lights now arcing about his room as the men moved. They were miner's flashlights, Vargas could see that, and the men themselves were hooded.

One of them, the one who had spoken before, held the Eveready beneath his chin. The light cast upward, and a huge shadow of the man rose up the wall and along the ceiling, and Vargas could well see that his hood was painted white and streaked with black stains that Vargas could not know were the spattered ink from the Santo Tomas murders. "Do you know who I am now?" he said.

"I do, yes," said Vargas.

He was steered toward the bedroom door. One man walked before him as he was marched down the hall, then as he was descending the stairs, he said plaintively, "What do you want of me?"

"What does anyone want in a photographic studio…but a photograph."

A light switched on. What had been a drawing room was now his studio. The front curtains were drawn tight so no one could see in. This had been done before they roused Vargas from his well deserved sleep. On one wall hung a decorative backdrop. And there was a table with cameras—a wood plate camera, a bellows, a box camera, a Kodak. There were tripods.

"We don't have 'God's light,'" said the Whiteman, "meaning, of course, the sun, but these will do nicely." He held up a mercury vapor lamp. "I'm somewhat of a photographer myself. And I am considered a rather good one."

Vargas had been watching one of the men. He was carrying a canvas sack. And God knows what for, or what was in it. The Whiteman ordered Vargas to strip down to the flesh.

Vargas stood there not believing, not willing to believe. "If it's about today…I was just hired to perform a funeral service. I had no idea those people meant to turn it into a political—"

"Strip, you bastard."

Vargas slipped off his shirt, bent and clumsy. He unloosed his drawers and they fell about his bare feet. He stepped out of them and back onto the cold wood floor. Fear had him righteously about the throat, and shaking he pressed his hands together to try and make it stop.

The Whiteman pointed to a beautiful highbacked cloth chair and asked one of his men to place it in front of the decorative cloth that hung down from the ceiling. "You," he said to Vargas, "go sit in the chair."

As the Whiteman looked over the cameras, Vargas did as he was told. He sat there, eyes downcast, staring at his shriveled manhood.

"I'll get enough light with vapor lamps. But…what camera would you suggest I use?"

"I'm not even Mexican," said Vargas.

"I thought you were."

"That was strictly a business move. I have no connection to those people. I just saw a chance to make money. You know people prefer to go to their own."

"I don't think people will believe you're not Mexican. Do you, Senor Vargas? I certainly don't. I think I'll use the wood plate camera."

He set the tripod up where he thought to take the photograph. As he crossed the room, Vargas said, "But I'm *not* Mexican."

The man tucked the wood plate camera under his arm and carried it back across the room and bolted it to the tripod. "One should never deny one's race or heritage. Where that is concerned, one should stand fast. After all, if you're going to be hated, you might as well take honor in being hated."

He looked through the lens. Studied the setting. Considered it artistically. "Of course, that won't change the fact of your being hated. Or because the reasons for being hated are real and true and earnest. A thing damned, is a thing damned."

He went to the corner of the room where there was a small end table. He lifted it and brought it to where Vargas sat and placed the table snugly by the chair. "You're shivering, Senor Vargas. There is no need. It's only a photograph." He then turned to the man with the canvas sack. "Put the skull right here on the table."

Vargas pressed back in the chair as the man came forward. He could feel the sweat accumulating around his groin.

"And besides," said the Whiteman, "who would pretend to be Mexican, if he were not? No matter what the money, who would degrade himself that way?"

The man opened the sack and from it took a human skull. Vargas watched it pass before his eyes, all white and shiny with its huge teeth. The Whiteman set it on the table, turning it, so it looked at Vargas.

He went back to the camera and peered through the lens. "Yes," he said, "this is showing promise."

He stepped back from the lens and slipped his hands into his pockets. He walked over to the wall with its tiers of postmortem prints.

"I looked at these before we came upstairs. And there is one in particular…" Where he stopped, he pointed.

It was a portrait of two young Mexican sisters, maidens, sitting in the spring grass above the banks of the Rio Grande. The sun on the river all glorious sparkle and upon their loose black hair, no less so. They sat side by side, these lovely young creatures. Each in the same lovely light patterned dress. One was living, the other dead.

"This photograph. This is Mexico," he said. "This is the Mexican…the Mexican people. They are sisters, yes? They look so much alike."

Vargas nodded that they were, indeed, sisters.

"Did you know when you created this, what you were saying? Did you mean to give it meaning?"

Vargas shook his head no.

"It just came out of you?"

"I guess," said Vargas.

"That's art," he said to the two men with him. "Pure art. I am envious, Senor Vargas. And I don't feel envy often."

Vargas watched the man just stare right into him. The eyes within the hood tight and flat, and the cloth moving slightly with each breath like some bloodless ink stained lung.

"Life blinds us with surprise, doesn't it, Senor Vargas?"

"I don't know what you mean," said Vargas.

"I would never have guessed what you've done possible from a Mexican."

"I'm not a Mexican. I swear it."

"You can fill the cup with sunlight but there's nothing there to drink." He looked to the man carrying the canvas sack. "Get out the rattlesnake."

CHAPTER 15

HE WATCHED THE HOUSE FROM A FILTHY ALLEYWAY like some conspirator, on the chance the men returned. It was past the witching hour, the clouds had settled in. There wasn't much but lonely drunks now and then making their solemn way back to wherever it was they came from, until he heard the rattling of a car motor. The vehicle came on and slowed as it passed the garden wall. His hand slipped down to the automatic he had tucked under his vest. There were two men. Anglos from the looks of them. They cruised around the corner and he heard that troubled gearbox shifting as the engine faded off into the night. The men he couldn't recognize, but that beat up Ford was another matter altogether.

The next morning John Lourdes left a letter at General Delivery for Cager Adams, letting him know he was staying at the Hamilton Hotel. Then he was to meet with Senor Barros at a Mexican food market by the bridge that crossed the river to Nuevo Leon where he would be given the list he requested. He sat at a quiet table with his hat pulled down low, drank coffee, and read Marisita's editorial which was titled: *The Confession of a Failure.*

She opened the editorial with an apology to the reader for her lack of journalistic discipline when it came to the funeral procession the day before. There was an astonishing fatalism to her asking forgiveness for becoming part of the story, for in doing so, she wrote, she had failed her first and foremost duty—objectivity.

She'd worded her emotions with cool dispatch, detailing the horror and tragedy without outrage or surprise. As for John Lourdes, this young woman had seemed so conventional, almost unadventurous, yet her descriptions of violence and inhumanity were fired with a fury that matched her actions on the street the day before. This Marisita Barros seemed, he thought, to be pulled in opposing directions at one time. And how did he assume that? It was a flaw, conflict, war, however you name it, that he carried around inside him every day, like a heart, or a pair of lungs.

"I have the list."

He looked up from the newspaper. It was not Eduardo Barros standing before him, but his daughter. He could not conceal his expression, and she said, "How should I take that look of surprise?"

"I was just—"

He held up the newspaper with her editorial.

She said, "My father couldn't make it. So he sent me." Which was not quite the truth. "Take a walk with me, will you?"

He folded the newspaper and got up and followed her. They walked over to Convent Street and the foot bridge there that crossed the river to Nuevo Leon. It was a wide plank affair with girder trusses that rested on stone pilings, and when trucks crossed the heavy boarding shuddered.

Before the chaos, it had been a more quiet, lazy bridge. But now families were leaving America because of the racism and threats, the loss of work, of being unable to work. Yet here came more families from a desperate Mexico, more single men trying to escape hopelessness, even parentless children, fleeing oppression from the totalitarian regime south of the Rio Grande. The world of people was trading one uncertainty for another, which shows you how far blood goes to beg the question.

"The world doesn't understand itself," she said, looking out upon the footbridge. "It doesn't know how to reflect. It lacks the quality of introspection. Its spirit is wearing out in one direction while it runs too hot in the other." She handed him the list. "And you?" she said. "How did you become what you are?"

"You mean by profession?"

"However you care to answer."

He unfolded the sheaves of paper. Her father had clear, plain penmanship. He glanced over the pages. "How did you?" he said.

"I was the determined child who did not fit into the plans of a determined father."

Looking up, he said, "You mean he wanted a son to carry on the tradition."

"Don't you all?"

She pointed toward the bridge. "That bridge is one of the most important places in my life. The border agent shack…I was in Mexico teaching for the summer at a convent school. My mother had taken ill, and I was called back home. When I saw my father standing by that building waiting for me, I knew. I felt him crying before I saw him crying. It was my mother who made him promise to give me the opportunity. Educate a woman…

and you teach a family…and so on and so forth."

He had watched her as she spoke, as a man will watch a woman, and she knew this and let it be. She found herself wanting him to watch her. It made her feel intimate and alive, and it didn't come as a surprise but more as a natural progression of what she'd felt the night before lying sleepless in bed.

He was lighting a cigarette when she turned to him and said, "So… How did you become what you are?"

He blew out the match. His answer was short and precise. "Hate," he said.

"Hate is a powerful emotion," she said. "And, of course, it has rules of its own."

"You wanted to have this talk because your father doesn't have faith in me. Doesn't really trust me."

"I saw you watched the house after you left us. As for my father… He believes that even God needs to be carefully watched by a good newspaperman."

CHAPTER 16

By noon the murder of Emmanuel Vargas had become the foremost news of the day. The *Laredo Weekly Times* had been secreted a photographic negative. And now copies of that original were hung by fine thread across the newspaper office windows for all in the street to see.

There was the funeral home director in death, sitting in the chair, his lifeless eyes staring. And a rattlesnake, coiled up in his naked lap, it too dead, its mouth propped open in that undeniable pose of readiness to strike. On the table beside the chair, the skull, and next to the skull a canvas hood with an empty set of eyes.

The sidewalk around the windows was mobbed with people trying to get up close to this grisly and obscene picture. Paperboys could not sell extras in the street fast enough. It went on like this all day. And somewhere along the way, men arrived and passed out fliers for the "Society," making their pitch for the hearts and minds of the people.

There were fights, and there were arrests, and they were as prompt as a coming dawn.

• • •

John Lourdes had weapons sent by train through Wadsworth Burr. His Winchester semi-automatic rifle, and a pump action trench gun with a sawed down barrel. On his way back from the baggage depot with the weapons in their carryalls slung over a shoulder he got wind of the circus going on over at the *Laredo Weekly Times*. He went to see the madness for himself. The Whiteman was the darkness come to life, no question about it. Even John Lourdes' own father, he thought, paled compared to this.

He sat in the hotel lobby like some real gent reading business reports as he went through Barros' notes, marking on a map the ranches where the haciendas had been warned, intimidated, threatened. A map he'd detailed before leaving El Paso with known and rumored crossing sites for drugs and contraband. Places where the Rangers and the private guards for Big Medicine patrolled. And these places, rough and barren where you sometimes found the wreckage of a wagon or scattered human bones, were not the place to come upon them. 'Cause being innocent was no better than being Mexican, or black for that matter, let alone guilty.

John Lourdes had coffee and watched the comings and goings in the lobby. There was a smoker where men drank and played cards or grouped together on comfortable couches and preened over their achievements. Most of the housekeeping staff was Mexican. Some, like the porter who had been to his room, had been relegated to this job when their previous lives were taken from them.

John Lourdes wasn't killing time, he was sizing up the porter to see about eliciting his services in taking down the Whiteman.

What had convinced him of the porter—an incident that occurred when he'd brought a couple of flush businessmen the liquors they'd ordered. One of them showed this Manuel Aguirre a newspaper. It seems the Schlitz Beer Company out of Milwaukee was getting ready to produce beer in amber colored bottles. They'd discovered that the darker bottle was superior to a clear bottle in keeping beer right. And they wondered what the porter thought of it. Amber being superior.

It was a bait and insult question. Whatever direction you go in, you open yourself to a racial body punch. So the porter did what John Lourdes had seen his own mother do, what he had been forced to do, what Mexicans were now having to do, what blacks had been doing for centuries to survive—deflect. Deflecting was a way to keep your manhood or womanhood and to keep a little shine on your personal dignity. The porter told them he thought the article fascinating and he thanked them for elucidating him on the subject. He actually used the word "elucidate." As he walked away, John Lourdes caught the older gent's expression. The look said Senor Aguirre might shit in the next order of hors d'ouevres.

Later, the porter brought John Lourdes whiskey and the newspaper. Entering the suite, he noticed the rifles laid out on the bed. They were neither in their scabbards, or carryalls. These were not sportsman's weapons, or those of the casual hunter. These were killing weapons and the expression on the porter's face said as much. John Lourdes was sitting in a chair and had an open envelope in hand.

In Spanish he said, "Senor Aguirre…Question…I need to find a livery out of town. Or a horse dealer. The mount must not be able to be tracked back to the seller, as I may lose a horse, or two. It would be best if the seller were not Anglo…But rather, amber colored. If you get my meaning."

The porter's expression filled.

"There will be risk," said John Lourdes.

He tossed the envelope on to the bed. A packet of bills partly showed itself.

"And from where does this risk come?" said Aguirre, stepping toward the bed.

"'The Society'…Big Medicine."

Aguirre took the envelope without even looking to see how much was there.

John Lourdes had not spoken to the Barros of this. His lie of omission was in part a matter of trust, but also, he did not want to put them, particularly her, at deeper risk. He did not want to exploit their vulnerability, unless absolutely necessary.

Sometimes a lie is the best measure of honesty.

CHAPTER 17

IT WAS THE THIRD NIGHT OUT ALONG THE RIO GRANDE that he came upon a gunfight. He could see down through a long trace of desert, bordered by jagged hills, the violent blaze of gunfire. He was so far yet from the scene he could not hear the report of the weapons, but he turned his mount and proceeded with haste toward the blue and white flashes that appeared and then disappeared like the cannons of lightning.

The first two days and nights he had followed a trail of haciendas and river crossings from burning daylight to pale evening. He'd followed men from Big Medicine as they patrolled the border. He spied with field glasses from cliff perches as they chased down immigrants, herding them back across the river in panic, firing into their fleeing shadows. He lived by cold camp and burro paths. He tried to remain invisible upon the landscape. The vista snaking elusively from sunless hillsides to dried out ravines. He would bring his mount flat to the ground and lie behind it, watching the dust of distant horsemen upon the desert floor djinn, then die.

But it was the Texas Rangers that evoked the most fear. They moved in small teams of two's and three's, and they didn't measure the law they meted out. They ruled in the terrible name of race and attitude. Not all— but many. They'd stop at ranches and often browbeat the tenant or jefe. They'd search the residence, question the workers over their citizenship. Intimidation was their stock and trade.

John Lourdes would creep about their nightcamps and listen to their boasts and travails, hoping for a lead on the Whiteman in a loose word. For a tell, a confession, a mistake, anything he could exploit to extort further information.

Then circumstances stepped in. He caught sight of headlights moving through dunes of sand along the river. A man came out of the high cane to wave the vehicle down. Two boxes of crates were labored into the back seat of what was a beat up Cadillac. The driver was black.

John Lourdes pushed his mount hard, chasing headlights through rugged brush and starlight. The Cadillac entered the gate of a walled hacienda. He scrabbled his way amid parched brambles and flowering yucca where he could see the black sitting at a table with a Mexican on a torch lit portico. John Lourdes had been weaned on this kind of suspect activity in El Paso, and it spoke of opium or morphine.

Not much later, riders appeared in the moonlight. He couldn't make out their faces, but they turned out to be Rangers from what John Lourdes could hear. Laughing and drinking together at that table, they were a motley crew of confederates, all right, proving the power of money trumps the politics of race. This was the first action that might lend itself to exploit in his hunt for the Whiteman.

That was until the evening of the gunfight.

A wagon road led down through a wilderness where he watched the blackened ridges flare from pistol fire. Pistols he could hear now echoing up through the folds of that canyon. He slipped the rifle from its scabbard and rested it across the saddle, and he leaned down low against the horse's withers.

Almost a half mile farther on, he could see the huge blue and white blasts of the gunfight. He led his horse into the brush and tied him off. Then he started down the road with his rifle.

He could make out the low roof of a scrapwood ranch house stenciled against the hillface. There was a corral with horses gone wild, pressing against the fenceposts in panic, trying to escape, their whinnying desperate. It looked to be a single firearm in the house, and at least two—no three— men with weapons assaulting the shelter from a triangle of directions.

John Lourdes could hear the men outside were Rangers, as they were ordering whoever was in that ranch house to "surrender to arrest." A scraggly, awful voice came back in Spanish calling them "scum 'Rinches...'" and "I have no intention of letting you run me off my own ranch no matter how piss poor it is..."

The firing kicked up again. There was a fierce volley from the firing Rangers. Big old blasts of white in the darkness. Puffs of grey smoke where the shells hit the skin of that shack. Whoever the character was inside had some real sand but was in dire straits, all right. And then that voice again, "I don't intend to be 'evaporated' by some Anglo trash. So why don't you boys come out and charge this place and let's have at it."

"You don't come out," shouted one of the Rangers, "we'll cook your ass in there."

"What? I can't hear you. I had my head up between your mother's legs."

Well, there wasn't talk after that. John Lourdes could see something was hurled in the air with a streak of fire attached to it. What sounded like glass shattered on the roof. He figured it was a bottle with kerosene or naphtha and a lit cloth as a fuse.

The roof must have had a lot of thatch in it to patch up any leaks because there was a wave of sparks that tindered right up. Long spidery flues of fire with the wind causing the flames to snap and yaw, and there was burning ash raining down on that strip of homestead and on the horses in the corral. They cried out and shook their heads and, in their madness, they tried to leap the fence, driving right through the holding posts. The smoke was getting awful, and the dust kicked up by the hooves of those escaping horses painted everything with a grim mist.

The ranch house door swung open and a choking figure stumbled out into the front yard and fell to its knees holding a wounded arm with the gun hand of the other arm. The Rangers approached the downed rancher from three angles. They were in no hurry now that they had their quarry down.

The fire was consuming the ranch house, and it was hard to hear over the crackling slatboards.

"You might as well shoot me, you 'Rinche' fools. I'm out of ammo."

"We're not gonna shoot you…We're gonna hang you."

No sooner were the words out of his mouth than he was shot. He grabbed at his side and went reeling backward and hit the ground gasping. The other two Rangers had no idea who had fired down on them and they tried to escape the attack like wild dogs, scattering, wheeling about and shooting aimlessly into the haze.

They were killed like meat. Shot down in the choking dust. Extinguished from this life without so much as a handshake.

John Lourdes came walking out of the grey and burning air. An apparition wearing bad intent. A bandana covered his face to keep the choking ash at bay. His eyes exposed, he looked about to see if anyone was left to return fire.

He stood over the wounded Ranger and kicked away his pistol that lay there in the sand. Blood seeped over the man's gold front teeth and out his mouth.

John Lourdes turned to the rancher who now stood cradling a wounded arm. "Whoever you are," the rancher said, "I thank the Virgin Mother for you."

It shocked him plenty to see it wasn't a man. But a tight faced rooster of a woman with long grey ratty hair and leathered flesh.

"You're a woman," said John Lourdes.

"You figured that out all by yourself, did you? And just by lookin' at me. Will wonders ever cease?"

She pocketed her revolver. She had a small ax in a belt strap which she grasped in her good hand. She went to lean over the wounded man.

John Lourdes took hold of her. "What are you gonna do?"

"I'm gonna chop his fuckin' head off once you give me the road."

He kept her back.

"Those 'Rinches,'" she said. "First, they put a lawyer on me, disputing my deed. Then they got me going broke hiring attorneys. So I fall arrears in my taxes. Then they send these. It's the Anglo game...to whiten up the Rio Grande Valley."

The house was pretty much consumed by then. The flames high above them. A pulsing color against the sky. Ash falling everywhere. The 'snowfall of hell' is what he remembered his father once calling it.

He leaned over the Ranger. "What do you know about the Whiteman? Who is he?"

The wounded man managed a few words through a grimace. "No one knows him, you fool."

"He had two men with him in Santo Tomas. Someone knows him."

"He's gonna be at the rally at Big Medicine," said the woman. "Every halfwit knows that."

"Be quiet," he told the woman. Then he grabbed the Ranger by the shirt front. "God help you if you don't answer."

As much pain as he was in, and all that he saw in the expression of that desert crone with her rotted teeth exposed, he spit in John Lourdes' face. "Lick that up, greaser."

He ripped the badge from the Ranger's vest. He then walked over to the other two dead men and tore loose their badges. He pocketed all three. He looked at the woman. "We're gonna have to bury all three of them. Where they can't be found."

She had covered her mouth and nose with her bloodied arm. She nodded.

"I'll go down the road and get my horse. I'll leave him to you."

CHAPTER 18

"WE ARE IN DANGEROUS TIMES, but all times are dangerous, aren't they," said Marisita. "As long as someone is in danger of losing their rights, of losing their place, being stripped of their dignity, livelihood, or of life itself. There is cause for concern, and so cause for action. And we, as *Mexican-Americans*, must rise to the challenge of such concerns."

There were about thirty or so women gathered in the garden behind the *La Cronica* offices. They sat in rows of chairs with cups in their laps and change on their minds. They were there to keep developing an idea they had—*La Liga Femenil*—A Womans League.

"And before I hand this moment to the next speaker," said Marisita, "I would like to close with one thought. To quote our dear friend and mentor Father Pinto... 'Even the well intentioned man needs to pay attention to what goes on around him!' Of course, now we need to expand that statement to include women."

There was polite applause, and then one lady among them expressed her own thought. "I can quote plenty of other statements, Bible and verse, that are in just as bad need of adapting. And I'll bet I'm not the only one here who can." Thanks to the bite in how she said it, this got a much more heady round of applause.

The ladies went on to discuss their blueprint for the league. The aims were simple enough. The first was to establish education for the poor and getting them into as many free schools as they could. To have food and clothes drives for the needy, create a nursing school for women using the steadfast idea that had been preached repeatedly in *La Cronica*—Educate a woman, teach a family. This would all be financed through private charities and fund raisers that sponsored auctions, concerts, book readings, and plays. Someone suggested putting on *The Wizard of Oz*, as the play had been a huge success and there was a motion picture coming out.

While the women moved about the garden in small packs of earnestness, there came a sudden blast that sounded like a shotgun firing. It caused a severe and stark silence among the ladies, and a moment of well-honed fear. Then a truck carrying junk came rattling around the corner backfiring as it left blooms of exhaust down the street.

The moment passed and Marisita said, "I'll bet we were all thinking the same thing."

She did not see John Lourdes watching her in the garden that afternoon. There had been rising threats of violence that week along the Rio Grande, and the fact that three Texas Rangers were missing, and presumed dead, had become the source of endless headlines and hideous conjecture.

She had walked to the Hamilton Hotel. She knew his room from what he'd told her. She could not shake the need to watch that shut veranda door with its shades drawn, but she walked home like some woman condemned to uncertainty.

Her father had noted her continual state of preoccupation and how she was suddenly prone to sleeplessness. To her father, John Lourdes was the shadow moving across the page of all the hopes and aspirations he had for his daughter.

• • •

The filtered light through the garden trees fell upon her white dress, her skin and hair all the darker for it. Surely the youngest woman there. A breath of good will among all that civilized determination. That was the way life was supposed to be. Long on heart, short on hatred.

From where he was concealed, John Lourdes could hear the women of La Liga using a term: Mexican-American. He'd never heard it used, had seen it for the first time in the editorial *La Cronica* published when Marisita was writing about the funeral. The term was meant to bring together all factions of Mexican—liberal, conservative, those for the revolution in Mexico and those against, the rich, the well-to-do, the poor, the immigrant, the illegal—to not only give them social and political power, but more importantly, a sense of identity. The value of culture, of history, of faith. A oneness. All of which, she had written, were being stripped away in this new world order.

A terrible loneliness fell over him that was too powerful to cast off. The longing for a life lost to him after his mother's death. When his own existence became the streets of survival where culture, history, faith meant little. Where he was a terminal outsider held together by a string of memories.

He should do what he came here to do and be done with it. To do otherwise was to be otherwise and what would come of it? He should stay away from all this because it would get into his heart and hurt him. So he left.

But he came back that night when the moon was upon the branches and the whitewashed adobe walls, and the crickets everywhere about the darkness. He picked up a tiny stone and tossed it at a candled upper window.

It tinged against the glass and soon a shadow passed, and her face appeared, peering out, unsure. Then her hand went up, fingers spread apart, and she disappeared.

He waited in the cold night air keeping to the dark side of the wall for the door to open. She was barefoot, her hair hanging loose about the shoulders of a sleeping gown, a candle held up high.

"You're all right." She led him inside and followed the light to the kitchen. "I've been so worried," she said.

"Have you?"

"Yes," she said.

He took off his hat. She set the candle down on the kitchen table and they whispered.

"I didn't mean to make you worry."

"It's been over a week."

"And I didn't want to come so late, but—"

"I understand."

"Do you?"

"For safety."

"That too."

What did he mean? She asked. He had no answer but a slight shifting of the head, as if it were not nothing. But she had a feeling, there was more.

"Have you seen the papers?" she said.

"No."

"You've heard about the three Rangers."

"More than heard," he said.

"I don't understand."

He slumped down into a chair at the kitchen table. "Could I have a drink? Whiskey...wine...anything."

She went to the cabinet where her father kept his whiskey and she took out a bottle and a glass and she blew into the glass to clear it of any dust. She set the glass before him and she poured, and she set the bottle down. She let her hand remain there close to his. He wanted to touch her, she saw that. Sensed it. She wanted him to touch her.

"I didn't know it would be so hard," he said.

"What?"

"I'm going to set something in motion that I hope…believe…will work in my favor. You must not be involved. Your father must not be involved."

He took the glass and drank.

"We are," she said, "and were, even before you."

He drank again.

"I was here today," he said.

"What?"

"Today."

"When?"

"You and the ladies," he said, pointing the glass toward the garden. "La Liga Femenil."

"Why didn't you—"

"You looked beautiful today," he said.

She was suddenly embarrassed, but very pleased.

"After my mother died," he said. "I grew up alone. I was twelve and living on the roof of a factory that made American flags. My mother had been a seamstress in that factory."

She did not wait. There was no point. She took his hand and then she slipped down into the chair next to his. And she did it with an impassioned simplicity.

"My father was an assassin," he said. "And a rather notorious one. He was Anglo. And I am the one who brought him to his death. The BOI doesn't know he was my father. You see…I had changed my name as a boy. I know about killing. I know what it begets, and I have lived it."

She hurt high up in her throat. The light measured the space between them. She bowed her head a bit and her raven hair fell across her face as she studied him. Like a painting, he thought, like a painting.

"Do you think you can redeem your memories?" he said.

"I don't know, John."

"I have something to show you."

Her head rose as he reached into his vest pocket and then he set on the table in the light three, star in the wheel, Texas Ranger badges.

CHAPTER 19

AFTER HE WAS GONE, Marisita took the candle and started back to the stairs and who should be in the dark there leaning against the railing?

"Father...you frightened me."

"Life around here seems to have taken a radical turn."

He walked to her and he took the candle and he went back to the kitchen and she knew to follow, that from his tone there was discontent.

"He just showed up, Father. It's been a week. He wanted us to know he was—"

"Us."

"...all right."

"And you didn't come and get me?"

He set the candle down on the table and surveyed the room.

"You were asleep, Father."

"You could have woken me."

"I thought...whatever he told me I could tell you myself."

He saw a used glass on the counter.

"Do you think..." he waved a hand over her attire, as if to remark "... this is appropriate?"

"I didn't think about it, under the circumstances."

"So...the hell with decorum...or class?"

"Urgency took priority."

"Don't you think that's rather disingenuous?"

"If you don't mind, Father, I don't appreciate how you said that."

He took up the glass, smelled. Knew it was whiskey, but just wanted to be sure. He set the glass down. "You were whispering for quite some time."

"So we didn't wake you, Father. But it turns out you were awake."

He got out a clean glass and blew into it to rid it of any dust. And then he looked at the whiskey bottle as if to see how much John drank. He then poured himself a glass. She, watching all the while, knew she had been and was being slightly disingenuous. For her own sake, and wellbeing.

"Why didn't you come into the kitchen?" she said.

He drank.

"It's not like you to be so…indirect," she said.

"I?" He shook his head. "The reporter in me says it's you who's being so indirect."

"Please say exactly what you mean, so I can answer accordingly. One reporter to another."

He emptied the glass then politely slammed it down on the table. "I mean you intentionally, and with forethought, allowed yourself to be dressed like that when he—"

"Father. I am twenty-two."

"Which means you are old enough to know better, and wise enough to admit better."

"I didn't think of it, Father. But if I had, I believe I would have done exactly what has you so angry."

"He didn't come here to just see this through."

"Here? You mean Laredo? Or this house?"

"They end up being the same thing. As they ultimately stand for and effect the same thing."

"Do they?"

"I understand that someday you will meet someone and there will be the overpowering urge that goes with it. Those emotions are not lost on me, or to me. I don't begrudge you your happiness, or your own woman-hood. But I believe I know this man—"

"Like you know me?"

"Now you're being coy…or at least clever."

Her back stiffened. She crossed her arms. "And where did I learn such things, Father?" I did not sprout from the ground fully formed, did I? I grew up in the shadow of a tree with long branches. But my branches must find their way to sunlight."

He saw this would go on and on. "What did he say that you did not see fit to wake me up for?"

"He has a plan to draw out this—"

"Which he discussed with you?"

"For our safety, he did not."

"I believe this Mister Lourdes has more trust in you, than he does in me. And that you have more in him, than you do in your own father."

She turned and started for the door. "We don't need more conflict, do we, Father?"

"Mexican-American," he said.

She stopped in the doorway. "Father?"

"Do you know why that term is so important?"

"I know what you know, since we talk about it all the time. And are of the same heart when it comes to that. Your point, Father?"

He held the candle close. She could feel the heat coming off it. "He is outside of us. He is…beneath us."

"Do you know…what you are saying?"

"It's not being racist. It's being honest."

He blew out the light.

CHAPTER 20

JOHN LOURDES RODE TO THE OUTSKIRTS OF THE CITY and dismounted. He walked a blue luminous landscape with an Eveready, scanning the rocks with his light where a rattler might lie in wait. He was alone in the pitched and crazy emptiness like a thing of stealth, coming upon tiny pyres of bone, turning boulders over, prodding loose wedges of stone upon the earth, exposing hidden crevices until he came upon a silent, coiled viper.

He put the light between his teeth. He removed a knife from a sheath belt and took off his Fedora. He knelt over the snake whose head now followed the heat of a living thing closing in.

They were eye to eye in a moment as old as time itself, and from the ranks of our bloody history. He began moving his arm side to side slowly, slowly, easing his hat closer and then the snake struck and when he felt the fangs hit the crown of that Fedora, he pithed the skull of that reptile with the edge of the blade in one swift and facile motion.

It was an old trick, for sure. And one that he had learned from the assassin who'd birthed him.

• • •

He was lying on his bed in the dark. One arm draped over his eyes when there came a knock at the veranda door. Well, there wasn't much traffic on the veranda at that god damn hour in the morning.

"Yeah," he said, without moving.

There was no answer. He slipped his arm away then shifted his head a bit. He reached for the gun on the table beside his bed. There came another knock.

"I said already…Who is it?"

A woman's voice. "It's Permelia. My name is Permelia."

"Who the hell is Permelia?"

"I'm looking for John Lord. This is him, right?"

"Jesus Christ," he muttered.

He eased himself up, swung his legs off the bed. He leaned forward and undid the lock. "Come on in."

The door cracked open a bit, then kept slowly easing inward and what should step into the room but the silhouette of a woman and when she took the next step or two, he could make out, thanks to a feathery bit of moon, that the young lady was quite naked. She also was, from the way she tottered, quite drunk.

She was looking around, peering into the darkness. "Mister Lord?"

"Lourdes," he said.

His voice from behind caught her unexpectedly, and she staggered a bit from surprise. "Mister Lord?" She was squinting.

"Lourdes," he said. "John Lourdes. Not Lord."

"Lourdes...like the place in England? Where the cripples go to bathe in the water at a shrine and get uncrippled?"

He just stared. "Yeah. But it's in France, not England. Unless they moved it."

"Can they do that?"

He stood now but he did not set down the gun. He had to get hold of her arm because she was starting to list a little too severely.

"I'm sorry, Mister Lord."

"Oh...forget it. You realize, miss, that you're swilled."

"I have an invite for you. Come on." She started toward the door. "Come on."

"Invite from who?"

"You want to know?"

She stepped out into the night and down the veranda she went. He looked out first to be sure. "Come on," she said, then slipped her hands together as if trying to entice a puppy, and there she went casual as if it were a Sunday afternoon in the park, totally unconcerned her ass was getting a full dose of the night air. She waited a bit for him to catch up. She was flouncy and half attractive and her hair was wild and matted, and she had a delicious grin.

"My sister and I come from Nebraska. Been here just two days. Was curious...How there's so many Mexicans in Texas?"

"Texas was Mexico."

"Texas? No."

"We took it from Mexico."

She looked around as if this was some kind of shocking news that nobody knew about. "Took it? …We did? …When?"

He shook his head.

"You don't need that gun," she said.

"Lady…I'm not so damn sure."

"Hey," she said. "If we took it, how come we didn't give them back all these Mexicans?"

He prodded her a bit to get walking.

"Are Mexicans Negroes? Or are they their own race?"

"The hell with it," he said and started off down the veranda without her.

There was a light from a doorway at the far end of the building. A woman's squiggly laughter, and a man's gruff whinnying. Once in the doorway, John Lourdes got the full view. There was Cager Adams on his hands and knees, naked as the moment of his birth. And on his back riding him like he were a wild mustang was who John Lourdes assumed to be Permelia's sister. And she was just as naked, with one arm scooped around Cager's neck. Not a sober inch between the two of them. Well, Cager must have got wind of John Lourdes' boots and legs, because he stopped bucking and looked up.

He saw him standing there with a gun in his hand and grinning wickedly, Cager said, "You here to put me out of my misery?"

"It's a tempting thought."

"I got your letter from General Delivery."

He shrugged loose of the girl who fell onto the carpet with a thud. He stood and motioned for John Lourdes to follow him out onto the veranda.

He pushed past Permelia who was just coming in. She asked where they were going and Cager told her, "I'm going to commit suicide." She had no idea if he was kidding.

"The rally at Big Medicine," he said. "Day after tomorrow. We're to be at their offices down on Flores Street that morning. We got invites. You'll be my guest. I told people about you."

He leaned into the wrought iron railing and sent a powerful stream of urine down upon Salinas Street.

"Yeah…What did you tell them?"

"How you saved our asses on that train. And that you got a nose for when there's killing in the air."

CHAPTER 21

A SMALL WICKER PICNIC BASKET was mysteriously left at the back door to the print shop of the Laredo Weekly Times. Someone had been banging on the door but when the night watchman finally answered, there was nothing but that picnic basket on the brick stoop.

The night watchman saw across the top a note was attached: TO THE EDITOR – IMPORTANT – PRIVATE.

The night watchman was Mexican and careful about his job, especially in these charged times, and though curious, he did not dare open the basket out of fear. He left it on the editor's desk, and it sat there until the man arrived in the morning. It was the same editor who had handled the whole matter of the Vargas photograph and hanging copies of it in the newspaper office windows. That he should be the recipient of this, was not a matter of chance.

His personal politics aside, the editor was pure capitalist, and when he opened the basket and discovered what was there, he called upon his whole staff to urgently join him. They surrounded the desk and he opened the basket lid and reached in and from it pulled a dead rattlesnake. And there it hung to its full four foot length and pinned to the carcass were three Texas Ranger badges. Holding the dead snake in one hand, he reached back into the basket with the other and took out a note that had come with it. This note he read to his staff with a newspaperman's sense of exigency:

—I have come to hunt the Whiteman—

Before morning the snake was hanging in the front window of the Laredo Weekly Times like it was a butcher shop. The badges had not been removed and the sunlight glinted off of them. Negatives had been taken, prints made and hung by fine thread just as the Vargas Funeral Home image had. And in a purely newsworthy and commercial touch, there was the wicker basket the snake had arrived in—and the note. The only noticeable difference between the two episodes was one had more Mexicans that came to see.

Eduardo Barros arrived with his daughter after getting a call from one of his paperboys. Her father was not shocked by what he saw, nor was he morally moved, but because he surmised this violent statement of fact was at the hand of the man his daughter desired.

She had already seen him. He was there, lingering at the back of the mob. He'd looked at her once, there in the clear light of day, then he looked no more.

You don't need a voice to say what you are feeling. Emotions like this you can't break down with words. They're just too strong. They move across time leaving regret and fear in their wake.

"You knew," Eduardo Barros whispered.

"We had this connection," Father.

"We have to write about this," he said.

"Yes," said Marisita. "I will...once I am clear what there is to say about it."

Clarity arrived on horseback. A troop of Rangers dismounted and went about dispersing a coiled rage of citizenry. And they were none too polite about it. There were Mexicans among the mob who were as appalled as the Anglos over what they were witnessing, either for show or fact. Others sloughed past the window silently grabbing a look and passing on. Something to tell the grandkids about, if and when the tide of society takes that inevitable turn. These Anglos sure hadn't shown much temper when the funeral director's exhibit decorated The Times' windows. Rangers stormed the offices and took down the snake and photos. They confiscated everything. They demanded the negative and prints and when the editor refused, they carted him off at gunpoint. And didn't he put on a show of indignation. Marisita had her story now. Even how to headline it—DEAD RATTLESNAKES.

● ● ●

An arm slipped over John Lourdes' shoulder. He crooked his head and saw it was Cager. He was all shaved and showered and his hair brushed. "What are you doing here...*Mister Lord?*"

John Lourdes glared at him.

"Well," said Cager, "Permelia is—"

"Low hanging fruit?" said John Lourdes.

Cager grinned. "That's rich. What are you doing here?"

"I can't resist a crowd."

"Wait till tomorrow at Big Medicine." He shook his head, he couldn't help laughing. "Low hanging fruit. How rich."

"What are you doing here?"

He pointed at the scene that had everyone's attention.

"What about it?"

"Blood," he said.

It was then Marisita and her father were herded along by the Rangers with all the others. Forced like sheep into the street. He avoided her glance, but she was watching. Taking in the man he was with in conversation. Young, handsome in a hard way, with a dirtied up Panama hat set on his head at a haughty pitch.

As they too were pressed by the mounted lawmen, John Lourdes said to Cager, "What do you mean...blood?"

"That's my business, John L."

MY COUNTRY
TIS OF THEE

CHAPTER 22

JOHN LOURDES WAS WAY DOWN IN THE MINE OF HIS THOUGHTS, making sure no circumstance was overlooked but remembering what his father had told him as a boy—good fortune is at least as valuable as good planning, and will probably keep you alive a lot longer. He was stepping up onto the sidewalk in front of the hotel when the short blast from a car horn stole his attention. There was Cager, sitting behind the wheel of a wretched car. He gave John Lourdes a hello brother salute and waved him over.

With a cigarette hanging out of his mouth, John Lourdes eyed this steel rubble. "What graveyard did you steal that thing from?"

"Courtesy of Big Medicine. At least until tomorrow. Let's take a ride and talk."

"Let's go inside to the bar and talk. Save our asses the abuse!"

"You're coming with me. We're gonna have a discussion about your future."

"Does my future warrant a discussion?"

"It sure does."

"And what do you know about my future?"

"I know it's looking brighter all the time."

John Lourdes took a moment. He was suddenly trying to look beyond the smile, to see into the lightless depths of someone, if there was foul play in the making.

"Come on, John L."

He went to get in, when Cager said, "Carrying your gun?"

"I hadn't planned on shooting down any of the local citizenry, so I left it in my room."

"Get it," said Cager.

• • •

Wherever we go, we carry our destruction with us…like luggage. Wadsworth had been talking about himself and John Lourdes' father when he'd said it. But he'd meant it in a broader sense. As some kind of universal truth for the young John.

Cager was driving them north, out of town. That Ford ran, but it was no cherry. Shadows lengthened, buildings grew more sparse. It did not take long before Laredo was just small squares of adobe through a veil of dust.

John Lourdes had not spoken the whole way. He was thinking on what Wadsworth had said as if this were one of those telling moments that might confirm the fact. It felt like it.

Cager bummed a cigarette and after he lit up, he said, "Let me tell you about my favorite subject."

"Which is yourself, probably."

"You are a marksman when it comes to observations, John L...which is why you're here."

He spit tobacco from between his lips.

"John L...I was born and raised in Nebraska. My father was in the army. He commanded a Nebraska regiment. Served with honor in the Spanish-American War. I still have his medals in my saddlebags. After... We got stationed in Los Angeles 'cause he was gonna be sent on to the Philippines. What a pisshole Los Angeles was.

"After the army helped the Filipinos defeat the Spaniards, what happens? They want us out. Can you believe those lousy bastards. My father wrote they weren't even wearin' shoes when we got there. They were practically livin' in diapers. Filipinos are just Spics swimming in a different ocean. The war against the Filipinos got pretty ugly before we whipped hell out of them. Maybe you know all that. They were animals. My father got captured outside of Manila. Him and a troop. You know what the Filipinos did when they got them a piece of a white soldier?"

He took off his hat and ran a hand through his sandy hair. The sunburn below the eyes accentuated the hatred there. He was too angry to look anywhere but the road.

"Let me tell you something else... My parents were straight up Christian Americans. My mother taught Sunday School. Still does, in Kearny. And I'll be damned if I let this country be turned over to Mexicans...Niggers... Jews...Or any other breed of socialist."

Cager breathed out cigarette smoke. He mumbled privately to who the hell knew who. "I loved my father," he said. "I worshipped the ground he walked on. I still ask his soul for guidance. He was everything to me."

He was consumed by his reality, that was sure. A rope stretched across half the world and pulled tight around his throat, and he was choking because of it. That was something John Lourdes knew about. But he was also envious of Cager Adams. His father was not a shameful albatross. And he didn't have to wash his mouth out every time he spoke the name.

The road suddenly appeared that John Lourdes had taken the day before. The car turned onto it. It was a turn that caught him flat. They were rumbling along through that same barren countryside, toward that same canyon where a pale dust blew and beyond it slender strings of greyish smoke.

"Where we going?" he said to Cager.

"I think I know what happened to those Rangers."

"And how did you manage to come by this?"

He started to sing a tune…" *I had a dog and his name was Blue and I bet five dollars he's a good dog too…I shouldered my gun and tooted my horn and I went to get a possum in the new ground corn…*"

At the edge of the foothills they came upon the smoldering bones of that ranch house. The Ford pulled to a stop. With the coming dusk shadows flooded the landscape.

"Smell the naphtha," said Cager. "This house was torched."

John Lourdes got out of the car. He surveyed the scene as if for the first time.

"Big Medicine sent people out last night," said Cager, "when they saw the fire."

In the failing light he could see there were many more tracks since he'd been there the night before.

"I think the Rangers were killed here."

"No vultures…no bodies," said John Lourdes.

"A woman owns this place. She's missing. Or she's—" He jerked a thumb toward that mass of scorched wood.

John Lourdes was staring straight at the spot where the Mexican woman had hacked the Ranger to death. The blood had dried and luckily the wind had scored away enough of it. But if you looked real finely—

"I got a letter in my pocket from the Chief Operating Officer of Big Medicine's Western sector giving me a job."

"Congratulations."

"Seeing you in Ulvalde. The trolley…Running down that shit coward of an engineer. You're polished, John L, and with sharp edges. I'll bet you even know what I'm thinking right now about what you're thinking."

"That's an awful lot of thinking, don't you think?"

"See... That's exactly what I mean. You know, John L, there's people who don't say too much because they're just plain scared. And there's people who don't say too much because they're just plain stupid. And then there's people who don't say too much because they're just too fuckin' smart, cautious, cunning and dangerous."

They stood by the car facing each other. A thin river of sunset along the hills behind them dying away. Everything around them turning cool and lavender in the silence. This moment of the world around them transcending both men.

"The letter states I've been hired to ensure the safety of all livestock, agriculture, property and personnel of Big Medicine's western sector."

"That sounds like legal talk for being employed to run to the ground anyone who defies Big Medicine."

"What the letter says, is what I mean. Which is why I brought you here. Why it could be important for you. You said...you can be either like the hunting dog in the song, Old Blue...or the *coon* that's hunted."

Cager was waiting for John Lourdes, what he might say, but he remained quietly distanced. His mind, you see, was on how providential it had been that he wore Brogans instead of his boots, because if Cager had brought him here on a hunch, and he was wearing his boots, some of those footprints in the road from the night before might have been the genesis for a little human bloodshed.

"I'm not brilliant at what I do," said Cager, "but I'm relentless."

"Let's go back to town and drink to the seas parting for your good fortune."

He started for the car. Cager followed.

"You didn't ask what the job is."

"It's not my business."

"But it surely is."

CHAPTER 23

THEY'D TURNED ON THE ACCELERATOR HEADLAMPS and started back. On that travesty of a road the lights rocked and dipped and listed like the eyes of a crazy drunk.

"They got to make better roads," said Cager, "or I'm gonna have to grow a lot harder ass."

The headlamps barely illuminated the ground ahead of them. You could practically spit as far as you could see.

"I'm sure glad you didn't suggest something as ridiculous as coming out here on horseback," said John Lourdes.

Cager ungraciously admitted this wasn't his finest hour. They had to damn well hold on not to be thrown clear.

John Lourdes caught sight of something. A teardrop of liquid silver just on the lip of the horizon is what it looked like in all that darkness. There, then gone.

He kept watching without mentioning it, but there it was again in those straights of rocky black. Cager was still cursing up a storm at his stupidity when John Lourdes said, "How much ammunition do you have?"

Cager glanced his way. "That's a hell of a question coming from nowhere."

"How much?"

"A box of shells in my pocket. Maybe thirty."

"I have three magazines."

"Should I start worrying?"

John Lourdes took out his semiautomatic and set it on his lap.

Cager saw, said, "Shit." He got out his revolver and did the same.

"What got you?"

"I thought I picked up sight of something well out there. A mile, maybe more."

"Should we turn off the headlamps?"

"What's the point? This damn thing you brought us out here in makes so much noise...Just keep going."

"They got plenty of outlaw greasers out this way," said Cager.

"They got plenty of everything out this way that would be more than happy to shoot us down."

It was too cool a night to be sweating, but both men were. The wagon track climbed a passage of low sandy hills and the Ford engine made this chappity sound suffering the climb, then started down onto a plat strewn with huge grey shiny boulders. That's when there came a man's voice crying out, a wounded plaintive voice, beseeching them for help in an English shadowed with a Mexican accent.

Cager stopped the car when John Lourdes put a hand up for him to do so. They listened.

"There's nothing I hate more," said John Lourdes, "than someone calling out for help in the dark."

"That's no more a wounded man than he is one of our fuckin' mothers." Cager wiped the sweat from his forehead that was causing his eyes to burn. "I'm sure sorry for dragging your ass out here in this wreck."

The man's cries grew more extreme.

"Shall we make a run for it?" said Cager.

A light flared on, bearing in on Cager. A voice from behind the light. "You could try to make a run for it. But you wouldn't get ten feet."

It was not the man who had been crying out. Then, from across the road a second light bore in on John Lourdes. "Get your hands up, gents," came this third voice. "Let's see those armpits."

More lights came on, piercing the Ford from different angles, half a dozen at least. There were men on horseback, others on foot, carrying lamps in wood battery cases. They closed around the Ford. One thing for certain—they were all hooded.

A man held out a lantern and leaned into the driver's door. "What you boys doing here...?"

Cager glanced at John Lourdes, unsure how to answer.

"Hunting," said John Lourdes.

A prolonged silence. The man by the door scanned the inside of the vehicle with his light. "In this ratty thing? One of these boys has a semi-automatic in his lap, and this character, a pistol. What could you be hunting?"

"We're hunting the men who killed those Rangers," said John Lourdes. "Which is what you all should be doing."

This tested the patience of his captors and one of them poised a shotgun up against John Lourdes' neck. In the darkness behind the light, a man on horseback issued a command. "Bring up the Mexican."

A couple of men reined their mounts forward out of the darkness. They had between them on horseback, a beaten and bound up Mexican. He looked like a fairly well dressed haciendado. Good mount, too. He had a nagging rope crimped around his shirt collar. The man on horseback who issued the commands did not carry a light. He said to the Mexican, "Look at these men. See if you know them. Put the light to those fellas."

The battery lamps were pushed into the car under the men's chins. They looked like bodiless apparitions with their deeply shadowed skulls pitched in a sea of night.

"Do you know these two men?"

"I do not."

"Are you sure?"

"If I knew them, would I not say so to save my life?"

The Mexican turned to the men in the car hoping to steal a last few seconds of life. "My name is Raphael Estaban. Please tell my wife I have been murdered—"

The rope wrenched and the man was taken from the saddle. He was not a hardened man or a strong man and when he hit the earth he cried out in pain. The horses around him reeled backwards or sidled and the lights their riders carried flared wildly, and for a moment, John Lourdes saw the man who gave the orders. It was a slashing and comet like instant where that dusty beam lit over him.

If it was him, these men knew him, they knew his name and they knew his face. And no secret, in the end, is safe. Not even his own.

That poor Mexican on the ground, flopping about like a fish, had shed all the skin of his manhood as he wailed for his life, knowing that he was now in the hands of the instrument of his own death. John Lourdes knew in moments like this, when the blood for murder is up, people start to kill, clearing the landscape, especially of witnesses.

So, he shouted out, "In case you gents are thinking about 'evaporating' everyone in the neighborhood. You better check the letter this man here is carrying. He works for Big Medicine."

This gave the men there something to consider. The one at the driver's door looked to the man on horseback. He must have nodded because the man leaned into the car window.

"Where's the letter, boy?"

"In my coat there," said Cager.

The man ransacked Cager's pocket. And sure enough there was a letter. He held it out, put the light to it.

"Read it aloud," said the horseman from the dark.

The man removed the letter from its envelope. He was a clumsy bastard. He put the light to the letter and read it aloud like a seven year old.

Then an order came back from the horseman, "Return him his letter. Let him go."

"What about the other one?"

"Does he work for Big Medicine?"

"No letter," said John Lourdes.

"Wait a minute here, if what you're thinking..." said Cager. "You all know about the Mex's attacking that train in Ulvalde? This is the gent that got it through. I was on that train. That's how we met. If it weren't for him, a flock of Anglos would be history...Now we're all whitemen here, aren't we?"

CHAPTER 24

When they returned to the hotel, the late nighters were still having at it. Gentlemen and ladies alike. Vignettes of small talk and bullshit. People solving the problems of the day in a few brief flashes of ego. And there was plenty to be said about the events at the Laredo Times and the ultimate wrongness of the Mexican race.

John Lourdes and Cager were filthy and tired crossing the lobby and Cager called out to the porter who was carrying a tray with empty glasses.

"Hey…You…Uncle Tom…Hey…Uncle Tom."

It happened to be Aguirre. The gentleman answered by coming over.

"We need a bottle of drinkin' whiskey sent to Mister L's suite."

Aguirre glanced at John Lourdes who nodded politely. As he started away, Cager called to him. "Hey…you know who Uncle Tom is? 'Cause you remind me a lot of him. Since I got here."

"I know who he is, sir. As a matter of fact, I know who he is in two different languages. Will that be all?"

He turned away. Cager shucked out a laugh. "I think that old greaser gentleman just stuck a knife in me."

"Yeah…I see it all right. Right where your heart ought to be."

Cager was watching the porter walk off. His jaw tightened.

"You better hope he doesn't poison your food some night."

"I better hope?"

When they got to the second floor, Cager asked, "I thought tonight we might 'get done.' And it had me thinking. If you could imagine any legacy for yourself…How would you like to be remembered, John L?"

He got the key out to his suite. He opened the door. "That across the whole West bartenders would know me. And they would tell stories about me. And people couldn't help themselves but listen."

He went into his room, turned up the lights. Cager remained in the doorway, thinking. About all those bars, and all those bartenders, all the stories and people paralyzed with listening. Talk about a trip down the road of personal vanity.

Cager entered. He slipped his hands into his pockets. "I know you're half being sly," he said. "But there's something to what you're saying. Something really grand."

"By the way," said John Lourdes, "if you ever try to get me back in that stinkin' body wrecker of a car…I'll kill you in a way you won't ever forget."

When Aguirre finally brought a tray with whiskey and glasses, he was reserved and trying to contain his anger.

"You got me before with that Uncle Tom crack," said Cager. "I might have to take you to task, old man."

He was reaching for money, but John Lourdes refused him. He peeled off some bills and set them on the porter's tray. "Go buy yourself a new sombrero," he said.

Aguirre saw John Lourdes was trying to get him the hell out. He nodded and then said, "Thank you."

Cager couldn't contain himself. "Buy yourself a new sombrero. Could you see that old fuck in a sombrero? That's rich."

Later, when alone, John Lourdes wrote a note to Marisita detailing events as they'd unfolded, giving her the name of the Mexican gentleman who had asked that his wife be informed of his murder. He could not swear to the man's death, though he was certain it had, in fact, taken place.

The last he'd seen of that poor soul was watching this caravan of lights head out into the frontier, moving along slowly, Indian file, into the blue black folds of the night until they were nothing, but distant looking fireflies suspended in the nothingness.

He placed the note in an envelope, sealed it, then addressed it. He called down to the desk for the porter. When Mister Aguirre arrived, John Lourdes held out the envelope and a neat packet of paper money. "Do you think you could get this to the *La Cronica* offices? It's important."

He took the envelope, but not the money.

"And be careful of that man I'm dealing with. He's a 'Rinche' without the badge, if you get my meaning."

"It's you who needs to be careful, Mister Lourdes…People here are devoted to their suspicions. And how they can make it profit them."

When the porter left with the envelope, John Lourdes went out onto the veranda and smoked. After what the porter had said, a question began to eat at him—Had he and the Whiteman both been witness to the instrument of their own death this night?

CHAPTER 25

MARISITA WAS AT HER DESK IN THE SHOP OFFICE after midnight finishing up her article titled—DEAD RATTLESNAKES LOOSE IN LAREDO. The article expressed how the acts of the Texas Rangers that day at the Laredo Times' offices were not only the most recent acts of racism toward the Mexican American, but the most severe. She did not blame The Times for their exploitation of the Vargas murder, or the possible killing of the three Rangers. Their business was news, and exploiting the news to their advantage—however callous or repugnant—was well within their rights.

The Rangers' actions would have been appropriate had they reacted in the same vein when it came to the Vargas murder, by immediately and professionally clearing out the window of the violent afterthoughts of a crime. But they had not.

And the reason was, to this reporter, obvious. The missing Rangers were white. Vargas, allegedly, was not. He was Mexican American, and a Mexican American was not considered white. And whiteness, as everyone knew, had gone beyond being a standard. It was now a sweeping declaration that had reached deep into the realm of absolute oligarchy.

Mexican Americans were to join the Chinese, the African, the Jew, and the Bohemian as the lowest remainders of society. Their future was the segregated bathroom and drinking fountain, the poll taxes established and levied by the Democratic Party of Texas to keep the poor from voting and so strip the middle class from the reaches of power.

It was whiteness that meant power, it was whiteness that meant the rule of law. But more than the rule of law, it meant sanctity, it meant heaven and it meant God, and in effect it turned the Mexican American into a dead rattlesnake.

But no one should forget that a dead rattlesnake can be just as dangerous as a living one—

She hesitated on that last sentence because she was concerned that might seem the newspaper was hinting that the ordinary citizen commit an act of violence, or as a threat to those in power, when what she meant was a cautionary inference to the present reality, for she well knew what violence had taken place.

She went to ask her father to review the article and offer his advice when there came heavy knocking at the garden door. Returning to their living quarters, her father was coming down the stairs in the dark.

"I saw out the window," he said. "It's Sheriff Rueda and his wife."

"At this hour?"

"Watch what you say and how you act."

"You also, Father."

As she put on the kitchen lights her father answered the door. The sheriff apologized for calling this late as he and his wife entered.

"Has something happened?" said Eduardo.

"Belen," he said to his wife, "you and Marisita go…Let me alone here with my friend."

Rueda was middle aged and always too thin for the clothes he wore. He was a plain looking man with many trepidations and uncertainties but not without courage, and he had bullet scars to prove it. But the world he now lived in was condemning him to be little more than a supplicant to his Anglo superiors. This was a private shame to his manhood that shaded his very being in all matters.

Eduardo offered him a drink, a chair, anything, but Rueda waved these aside. He had urgent things to speak of. "There are rumors," he said, "that the killers of the three Rangers are here in the barrio."

"Do they know they are dead?"

"Listen to me. And since your paper has many sources of information their suspicions are you might be aware of this."

"And who the killers are."

"And who the killers are? Or where they may be? Who may know them."

"No one in the barrio has come to me with such information."

"This is good. Because Captain Asa will be coming to question people in the barrio. And you know how that one is."

"The Christian wolf is well known among the living and the dead. But means little to me."

"He can make one's life very unpleasant."

"Rueda," said Eduardo, "do you feel threatened?"

• • •

The two women remained in the hallway with a single light on. They stood close together like two people gossiping.

"What are they talking about in there?" said Marisita.

Belen pointed to the sheet of paper in Marisita's hand. "Working so late...Or is it a note to your lover?"

"Excuse me?"

"I have heard rumors of a gentleman caller here late at night."

"Marisita put forth a look of complete disbelief. "A gentleman...here? If that were only true. But could you imagine, with my father in the house? Though I have thought about it."

She saw the woman did not believe her. Belen reached for the paper. Marisita thought to keep it from her, but that would only arouse her suspicions. Belen was decent enough. She was there for *La Liga Femenil*, there for the charities and the good will, but when the winds of change blew, she was prone to being carried off in the wrong direction.

Marisita handed over the single sheet of writing. "It's to my love. Would you look it over to make sure all the spelling is correct?"

Belen held it to the light. Read with anticipation that began to fade accordingly.

"I would be frightened to write such things publicly," she said.

"It frightens me sometimes. I say to myself, 'Marisita, who is the young lady using your hand to write such frightening things? I don't know, I answer back...But God bless her.'"

Rueda called to his wife. She handed back the article. In the kitchen, goodbyes were said. Once the door was shut and bolted and Eduardo saw they were by the gate, he turned to his daughter. "Captain Asa will be paying us a visit."

"Belen said there were rumors of a man coming here late at night. She asked if he was my...They're suspicious, Father. Will they act upon their suspicions?"

He was overcome with concern and some degree of sadness at the weakening he saw in a friend. He went to the cabinet where he kept his liquor and then thought the hell with it and said to his daughter, "The urge to save humanity is sometimes a front to control it. Even in something like this. So, yes...It would not surprise me at some point if the Ruedas succumb to their suspicions. Ohhh...they will feel sorry for it later, then they will put flowers on our graves to make amends."

CHAPTER 26

MEN WERE GATHERING UP outside the Big Medicine offices on Flores Street. There were about a dozen trucks and cars ready to caravan them out to the rally. Most worked for Big Medicine or were connected to 'The Society.' As a matter of fact, 'The Society' had headquarters in the Big Medicine Building. The men were drinking and talking among themselves. They had 'gented up' some—which meant a shave and shower. John Lourdes was among them, smoking, keeping to himself mostly, listening for what he might learn about the man he was hunting.

There was a sudden rush of hoots and catcalls and even whistling and John Lourdes turned to see what was feeding all this excitement.

Here came Cager Adams in a tuxedo. He was a sight, with a top hat and waistcoat with black satin lapels. And the trousers, they had beautifully stitched side braids. His black shoes were all shiny, and to top that costume off, he wore a Henley undershirt. A god damn undershirt thought John Lourdes. If that doesn't take you right over the edge.

Cager moved through the crowd like God Almighty, absorbing all the cheers and mocks and the stabby comments, arms raised. "I understand your envy, gentlemen. I would be too, in the company of greatness."

When he was finally standing before John Lourdes, he said, "What do you think?"

"In the magazines, they would call that look 'the peacock male!'"

"No kidding?"

John Lourdes leaned forward and sniffed. "What's that odor?" He sniffed again. "That's god damn—"

"Quiet," said Cager. "I was broke last year and worked as a grave digger for a while."

"You didn't—"

"He was going in the ground. And we were about the same size."

• • •

The western sector of Big Medicine began about ten miles out toward Salado Creek. In Webb County the company produced cotton and Bermuda onions. There were cattle and sheep...and oil. The men were packed into the back of the trucks that rumbled through the stone gates where guards kept watch against trespassers.

Cager had hold of his top hat to keep it in place, or else—

"Word is," John Lourdes said, "the Whiteman is gonna be there today."

"That so?"

"My gut says it's Captain Asa."

"The Christian Wolf?"

"One and the same."

"I'm more interested in the man that 'evaporated' all those Rangers. They're gonna put a bounty on him, I hear."

"That'll bring in all the trash."

"You know what else I think?" said Cager.

John Lourdes could smell the thought on him as clearly as he could the embalming fluid on that tuxedo. "You think the fella that did in those Rangers might try and be here today."

"You got that right," said Cager. "But how?"

"Because it's something *you* would do."

"And something *you* might do, John L. And you know why? Because we're slicker and more daring than these...rednecks."

"And better dressed."

• • •

The place of the rally was a sight to behold. It was set upon a huge plain where a stage had been built and covered against the sun by a white tarp that rippled and rose with the breeze. There were acres of trucks and cars, wagons and carriages and horses staked off. Stalls had been erected where vendors sold liquor and food, ice cream and sodas, and treats of all kinds. There were banners and placards to 'The Society' and American flags and the flag of Texas. It was a carnival designed for the heart and soul of a people, and their version of themselves.

Upon a hill overlooking the scene was a house. "The largest in Webb County they say," Cager said. It was where the C.O.O. headquartered and lived, and that was just for the southwestern sector.

There were about a thousand people John Lourdes and his tuxedoed friend walked among. The house held no interest for him, but all that strange equipment on stage did, with their dials and switches and toggles and where cables reeled out to the edges of the stage and were strung from posts fifteen feet high at the least in every direction like the spokes of a wheel, well into the crowd where they connected to what looked like black metal boxes with one open side.

"That's him," Cager said. He got John Lourdes' attention and pointed. "Captain Asa."

Asa led a retinue of Rangers through the crowd in his white shirt and tie and formidable Stetson. Clean shaven and level eyed, he looked like the type to breakfast on your soul, then get on with the day like it was nothing.

One of the men with the Captain spotted Cager and shouted him over. Then there went this oddity in a tuxedo, who fell in with a phalanx of drab looking hard case Rangers. John Lourdes wondered who would be in for the greater shock.

There came this booming, scratchy voice from seemingly out of nowhere. "Ladies and Gentlemen...Good citizens of our Beloved Texas... Americans all...May I have your attention, please?"

John Lourdes looked up, as did those around him. There were measurable looks of wonderment. The voice was coming from that metal box and from the others on posts in a vast circle around the stage on that open stretch of prairie.

He turned his sights on the stage where a man sat at a desk by all that machinery. He spoke into a piece of equipment that he held in his hand.

"What you are listening to," he said, "is called an enunciator. It was invented by the Automatic Electric Company out of Chicago. The executives at Big Medicine have been given the opportunity to test the enunciator at this event to see how it works outdoors. So...If you all can hear me, please give out a round of applause."

There was a charged wave of it. Adult and child alike. You could feel something new and wonderful in the air.

"Well," said the voice, "let's gather up...Because this great rally is about to get under way."

CHAPTER 27

THOSE THAT HAD BEEN LINGERING ABOUT began to pay attention. The food stalls started to empty. Small packs of men got down that one last swig. Children dashed through the crowd toward their calling mothers. Women stood with parasols against the sun to be joined by their husbands. The old sat on chairs they'd brought, brushing back the heat with the brim of their hats or brittely fans. It could have been Sunday anywhere in these United States where hopes ran high and God came calling to lift one from misery.

A handful of men gathered upon the stage. John Lourdes noticed that the one who had done the speaking set the piece of equipment that had been in his hand beside a Victrola there on a table. A moment followed he had never been witness to or heard of, and he was not alone. There came this woman's voice, this beautiful, emotional voice, singing through that metal box, through all the metal boxes strung across that vast expanse of Texas prairie... *"My country, tis of thee...Sweet land of liberty...Of thee I sing..."*

It was a moment that held the people there spellbound. They looked up to those metal boxes in awe. One by one they put a hand across their hearts. Fathers shook their children to do the same. The old struggled to stand and pay honor to a world that had birthed their dreams, those who could not lifted a shaking hand to ask for help.

"Land where my fathers died...Land of the pilgrims' pride... From ev'ry mountain side...Let Freedom ring."

It was like a scene from a picture book, with the breeze blowing and the tarp covering the stage undulating like some oceanic wave and the flags everywhere alive against shimmering endless blue.

Vanished scenes from John Lourdes' childhood came flashing back. He was with his mother on the Fourth of July. At the park downtown where they celebrated the country with parades and fireworks. The country—his country. He did not know when he'd put a hand across his own chest. It had just happened, this unconscious act rising up out of the very soul of him. And one that fixed him in the world, that gave him an anchor against heartless grief and prejudice, and that placed him where he had identity.

"My native country thee…Land of the noble free… Thy name I love…"
With all that was about him, what he would have given to have this dream completely. To be one with it. But he knew in this America, on that day in the year of our Lord, he could not. He was struggling to get aloft on what might be a sinking ship.

But he refused such thoughts. Because refusal was an act of hope. And a commitment to refusal demands defiance. And for him, defiance was born humbly in the endless miles his mother had marched across the Mexican desert toward a toiled freedom when she was not much more than a girl, just a poor and uneducated peon who knew nothing of the world, and who wasn't worth a drink of water to it, or to anyone for that matter, except maybe a soul dying of thirst. She was a child mother who'd spent years stitching together American flags that in part were for those who quietly despised her.

This was a truth he always wrestled with. Human struggles always take you uphill, where there is no view as to what lies ahead.

That hill being his life trying to stitch together the facts to the job that brought John Lourdes to this place and time in the year of our lord, where part of him was quietly despised by the people around him,that he so much wanted to be a part of.

They were singing now, voices rising across that American plain and on into an untouched sunlight and sky. And that deeply emotional woman's voice coming through those metal boxes, echoing until it was no more. There was something noble and wonderful, something heart wrenching and beautifully affecting, that so confounded him because he knew many of the people there—good people basically, decent people, caring people, religious, hardworking, sincere and sacrificing—were there because they carried an ugliness around with them in their day to day lives. It was not a flood of injustice or hatred or disdain, it was more of a trickle really, a vadose stream, if you will, just below the surface of their goodness.

It was an ugliness he knew about all too well. He'd drunk from that vadose stream many times because he was one half of each whole of the world. It was a whole he could not complete or climb out of.

Wadsworth Burr, in his own kind and soul failed way, had told John Lourdes, "Be aware. The soul sometimes shrinks from fatal choices. Then tries to convince you that those choices are all a dime a dozen. They are not. The world is built on fatal choices as they are the ones that see us

through the blackest air. And that is when a man truly sees himself for
what he is. I know this…because I failed this."

"…*Let mortal tongues awake…let all that breathe partake… Let rocks
their silence break…*"

John Lourdes looked upon his own shadow. What fatal choices lurk
there, my friend? He was singing now with the others, but about a country
that was still somewhere yet down the road.

CHAPTER 28

WHEN THE SONG WAS FINISHED AND THE CROWD PEAKED, the man who had spoken earlier stepped forward and with the same device in hand addressed the rally. "Ladies and gentlemen… it is with gratitude I get to introduce to you a great American. And the man who created the Social Committee for an American Republic known across Texas as 'The Society'…Doctor Elijah English."

Of the half dozen men on stage, the most unassuming, to John Lourdes, stepped forward. The Doctor was neither a tall man nor a short one. He wore a plain linen suit in need of pressing and an indecorous tie and his brogans were well worn. He looked as if he did not take in much of the sun, and his pure blond hair was thinning. To look at him you might see a clerk who passed his whole life unseen while in plain sight.

He unbuttoned his coat and with a handkerchief wiped the sweat from his brow while he waited patiently for the people to quiet. The device he talked into was placed on the dais he stood behind. And when he spoke, his voice was as unassuming as he was.

"My father," he said, "was a missionary and doctor in Mexico. He was murdered by the natives he served. Hacked to death and thrown into the fire. Some of his organs were eaten.

"My mother was a nurse and missionary. She was pregnant with me at the time. She escaped in a boat and was chased by these same natives for a day and night. But she escaped and so I was born. It just goes to show you what a white woman of faith can do. I think that about sums up the nature of Mexico and the Mexican."

He wound the handkerchief around one hand and placed both his hands upon his hips. He looked about. He spoke in a smooth flat cadence.

"I became a doctor because of my father. I served in Cuba during the war, and in the Philippines. There I learned about our brown brothers. And the diseases they carry. After the war, I served at a leper colony in Louisiana…and then in Texas. A small private colony not thirty miles from here. It's a horrible disease. And do you know where it comes from in this hemisphere? And how we Anglos can contract this disease?"

He walked over to a table and took up a burlap sack that seemed to be weighted down and returned to the dais. John Lourdes watched this silent play. He watched the people crane their necks and get up on tippy toes. He watched children squiggle their way through the crowd to get to the edge of the stage. The Doctor, unassuming as he was, had a flair for drama. He opened the sack and reached in and from it he slowly lifted a dead armadillo he held by the tail. Its skull had been blown off and the head now was just so much stringy flesh. You could hear the moans of disgust among the rallyers all the way back to where John Lourdes stood.

"Experts are starting to piece together a theory that these little creatures carry leprosy. You can actually see signs of the disease on their bodies. And they believe this is how humans come to be infected. And do you know where these creatures hail from?"

He looked about the audience. He was waiting intentionally for an answer, or a stab at an answer, when someone in the crowd finally shouted, "Mexico?!"

The good Doctor speared an arm in the direction of the crowd.

"Most armadillos," said Doctor English, "have their genesis in the desert provinces of northern Mexico. And this—" He held up that dead bloody thing— "perfectly symbolizes Mexico's legacy to us."

He tossed the armadillo aside, so it lay there on the stage at his feet. He wiped the sweat from his face. His voice rose in pitch. It now had force and range, and it even ruled over the scratchy flaws in the equipment he spoke through to the crowd.

"We are in crisis, people…Do you know where the greatest threat to our democracy comes from?"

He waited until someone finally yelled, "Mexico."

"Yes…Do you know where most of the illegal morphine in Texas comes from?"

Voices spread among the rallyers, shouted, "Mexico."

"Do you know where most of the illegal contraband in this state comes from?"

From everywhere, voices shouted, "Mexico."

"We are besieged, people. At the rate Mexicans are flooding our borders, there will be more than a million of them here in a few short years.

"One million…Think of it. Santa Ana brought six thousand to try and take Texas from us. Could you imagine if he'd had an army of one million?

"Do you know what that many Mexicans represent? They represent a cancer on the body politic and the well-being of this state. They are a cancer, and there will be no way to cut it out. It will have metastasized in the cities, and in the towns, and across the countryside. Because where the Mexican goes, he brings decay and filth with him, he brings corruption with him, he brings criminality with him. He comes with a hand out and a lie within.

"They will destroy the ability of the poor Anglo to have a livelihood because the Mexican will always work for less, just as he will commit a criminal act if necessary, to survive. He doesn't care, because America is not his country. America is an Anglo country.

"But beware if you doubt what I say. Take a look across the river. Mexico is led by a corrupt dictatorship that is crumbling before our eyes, and then what? They'll have no president. No true government. Just someone named Madero who they call 'The Leader of the Revolution.' They have always been a country of corruption and failure. They would have no railroad and no oil industry if it weren't for Anglo-American money and know how. What if after the government falls, half the population scales the banks of the Rio Grande with claims of desperation and poverty?"

John Lourdes watched with taut anxiety as Doctor English wiped the sweat from his face time and time again, and how he wound the handkerchief around one hand while he made a point and then unleashed it like a whip. Whatever John Lourdes had thought about the Doctor, that unassuming man carried a volcano around inside him and the people there felt it, and they experienced it, were deeply connected to it. John Lourdes could see that in their expressions, in their posture, their gripped hands, and raised voices. Because the man on the stage expressed their hidden fears and most hateful terrors. And he was showing them the dawn of a future without them.

Doctor English held up a pack of newspapers. "Mexican newspapers, published in Laredo." He singled out one and the others he tossed aside. "*La Cronica*...Read it and learn...In this newspaper, the editors refer to Mexicans as...Mexican Americans. It is a strategic turn of phrase meant to craft the idea that Mexicans here are wholly American. That they are equal in the social order. And if you read these newspapers and eavesdrop on their thoughts you can see their intentions to pull together every political, cultural, rich, poor, peon, mestizo, Tejano and full blooded group into a unified whole.

"Their aim is obvious...Power. Understand, people, they hate us. They hate our being white. They hate that this is a white country. That it is a privilege to be white. A privilege that built the greatest nation the world has ever seen...A privilege they can never truly enjoin, and so one they will try to take down. Mark me, now. There is a revolution happening, and I'm not talking about the one across the border...I'm talking about the one that is aimed at the heart and soul of who we are."

CHAPTER 29

JOHN LOURDES GOT A GOOD JOSTLING from an elbow in the back and turned to face a grinning Cager. "Before the fuckin' revolution runs us Anglos off the face of the earth," he said, "there's good people what want to meet with you."

Cager led John Lourdes through the crowd. It was pretty intense by then. Even rowdy, with all the applause and calling out. Every time Cager was instigated to applaud he held his hands over his hat to do it. John Lourdes thought he cut a pretty ridiculous looking figure of a man who would slit your throat in your sleep.

He was led up to the big house. There were a dozen men congregated on the porch around a cart with an assortment of whiskeys. Cager made the introductions. To a man they wanted to shake John Lourdes' hand for the action he took at the Ulvalde depot killing "greasers." And when these gents shook your hand, it was all about manhood.

The Captain was sitting in a highbacked wicker chair at the far end of the porch. He had an envelope in one hand and was tapping it against the fingers of the other. When he shook John Lourdes' hand, he said, "I was told by this character here," he glanced at Cager, "is that you intend to hunt down whoever it was that killed those Rangers."

"It is my intention, yes."

The Captain looked over at a man who leaned back against the porch railing. He had a calculating stare. His hands were tucked into his suit trousers. John Lourdes would learn he was an executive who served under the COO of Big Medicine. He nodded.

"You can," said the Captain, "consider yourself in the employ of Big Medicine as security."

"I thank you, sir…" said John Lourdes, "but when you are in someone's employ, it means you have to rightfully take orders. If you don't mind, I hunt best when I hunt on my own. I will, upon delivery of the body, expect a reward."

The man looked to the Captain. The Captain nodded silently. The man said, "The newspapers are in the process of being notified that Big

Medicine will be putting up a substantive reward for information that leads to the capture and or killing of the suspect or suspects who committed this vile act."

The Captain reached out, handing John Lourdes the envelope. It contained a letter which he read under watchful eyes. It stated that he was an active member of 'The Society' and therefore privileged to all its protections.

"It's important you carry it at all times," said the Captain. "It might keep you from getting killed if you have to prove where you stand."

He put the letter back into the envelope and the envelope in his trouser pocket. "Unless some Mex catches me with it."

"If they can read," said Cager.

One of the men on the porch called for everyone's attention. He'd spotted a car on the far side of the hill, and it was coming on fast toward the house. You could hear the horn as it got closer, and see a man leaning out the shotgun door window. He was waving and pointing. About a mile out there were flames coming up out of the earth.

"Mexicans," the man shouted. "They're torching the northern warehouses."

The men with horses and arms were quickly sent out with the Rangers in a strike force. John Lourdes and Cager both were given mounts and rifles from a private armory on the property that was unmatched in western Texas. They came upon the scene of the fire where three huge warehouses stood burning. A blight of black smoke everywhere. Men who worked for Big Medicine were trying to save what they could.

They pointed the way, and the two riders cut across a hard scrabble plain. At the edge of windy foothills came the report of gunfire. It sounded like a standing battle. The ground they traversed was scattered with pieces of broken rock. John Lourdes was veering away from the gunfire and Cager confronted him on it.

"If it's a standing fight we might be able to swing in behind them," said John Lourdes. "And don't ride so damn close to me."

"What are you talking—"

"You're a target in that god damn outfit, and I won't be killed because of it."

As the threads of gunfire grew more sharp, they slowed their approach, and soon after John Lourdes dismounted and Cager followed. The two men slinked their way along following a path of goat tracks amid the rocks. Then there they were, their hatless foreheads and eyes peering over a ledge and down into a fortification of stony juts.

It was a standing fight. There were about a half a dozen Mexicans, it looked like, and from their position they could hold off the whole city of Laredo, let alone the fifteen or so men Captain Asa had with him.

Cager jabbed at John Lourdes' side and pointed. In a sandy draw back from where the fighting took place, a lone Mexican with a pistol held the reins of six mounts.

"A Mex afoot is more likely to give it up," said Cager.

"I'll flip you for who gets to kill him and who runs off the horses."

"You take the horses," said Cager. "I want to show off a little."

They walked their mounts down through a craggy maze of ravines, their hands over the horse' muzzles to keep them quiet. Reaching the flats, they remounted and pulled forth their rifles. From the mouth of the canyon they charged up that sandy draw firing their weapons and howling. The horses startled then skittered at the gunshots pocking the ground around them. They trampled over each other trying to escape and the Mexican was nothing but drag marks until he managed to loose himself. Bloodied and wobbling, he got upright only to have Cager ride past and swash him across the face with the rifle barrel breaking his jaw and shattering teeth.

John Lourdes drove those horses into the reaches of that bone dry playa. The men saw the dust of their mounts trailing off into a wretched wasteland, and they broke rank and scattered. Some were shot down, a few managed to lose themselves in a confusion of stony abutments and desolate gullies, and vanish.

It was Cager who kicked and prodded that renegade Mexican back to the Rangers. Captain Asa was looking over the dead who had been laid out in the sun. He was going through their pockets to see what he might learn. They weren't bandits, that was certain.

When John Lourdes rode back among them, they had the Mexican upright. He was a tottering waste with a swollen jaw and one eye shut and black with blood from the beating he took. He was being interrogated by the Captain in sharp Spanish. When he would not answer whether he was part of some subversive group, he was bludgeoned to his knees. He looked up and flashed a row of serried teeth, and there was no measuring the defiance John Lourdes saw in the man's expression. The Mexican knew he was coming to the world of death, and he meant to meet it with blessings of hatred.

He told them how his people would take this country back. That they would keep coming across the border until Anglo power was shaken, then broken. That the whites would come to be our cattle and sheep. That your children will come to serve our children. That your grand sense of privilege would be ground into the dust when we make the laws. That as far as the 'Rinche' was concerned, we would match you blood for blood. And the fact that you have to demean and destroy us, is because you are already defeated, and it enrages and frightens you. That you hold onto your white country like a drowning man holds onto the air.

The Captain ordered all those who were not Rangers back to Big Medicine. Before the men rode off, he thanked John Lourdes and his tuxedoed friend for their strategic actions. As the riders made their way Indian file up through the rocks and back to the road there came this sudden and horrific volley of gunshots. Then there was just the wind. The men glanced back at that silent entry to the canyon. Still as a painting it was, when there came the single echo of a pistol being fired.

Cager was wiping the dust from his top hat with the sleeve of his coat. "Sounds like the Mex was trying to escape."

CHAPTER 30

Marisita was standing beside their Hoe printing press as it turned out pages of the upcoming issue of *La Cronica*. It was noisy and hot with the gears turning and the rise and fall of the slat teeth that kept the pages in place as they passed over the copy blocks. She was reviewing the front page to see how her article appeared in print. She and her father had decided not to edit it, but rather let it stand as is.

Immersed as she was, she could not hear over the ratchety turning of the rotary that she was being called to, until the paper feeder leaned down from his post, sliding pages onto the rotary and practically whistling in her ear. When she looked up, the feeder jutted his chin toward the front of the shop.

There by the desk at the entry was a rather distinguished looking soul who their office secretary was pointing at and making a talking motion with her thumb and fingers.

As Marisita stepped through the wooden gate that separated the entry from the print shop, she wiped the ink from her hands with a rag she kept tucked in the belt of her skirt. "Can I be of assistance?" she said.

"You are Senorita Barros?"

"I am."

"My name is Manuel Aguirre." He glanced at the desk where the secretary sat watching. "May we speak privately?"

In these times, there was no telling what that meant, so she led him out into the daylight.

The sun bleached the front wall where they stood on the sidewalk, eyes squinting against the brightness. She watched Aguirre retrieve an envelope from his coat pocket and hand it to her. "Mister Lourdes asked that I give this to you. I sense some urgency."

She stared at the envelope. She was unsure. "How do you know Mister Lourdes?"

"I work at the hotel. I am the night porter there. I assure you what I say is the truth."

She studied the man a bit. She took the envelope. She held it in one hand and tapped the fingers of the other with it. There was something about this man.

"Have we met before? I feel there's is something about you—"

"A year ago, Senorita. *La Cronica* did a series of articles on that strip of Mexican owned businesses along Matamoras and Saint Augustine—"

"By the fire house," she said. "All the businesses burned. Arson…"

"You interviewed the owners."

"Yes."

"I was one of them."

"Yes."

"They are all Anglo now, as I'm sure you must know. This morning, coming here, was the first time I have been on that part of the street," said Aguirre. "There is a café where my business once stood. In the window there is a sign that says…Mexicans not served here. Whatever you do, make sure we do not die quietly."

They shook hands and parted. She watched him walk off into the everyday street traffic. Quiet, and straight backed. One of the forgotten.

She read the letter and it disturbed her to no end. She showed it to her father. The address of the wife would not be hard to find. Her husband had been one of the outspoken.

The residence was a few miles out of town toward Las Minas. Her father thought it best he take the ride. She didn't want to argue so while he went about his duties, she took a pocket Colt that he kept in his desk at home, slipped it into her purse, and told the office secretary that she was going out for a few hours with their cart.

Since most, if not all, of the local troublemakers would be at the rally at Big Medicine, she thought it safe, or at least safer, even travelling alone. She kept the Baby Patterson on the carriage seat, hidden neatly by her skirt.

She went alone as a point of order, as something she intended to write about. In this version of the world, bravado and defiance were just as necessary as quiet and reserve. The country she rode through on her single horse cart was stark and burnished with sunlight that made the vast emptiness all the more sinister.

This kind of trip was considered nothing more than difficult for a man. But for a woman, it was made out to be the end of the world. A testing block of character. These kinds of thoughts caused her to wonder—what if

God had created Eve first? And what if Adam had fallen prey to the apple? How would our view of history be different, how would it have affected woman's selfhood?"

Even though her wide brimmed hat staved off the sun that beat down on her, she still had to hood her eyes because in the distance there appeared this rising train of dust. It was singular and snakelike and fast approaching. If it were riders, there were many of them, but it wasn't. They were trucks, and they were coming on through intense wrinkles of heat.

The trucks—there were about a dozen of them with slatboard railing and filled with Mexican workmen, packed in like crated chickens. She'd seen all this before. These were Big Medicine trucks, with armed guards in the vehicles that bookended the caravan, taking immigrant labor out to grub camps where they would spend weeks going about the back breaking business of clearing brush to prepare the land for crops. Then these illegals would be shuttled back across the river with nothing, but desperation pay for their efforts, while poor Mexican American laborers were kept from being hired, so they'd ultimately be driven from Texas.

As the trucks sped on toward her out of their own dust, she veered the cart off to one side. The lead vehicle went rumbling past and the men, armed with rifles, saw it was a woman. One of them fired a shot into the air and the driver worked the horn and the men in the back of the trucks saw now it was a Mexican woman and a young and lovely one at that, and the things they shouted and the actions they mimicked, truck after truck, was enough to fill a lifetime of bad taste and crudity. Some just doffed their hats and waved or grinned, while others grabbed their cocks and made aberrant and almost impossible motions with their pink tongues. And all through a thin veneer of choking road dirt, until the last vehicle with four armed men slowed considerably, and as it eased alongside her one of the men shouted, "We're busy right now, but don't be surprised if we come back this way later to make your acquaintance."

She watched them rumble off into the drifting dust after that. They'd meant to scare her, and they'd succeeded.

Her cart pulled into the walled yard of a ranchero on a slight rise near the road to Las Minas. There were chickens and hogs about and a wheeling dog that barked and nipped at the cart wheels and the forelegs of the horses. And there was a barn and a stable where two Mexican laborers spread hay and a couple of little ones who stopped playing at a trough of water to watch. It was a portrait of silent suspicion as this young woman stranger stepped down from the cart seat.

In Spanish she said, "I'm looking for—"

"We don't want you here," said a woman.

Marisita turned and here came this full bodied matron in a black smock and toting the raised barrels of a shotgun.

"Are you Senora Estaban—"

"You're not the first whore they sent up here with some story—"

"Senora Estaban? I believe I have word about your—"

"Another whore with another story."

"Senora Estaban—"

"But you will be the deadest whore if you don't get back in your carriage and be gone."

"I don't know of what you speak, but I—"

The woman fired a shot into the air. This sent the chickens scattering and the hogs and the dog began this wide circle around the yard barking crazily, and snapping, the white hairs on his back all risen up.

Marisita climbed back into the cart and made quick work of getting horse and cart turned around. As she started out the gate, her voice rose, "I work for *La Cronica*. My name is Barros and—"

Another round was fired, and the woman took two more shells from her smock.

Marisita whipped her horse and shouted, "I have word your husband might have been murdered…by the Whiteman."

CHAPTER 31

HE RETURNED TO HIS ROOM EXHAUSTED THAT NIGHT. He needed a bath to clean his flesh of the day, if he could. We do what's necessary. It is the ultimate caduceus of necessary and right. The snakes intertwining for as long as there's man. 'The cure's in the killing' was something his father had said. How many times? 'The cure's in the killing. Remember that and be done with the rest.'

There was a knock at his door. Please don't let it be Adams. It was the porter instead. He asked if he might enter, and handed over a note. On it was written an address and how to walk there.

"What is this?" said John Lourdes turning over the note.

"You need to go now."

"What?"

"It is my home and how to walk there."

He did not understand, but saw it was urgent.

"She is there waiting."

• • •

It was a squat two room house down a dirt walkway of squat two room houses. Gas lamps, burlap curtains. A child crying somewhere behind those adobe walls, people laughing, prattling in Spanish. A door here and there open to the edges of everyday poverty. A face with a cigarette in hand stared at his passing, an expression tailor made for suspicions. A mobile of metal crucifixes jangled beside the door where he knocked and waited.

He glanced back up the walkway. A feeling of being followed had settled in, a feeling that would be part of him now. The door opened, however slightly, and there she was in shadow, pulling him into the darkness, closing the door behind him.

Before he could speak, she had her arms around him. It had happened spontaneously, just before he got out the question, "What's wrong?"

"I went to see the woman today whose name you gave me."

"The wife?"

Marisita explained how she was confronted. The woman, intense, enraged, nothing but threats and a shotgun. All willingness to listen had been stripped out of her. What in God's name could people have told her to exploit her and get her to such a faulted place?

"There's a madness," she said, "that seems to be expanding, filling up everything we know or experience, that we believe or have faith in, that has become a factor in all that happens, or could. That exists in spite of us, that is more powerful than us.

"I'm frightened, John. Because I don't know what it will take to confront such a madness."

He just kept holding her as much for his own wellbeing as for hers. He could smell the night on her hair, the scent of woodsmoke on her shawl. He wanted to rest there, from a world that didn't count, or little mattered. What she had said could just as well have been taken from the page of his own being.

"I helped kill a man, today," he said.

Instead of leaning back to try and see his face, even there in the dark, she only held him all the more tightly as if to assure him she was there to listen.

"The rally?" she said.

"I saw the future today. And it was as inspiring as it was unsettling."

He pulled himself away from her then, "I need to tell you," he said. "Is there a light somewhere?" He took from his vest pocket a match and struck it on his belt buckle.

She had made her way to a table where sat a kerosene lamp. The match like a firefly as he crossed the room. He lifted the lampglass and lit the wick. Her eyes on him the whole while. He set the glass back down in place and a goldish bloom cast their shadows up the wall and onto the ceiling of that tiny living quarters where they touched.

He sat in a chair beside the table and stared at the light that she saw burned in his eyes.

"About half a dozen Mexicans raided Big Medicine. They set the warehouses on fire."

"Right during the rally?"

"Yes. They were organized. This looked like a political statement to me."

"There are groups all along the river on the Mexican side. They send us letters and manifestos to publish. They want our government brought down."

"I had a hand in their capture. That Captain Asa...He interrogated the one survivor. They beat the flesh off that boy...All he said was this is a white country that needs to be brought down...and that one day they'd take over. That's when the Captain sent us all on our way. Except his Rangers. I don't think we'd gone a quarter of a mile before we heard this slaughter of gunfire. We do what's necessary to get to what's right. We do what's right to get to what's necessary. It wasn't right, but it was necessary."

She came up alongside him and rested a hand on his shoulder. He seemed too young, she thought, to have seen so much. She moved her hand, so the fingers drifted across the back of his neck. "We might have done you harm, bringing you here."

He looked up.

"Your father doesn't much care for me, does he?"

"You bring out a struggle that's going on within him."

"I'm not what he bargained for."

"No," she said. "I'm not what he bargained for."

He reached and took hold of her wrist. Her hand snaked back to reach for his.

"I'm my father's right hand man...except I'm not. I don't want to disappoint him, and yet that's what I do. He wants me to be happy, but not 'til he's ready. He needs me more than he wants to admit, but I need him less. And where I feel heartbreak, he feels anger."

He tugged at her hand a bit and her head slowly came to rest against his.

"I was foolish in a way," she said. "I never realized."

"Is it me?"

She took a long breath, her voice a mere whisper.

"I believe in simplicity," she said.

He closed his eyes for a moment.

"It even sounds foolish just saying it."

A silence followed. She saw their shadows together. He reached up and stroked her face with his hand. Her eyes closed as he eased up to kiss her. She could hear the chair as it creaked, and the lick of the flame and their unsettled breathing.

"If we allow ourselves to feel this," she said, "will we be destroyed?"

He did not know what to say. With all the hurts in the world, how could he answer? And so, he just held her with only that mobile of small metal crosses the breeze blew upon like a convene of voices.

CHAPTER 32

When Marisita returned home, her father's whiskey bottle was on the kitchen table and a light on in the shop. It was well past midnight, but he was at his desk. When she entered, he was sitting back and staring, as if waiting on her.

She remained on the landing. "Writing, father?"

"Proofing."

"Can I be of assistance?"

"You didn't mention you were going out."

"No, Father."

"So I didn't know where you went or when you would return."

"That would hold true, Father."

He stood. He crossed the shop and started up the landing stairs. She saw that red faced and watchful stare which meant he was trying to contain his anger.

"I see your hair is down," he said.

"My hair?"

"Yes."

He faced her from just feet away. Hands pushed deep into his pockets.

"My hair was down most of the day, Father. You just didn't notice."

She turned and started back into the house. She was going to go to the kitchen but decided it would make for a shorter interrogation if she went up to bed.

"So," he said. "This is it."

She stopped partway up the stairs. "I don't feel you need to ask questions you have the answers to."

He found himself shocked. "The world is moving too fast."

"That's all relative, Father. It may well be we have been moving too slowly."

"You're just tolerating me, aren't you?"

"Maybe we've just seen each other too narrowly for too long."

"What you can say to me so congenially."

"Isn't that best?"

"Where did you meet with him?"

"Where?"

"At his hotel?"

"I did not go to his hotel. And not because of some social stigma. But because it wouldn't be safe. We are concerned about safety, are we not?"

"You had to meet him somewhere."

His voice raised a nasty touch's worth.

"At the rally today, John told me that Doctor English referred to *La Cronica* to make a point. About how we use the term *Mexican American* to *incite* unity and organize for political power."

"Doctor English means to turn us into 'niggers.'"

"He means to use us as scapegoats, that's for sure. I'm going to bed."

"We are targets then."

"Yes, Father, I believe we are."

Again she started up to her bedroom.

"Maybe it's best I send you to your aunt's."

This caused her to not only stop but come back down the stairs to where he stood.

"In Mexico City? This is my home, Father. I start my future from right here, thank you!"

"I could make you go."

"You could force me on the train, but you could not make me go. And don't forget, Father. I am a trained teacher. And a credited nurse. I could get off at any station along the way and start a new life."

"There wasn't invective in the words," he said. "But in your tone—"

"You are trying to reach down inside me and pluck out my heart. I won't have it, Father. I am of the age where I can challenge for my own happiness...or misery."

"He's a murderer."

"Yes," she said. "And that is why he was asked to come here. By us, by Father Pinto, and by the Bureau he works for."

"The same people he's lied to."

"Lied...how?"

"He was not honest about his own father being—"

"So you were eavesdropping that first night."

"A man cannot eavesdrop in his own house."

"There are such things as boundaries, Father."

"And how many more lies is he living with?"

"You should read your own newspaper, Father. Boundaries are much discussed there."

"You'll want a husband one day and a father for your children. He is no man's land."

She would have no more of it. She went to her room and lay in bed in the dark. With her pride and expectations intact, and when her father knocked, she did not answer. She was glad when the door to his room shut. She hated him at that moment because she saw in him a mounting reality of how it would be. The same words being said, the same crystallized thoughts, the same antagonizing one just uttered, but from different faces.

GRACING HEAVEN

CHAPTER 33

THE NEXT DAY JOHN LOURDES RODE OUT OF LAREDO fully equipped for the search and pursuit. Cager leaned over the veranda railing in his drawers and shouted to him, holding up a copy of the *Laredo Times,* and pointed to the front page posting of a ten thousand dollar reward for the capture or killing of the Rangers' murderer. "I got my name all over that reward," shouted Cager.

John Lourdes nodded and waved him goodbye.

He had become familiar with the country. Its scored dusty roads, the slivery back trails. Places to roost where he could surveil the land in safety.

He came upon the wretched and the poor afoot or in wagons, after their secret crossing of the Rio Bravo. Often, they'd run in fear, or hide behind their wagons to make a fight of it. John Lourdes would just doff his hat from a distance and ride on. One dusk he noticed spindles of dust moving against him. Through field glasses he saw a filthy and haggard bunch of Mexicans with machetes where their rifles should be. They had the look of border trash who were coming on to run him down then strip his carcass. He made a stand on the last low sandhill before the desert. He had halved their number before the survivors scattered.

He walked among the dead with pistol drawn. One of their number still lived. He sat splay legged with his head back against the bulk of his fallen mount. He was holding his stomach where the blood had seeped between his fingers and down his pantleg turning the sand to its color. He was ill fed and pale. He looked up at the shaded face.

"Are you him?" he said in Spanish.

"Who?"

"The Whiteman."

John Lourdes said nothing.

"If you could please be a good Christian...and kill me."

He had a holstered revolver which John Lourdes pointed at.

"I have no ammunition. The others...very little."

"Then how did you intend to make a fight of it?"

He shrugged weakly, "Desperation."

The man bowed his head and angled it to make it easier for John Lourdes. He took a step closer and then sent this ragged soul on its way.

He lay in wait at each on the list of threatened haciendas. The Estaban ranchero where Marisita had been run off drew his deepest interest. He would sit cross legged in the dark wrapped in a blanket and waterproof tarp, no matter the cold or flash of rain. And the day was no different with its relentless sun. He was the solitary wolf watching tirelessly and when he thought it safe, he let his mind go to her. He imagined scenarios of awkward grace and longing to help him with the loneliness.

Each night he had to cross through Big Medicine. Past the endless prairie that was being put to the torch to clear the land. The flames riding the heavens for miles and where the silhouettes of men against the orange pulse of the fires worked—the undesirables brought here from Mexico in trucks, their faces bound up like mummies in wet rags so they might survive the heat and endless smoke. Exhausted men trudging along, hunched under the weighted stacks of dry and rotted brush. It was like looking into the fire pits of hell where there was no beginning and no end.

When the moment came, the proof lay in the nights of waiting and readiness. Riders appeared upon a cloudy bluff and approached the Estaban ranchero. Three, four, five of them, riding parallel to the wall of that sleeping compound stopped at the closed and barred front gates, as John Lourdes followed their actions through field glasses. They were deeply shadowed figures, but one thing was certain—they were hooded. One of their number sidled his horse up to the wall while another took hold of its reins. The rider stepped up onto the saddle then lifted himself over and into the compound.

John Lourdes moved quickly now. He got his mount saddled, the blanket and tarp bedrolled and tied off. He sat atop his horse and slid out his rifle and slung the strap over the pommel. He then went back to watching with field glasses and the gate opened and the riders silently disappeared within.

There was a warm sweeping wind when the gunfire suddenly erupted. The men in the compound were in all out war with a rabble army of hogs and chickens, a barking dog and panicked goats. A light flared on in the house. There was a shotgun blast, a woman's tortuous cry. A man somewhere began to plead for the life of his children. Endless pistol fire and flashes of blue lightning from the muzzle of gun barrels. Then there was just nothing. The riders came roaring out of the compound and down the bluff and there was just dust rising above the ranchero wall and that lone light to mark the place there in the dark.

John Lourdes swept through the gate and came upon a death scene. Whatever beast lay in men's hearts had bared its soul in all that bloody stillness. He reared his horse about and started out the gates and down the bluff, but at an angle to the riders' dust, so as to fire into them when opportunity unveiled the moment.

The riders trailed along single file unsuspecting, over stony and wild terrain, and as they crested a sandy incline they were overtaken. With the sky and its stars behind them, their black images were marked for a weighted moment.

The men had been talking among themselves as lighthearted as could be, like gents around a card table or in a bar somewhere, sharing the inconsequential banter of their lives when he fired into their ranks.

CHAPTER 34

JOHN LOURDES MADE HIS WAY TO BIG MEDICINE after he had escaped the wrath of those hooded riders. He knew they would take the wounded and the dead to the main house. There was always a doctor there on duty for the executives and white employees.

He had hit the lead man in that long column. He saw him twist violently then come down hard on his horse's withers. The animal must have spooked because it veered then charged over the crest and disappeared down the dark side of the hill. The second rider was taken clean from the saddle. He was there one moment against the skyline and then it was just his mount pitching sideways after that.

The men rallied quickly around their fallen comrades and returned fire in the direction they believed the shots had come from. They were hard cases and not afraid to get after it. John Lourdes could see flashes of pistol fire as they widened their path of attack. He had lost his advantage and disappeared into that remote river country.

He came upon the main Big Medicine gate, lit as it was with lanterns. There were three nightguards at the entry shed and they were loaded down with weaponry. There was a tension in the air as they ordered him to stop, and then surrounded him. He had to show his letter. As he waited, one of the guards said, "You with the men what got shot up tonight?"

"Men were shot?"

"It's bad," said the guard.

"Bad," said the third. "It's a fuckin' war."

The one who'd reviewed the letter handed it back to John Lourdes. "Big changes up at the house. So don't go being shocked and act foolish."

"What? What kind of changes?"

The men laughed among themselves like it was a private joke.

• • •

He knew there was a risk breathing down the neck of a disaster by just appearing like this. But it's the chaos of the moment that sometimes lends itself to the clearest answer.

It was the Whiteman that he'd come for, and the one that he meant to have.

The house was about two miles in from the gate, but it wasn't long before he saw this huge arcing light in the sky. It was panning across the prairie, moving slowly in one direction before turning back in the other. This cycloptic beam reaching far into the night.

A search light had been moored to the third floor roof of the main house. And as John Lourdes came up the road and the light washed over him, it was as if he had ridden directly into the day.

At the top of the hill, machine guns had been set up on both sides of the road. The black and brass Maxims were placed behind a barricade of sandbags. Lights had been strung from wires above each post where gunners kept watch. As John Lourdes rode past he nodded to them, but they only stared back coldly.

There were groups of men all about the lit porch. There was a heightened state of anger in their dialogue. He was taking a small cloth sack from his saddle wallet when Cager came along. "John L…what brings you out here, boy?"

"He held up the clothsack. I had some company last night on the road. What gives here?"

"A security patrol was attacked tonight." He pointed to a truck by the side of the house. Light through a screen door fell across a body lying back in the flatbed and covered by a tarp. The men around the truck were riled all to hell and talking revenge.

"There's another one upstairs," said Cager. "The Doctor is trying to keep him breathing."

"Who attacked them?"

"I guess you could answer that as well as any of us," said Cager.

"Me?"

"Damn right."

"I just rode in on this party."

"John L…My grandmother was a pretty slick old creature, thick eyebrows, and not a shred of kindness. Saw right through me. Would say… 'Boy, there's some people living in Springtime while the rest of the world is bogged down with Winter.' She could have been talking about you, Springtime."

Cager took hold of John Lourdes' shoulder. His eyes got this slinty look. "One day, when that reward gets righteous enough for the fella that killed those 'Rinches,' we'll have to engage in a serious talk."

John Lourdes paid him no mind. He pointed at the house. "What goes on there?"

A bay window opened to a room of paneled wood and bookshelves where Captain Asa was in intense conversation with four men and the executives for Big Medicine that had given John Lourdes the letter. He'd learned the wounded young man's name was Evans, and his family, a major stockholder in the American Enunciator Company out of Chicago.

The Captain was pounding his fist, going back and forth in dialogue with those in the room. There was a terrifying authenticity to the Captain. His rage unharnessed. And when he turned, John Lourdes saw that the front of the Ranger's shirt was spattered with blood.

CHAPTER 35

CAGER CALLED OUT TO THE CAPTAIN. He and John Lourdes were up on the porch. The Captain's fury was only matched by the sorrow bleeding out of him. He was staring at the truck when Cager told him, "Lourdes here got into a shooting match last night."

"Where?" said the Captain, now glancing at him.

"On the road about two miles west of the bridge that crosses Los Olivos Creek. Killed a couple of them."

"Radicals? Revolutionaries from across the border?"

"They looked pretty poor to me. Bandits, I'd say."

He handed the Captain the cloth sack. "Took their possessions for you all to see. Pretty meager."

The Captain took the sack and went over to a table, pushing men aside to make way. He poured out the remains. It was mostly junk. Coins, a rosary, utility knives, a tintype, a compass, some poor brand of tobacco, a pocket watch with the front lid missing. Nothing to show these were men of thought, men of meaning. The Captain used the back of his hand to wipe it all from the table.

"How many?" he said to John Lourdes.

"Three. I left the bodies on the road as a warning."

"Good work," said the Captain. "And God bless you."

A car pulled up. The driver shouted, "I got the reporter here."

The man who stepped from the vehicle with a notepad and a derby worked for the Laredo Times. He wore glasses and a plain suit, and to John Lourdes looked the type that could barely handle a toothache, let alone this crowd. The men were all over him, spewing out vulgarities about the murder and the state of Mexicans in general. They were talking over each other, wanting the world to get a record of their mighty opinions.

Then the Captain was all over them, ordering them with Christian charity to shut their damn mouths.

"I practically raised Bucky," he said. "Got his blood right here on my shirt. And I'll be damned, but you'll shut it down."

The Captain got out a bandana from his back pocket and took to wiping his eyes. This quieted the men down all right. These were not the kind of men that cried in public. They held their sorrow like they did their liquor. The seeds of human vulnerability were planted deep within them on account of all that worldly hardness, and sometimes it took decades for it to surface. But when it did, they were like man of war fighting ships coming too close to shore and breaking apart on the reefs.

The Captain had walked over to the truck, the reporter followed along. He had his pad out and was taking notes in a chickenish looking shorthand. The Captain clasped the dead youth's left hand.

"Not having a son of my own, he came to be like my own child…I bought him his first Hercules bicycle. Taught him how to ride the thing."

He shook his head like some great weary beast and stood there. At that moment, death was his emperor.

John Lourdes wasn't ten feet away on the porch steps. Just one of that silent majority watching. He had shot the boy with impunity, but he felt sorrow for the Captain. For the ghost of a feeling that was now gone to him. The unreckoning heart is all that is sometimes left behind, sadly. Ghosts and unreckoning hearts were something John Lourdes knew about. And it was what connected him to the Captain at that moment.

He also knew all that pain the Captain was suffering tonight would mean hell to pay tomorrow.

That was when Doctor English appeared on the porch. He stood under a singular light. His sleeves were rolled up and he was wiping blood from his hands and forearms with a strip of white sheet. He was told the reporter was there, though he could see that for himself. His greatest concern was his dear friend over by the truck.

"I want you all to know," he said, "I took a few shells out of that hard-charger upstairs, but he should be ready to go by Christmas."

This got the crowd rousing. The Doctor came down the porch steps slowly. He had to walk right past John Lourdes who glanced at the sheet. All that blood, he thought, and the son of a bitch lived.

"God makes great souls," said Doctor English, "but America makes great men."

He walked to the truck, moving through that gathering of men, wiping and rewiping his hands and forearms. He wanted them to see all that blood.

"Charles Bucky Warren was taken from us too soon," said Doctor

English, "But he was already a valedictory speech of what it means to be American and a proud member of 'The Society.' Charles Bucky saw that this was a Christian country of hope and promise. Built on the backs of our European ancestors who themselves were a vision of hope and promise.

"He saw the Spanish had gone to Mexico and mixed their seed with the native Indian, and what did they create? A race known as the Mexican. As lazy and corrupt a people as has ever existed. Just look at the state of their nation. The people of that state of the nation are the nation. They are the children of the children of the children of that flawed breeding. That has left us with a corrupt dictatorship of crumbling morals just across the river. And the people that cross here illegally…Charles Bucky knew what they bring here…they bring defeat. They carry it like a disease.

"As I said at the rally, we are starting to see the term—Mexican American—used to define a people. It is not a term of purity, but a term of art. It is a fiction.

"Charles Bucky saw that. Because a Mexican is in and of itself a mixed breed race. And it cannot attach itself to the concept of America like some parasite and hope to find purity.

"Charles Bucky saw that. That's why he was guarding the gate to our dreams, why he was manning the barricade to defend the security of our future. For twenty-four years Charles Bucky Warren graced our lives… Tonight he is gracing heaven with his own. And it's left to us to contend with the present."

CHAPTER 36

Sitting at the desk in his hotel room smoking, John Lourdes looked out the veranda doors into a dawn coming on with beautiful simplicity. Pencil in hand, he finished writing up a series of names:

Ranger – Captain Asa McLowry
Ranger – Harry Hughes
Ranger – Denis Ahearn
Citizen – Jon Pettyjohn (The Society)
Citizen – Leonard LaShelle (The Society)
Citizen – Charles Bucky Warren (The Society) Dead
Citizen – K.J. Caparell (The Society) Wounded—Laid up at Big Medicine

He made a copy of the list. He folded it and tucked it into his vest pocket. He sat back and sipped coffee and let the day just come to him, all soft and lovely with promise.

• • •

Luis Perez was a retired sheriff. He was arthritic and slow and lived in an unforgiving body of fifty. He carried a pistol in a shoulder holster and sat out front of the *La Cronica* offices at a table the Barros had set up with an umbrella to keep the sun off this former sheriff's neck and shoulders. He was, for all practical purposes, hired security.

Senor Barros had gathered the staff together a few days prior. He need not explain the growing political hostility and how it might affect his employees' safety. He promised there would always be a job for anyone when they decided to return.

He learned that day a few were already carrying weapons. Those who remained did so because of loyalty, their belief in the value of a cause or in deference to a paycheck. Senor Barros did not ask, as a matter of pride. Not only theirs, but his own.

Sheriff Rueda appeared at the *La Cronica* offices under the guise of

142

a courtesy call. Perez hated Sheriff Rueda and privately called him "The Spider." In the editor's office with the door shut, Rueda confirmed a rumor. The Captain would make a sweep of the barrio, questioning civic leaders as to the identity of the man who'd killed the three Rangers. Rueda then added that he'd heard the Captain already had pertinent information as to the murderer's identity and was testing the different parties as to their veracity. He would then indict these people as co-conspirators to murder.

Rueda looked out the glass partition in the door to the press room and studied the faces of the people working, fellow Mexicans who avoided his stare. He spoke as if in secret, "If you should know this man, Eduardo... there are people who will help you in this matter...Our people."

Barros took Rueda's hand in both of his and held it in deep friendship. "How fortunate I am to have you as a friend...I thank you for this warning...But I have nothing to offer, because I know nothing."

"The Spider is watching," said Perez. "He is crawling around here somewhere. Or he has people crawling about."

Barros sat at the table outside with Perez. Perez sat back with folded arms, his bulky frame shaded. He was like a coarse Mexican Buddha, taking it all in.

"If you have information," he said, "The Spider means to coerce you into the grave with it."

"I do not like the sound of that," said Barros.

"You might consider having him killed."

"What?" Barros looked into this shaded, placid face. "What have we come to?"

"It's just a thought," said Perez.

• • •

There was a roofless motion picture theatre up on Flores Street that the women of *La Liga Femenil* had rented for their meeting. Many of the women sat with parasols to protect themselves against the sun. Others, like Marisita, used their rebozos. A woman on stage, and behind a makeshift podium, read from her notes. She managed to turn provocative life issues into drab reportage. But her dull representation did not utterly defeat the fact that women in America were becoming more and more part of the workforce. They were earning professions, taking jobs, starting businesses and so became less reliant on the same old rituals. Rituals that tied them to the past.

The question—could a Mexican woman achieve that freedom better in Mexico or in the United States where she had to face the adversary known as racism? It was an idea that seemed to have left Marisita hanging from the top of the question mark.

Outside with the other women, listening to their exigent opinions, even knowing that she, probably more than any of them, had slipped the bounds of convention could not be certain whether freedom was more attainable in—

She was bumped into slightly from behind. An apology was given as she turned to see that half smile of the innocent stranger. He proceeded up the block, looking back once.

She followed after him. He crossed the street and when he turned onto Matamoros she knew where he was heading and she did not need to catch him, though she badly wanted to, because he'd be there…in that open doorway, wearing the smell of manhood and consequence.

Holding the rebozo with her long dark fingers tight around her head and shoulders, down that walkway of sunlight between whitewashed mud-brick shanties she went, past where women sat on stoops and watched their fat and barefoot children play in the dirt. The door at the end of the walkway open, exactly as she expected. And there, back from the light, he stood, a shadow of anticipation.

In the cool dark quiet of that adobe, the door swung closed and with the latticed wood shades shut tight and the air still and heavy with silence, they kissed.

It was the fugitive dream she'd imagined in the dark reaches awaiting sleep. The unreal unleashed to the sounds of their breathing and the rustle of clothes as they fell away like bits of colored cloth she'd seen a thousand times in her mind dropping slowly through a perfect sky.

CHAPTER 37

WHEN DUSK CREPT THROUGH THE BORDERS OF THE WINDOW, she sat on the edge of the bed where he knelt before her strapping up the laces on her boots. As she watched, she had no notion such a moment could please her so. His hand stopping now and again to caress her leg.

It wasn't just the act itself, or the feelings the act involved. It was the freedom, the independence to satisfy one's want for happiness at the moment of their choosing.

She brushed at his hair with a hand and whispered, "It will never be the same again."

"What?" he said, looking up.

"Everything."

"It never is again, is it?"

They remained like that, just looking at each other, as if seeing each other for a first time once again. But when he stood, there was work to be done.

He handed her the list of names he had in his vest pocket which she looked over with wrinkled eyebrows.

"Seven hooded men," he said, "invaded the Estaban ranchero where you were thrown off. They killed every living thing…man and beast alike."

"When?"

"Last night. I followed after them. Shot two. One of them on the list is the Whiteman."

"The Captain? Do you think?"

"Find out what you can about them. Maybe they have a Mexican housekeeper or cook? Someone who will confide to you about their habits, and such."

"What are you planning?"

"I'm going to kill them all."

He slipped on his vest, buttoned it. She watched him. How matter of factly he'd said it. She thought it unreal, what he'd said, if not impossible. Just something a man comes out with when confronted by an overwhelming atrocity.

"Have you seen the newspaper?" she said. "The Laredo Times?"

She rose from the bed and he followed her as she went to the living room where she had left her cloth carryall on the sofa. From it he took a copy of the newspaper which she offered him.

"The two column headline…read it," she said.

He glanced at the front page. Caught a headline in bold lettering:
BRAVE RANGER NOW GRACING HEAVEN

The words were straight out of Doctor English's mouth. He shook the newspaper which he held in both hands to uncrimp the page.

He began to read. The article claimed a gang of about forty militant Mexicans had illegally crossed the border and attacked a squad of Texas Rangers traveling with employees of Big Medicine. Captain Asa McLowry was quoted as to how the Mexicans had opened fire from a place of cover, shouting racial obscenities and hatreds for our government and people. A violent gun battle ensued. Facing overwhelming odds, it was the incomparable courage of Ranger Charles Bucky Warren and K.J. Caparell attacking the enemy position that turned the tide and drove the Mexicans—

He took the newspaper and crumpled it in his hands. "This isn't true. This isn't news. It's a fake…a fraud. A dime novel passing as—"

"There's more at the bottom," she said. "About the funeral and a candlelight vigil they'll have outside the Big Medicine offices on Flores."

"What have I done?"

He shook his head.

"What have you done?"

"I've made heroes out of—"

He went to tear the newspaper to shreds to get rid of a little of that white hot rage. Then he realized you can't get even with a few pages of newspaper. That's the fool's passage. He tossed the pages aside.

"I've failed," he said.

"You failed nothing."

"I made them bigger—"

She took him by the shoulders. "They are bigger…for now."

He looked into her eyes to see if she could rid him somehow of this unsettling actuality. She brushed her hand across his chest and shirtfront with slow care, as a mother or wife might do to get her child or husband ready for the world.

"You're not just trying to bring a man to justice," she said, "you're trying to bring justice to man. And this is not a single mountain to climb as you go. But a range of mountains risen up through years of racism and privilege…and that mean to defy our will."

CHAPTER 38

CAGER ADAMS SAT IN THE TUB IN HIS HOTEL ROOM with his knees pulled up. Between his legs were his trousers and shirt. He was washing blood and bits of human flesh from them while he bathed. He scrubbed them hard with lye soap and then just let them soak. A cigarette burned in an ashtray beside the tub. While he sat back and smoked, he studied a ruined piece of lead about the size of a peanut he held to the light. There was a knock at the door, and he shouted, "Enter!"

It was the porter, Senor Aguirre. He carried a tray with a pot of coffee and breakfast. He was setting it down on a table by the bed when Cager shouted, "Bring it here, Tom."

The porter entered and set the tray on the floor by the tub where Cager pointed. He held that piece of metal up between two fingers.

"You know what this is…Uncle Tom?"

To the porter's eyes, it was no trinket.

"It looks like a spent bullet, sir."

"I'll bet you knew that in two languages, didn't you?"

"Is that all, sir?"

"No…" he said and sat back.

The night before, Cager had offered to drive Bucky Warren's body to Laredo. The ranger had rented a room attached to a garage out back of a brothel where he'd tended bar in his spare time. The undertaker was not due till morning, so Cager laid Bucky out in the garage on a sofa that was practically falling apart. Some of the whores were in there gasping away at the body until Cager ordered them out. One of them said, "You gonna cuddle up with him, honey?" They were giggling like idiot geese when he kicked at their asses.

He got the garage door closed tight. From his pocket he took out an ice pick he'd stolen from Big Medicine, once he knew he'd be driving good old Bucky back to town. He brought a lantern over and set it on the ground by the sofa. He sat beside Bucky and unbuttoned the youth's shirt. The wound was pretty high up in the breastbone. A kill shot, for sure. Well, he took that ice pick and shoved it down into the hole in the youth's chest. Thank God, so much bone had been blown away because it took no time poking and prodding for him to feel metal scrape on metal.

He then began to hack away at the edges of the wound as if it were a chink of ice, trying to expand the ravaged tissue, and when he thought it enough to dig the bullet out, he set the pick aside and went to work. He wormed the index finger of one hand down into the gloppy cavity. First the index finger of one hand and then the index finger of the other, wrestling and forcing their way, and then two fingers of one hand, blood and gristly flesh oozing up between his knotted hands until finally—

Cager made the porter stand there a long while, and for no good reason.

"I'll bet you'd like to drown my ass right here in the tub, wouldn't you?"

The porter said nothing. He just stared at the soaking clothes there between that pig's legs.

"When you die," said Cager, "which language do you think you'll die in?"

"Dying only comes in one language, sir."

Senor Aguirre then walked out of his own accord. Cager sat back and laughed out loud. "That's rich," he said. He hauled up his trousers and shirt dripping reddish water and squeezed the blood out of them. He shouted, "Hey…Tom…you're all right."

• • •

In clean shirt and trousers, Cager drove that borrowed jalopy out to where John Lourdes had said he'd killed those three Mexicans. He scanned the searing horizon with field glasses till he spotted the black cutout of vultures riding the thermals. "Not exactly the star of Bethlehem, is it?" he said aloud to the emptiness around him.

The bodies were swollen and foul looking when he came upon them. He stopped the car and stepped out with a pistol in hand. There was what looked like a barroom of stoop winged and knotty headed scavengers feasting on the corpses. He cleared a path with a few well placed pistol shots. He covered his face with a bandana.

That stench could last all the way into next week. The bodies so bloated from the heat, one nearly burst apart where he kicked it. He couldn't keep from gagging and bent over to fight the need to retch. He got out the icepick. And spitting up bile, he said, "Gentlemen…if you don't mind."

A carreta pulled by two donkeys came slowly out of the heat. Cager was kneeling over the torn open chest of one of the bandits as the cart approached. In it, a family of Mexicans and all their belongings stacked up and tied down. A rattling of pots and cooking pans. Shock could barely describe their expressions as they went past.

Cager, with a bloody forearm resting on one knee, said, "What are you greasers staring at? Ain't you ever seen the devil?"

CHAPTER 39

THE FIRST OF THE MEN ON THE LIST that afforded John Lourdes the opportunity of gracing heaven was Leonard LaShelle. He was coursing the sidewalk out front of the Big Medicine offices handing out fliers to everyone
that passed, everyone except Mexicans, of course. Those people he forced
the fliers on. John Lourdes picked one up that had been cast into the street.
It was announcing the vigil which was being sponsored by 'The Society.'
John Lourdes folded up the flier and placed it neatly in his pocket.

LaShelle was about ten years older than John Lourdes and his life was
SCAR. He didn't talk much, and he didn't drink at all, and he was a dea-
con at the Baptist Church. He wore a funny looking railroad cap which he
kept pulled down low. But about his only outstanding characteristic was
the Webley Top Break he carried. And he was considered a fuck of a good
marksman, or so John Lourdes heard.

A car pulled up and in the back were crates of canned goods and food-
stuff. LaShelle handed off the fliers then climbed into the car which took
off up Flores.

"Where's he going with all that?" John Lourdes said to one of the men
there.

He answered, "The leper colony."

• • •

About eight miles out of Laredo on the way to Torrecillas was a wood
sign hammered to a post, and there were cans strung to the post from
ropes so it would be impossible to miss. The sign said: GRASSLANDS
SANITARIUM.

A wagon path tracked its way down through about a half mile of dead
brush that rose to near as high as a man. It led to an enclave of buildings
that faced a pale and shallow pond with a few tired looking trees in that
deathly warm afternoon.

John Lourdes studied the scene through field glasses. There was a ranchero that looked like it had seen better days and about a dozen one room

adobes and clapboard shacks with thatched roofs. It looked like an old fashioned Mexican village. There were a few cooking fires where slivers of grey smoke rose into the lifeless air. People moved about, a few anyway. Some were lepers and bearing the sign of the disease.

The car he'd seen in town was parked in the ranchero courtyard beside a second car. LaShelle and the driver were unloading the crates of food.

He set the field glasses down on his thigh. He looked about him. Miles of brittly grass. He could kill LaShelle easy enough on this road. It was just a matter of the right spot where his escape from the scene was secure.

"Not exactly the location one might choose to put on a postcard."

Startled, John Lourdes came about in the saddle to see who had spoken. A man walked toward him with a book tucked up under his arm. He wore a plain white shirt and light colored linen pants. It was Doctor English. When he got up alongside John Lourdes, he put a finger up. He seemed to recognize the youth.

"Yes, sir," said John Lourdes. "Last night at Big Medicine."

"Ahhhh…do you work for them?"

"Well, sir…I'm assisting them…in a matter of some importance. A safety matter."

The Doctor studied John Lourdes with a sure eye.

"I assure you, it's safe."

"What?"

The Doctor pointed. "The lepers. You knew it was a leper colony."

"I did, sir. I'm hunting someone. So I thought it best to learn the country. To see where someone might safely take rest."

The Doctor glanced at the saddle, at the rifle scabbards.

"Can we offer you a drink? Something cool, perhaps? We have a small ice house down there, believe it or not. Or are you afraid? They're not contagious, I assure you."

John Lourdes climbed from the saddle. "I'm not afraid, sir." He introduced himself. The two men shook hands. He walked with the Doctor down the road to the compound.

"My mother is here."

"I heard you talking about her at the rally."

"I come here as often as I can." He held the book out. "I read to her. Her eyes are bad. It gives us a chance to be together. Are you a member of 'The Society?'"

"I find it best, sir, to do what I do alone."

The Doctor thought on this for a few moments. "You are him, aren't you? The one the Captain told me about."

"I'm here to kill a man, if that's what you're asking."

They walked on. The crusted earth cracking under their boots. The only other sounds, birds somewhere calling out to the world.

"You may destroy the man...but the darkness remains."

John Lourdes wasn't sure what he'd heard. "Excuse me, sir?"

"You need to remember that," said the Doctor. "It's something I learned in Mexico as a boy. And I've seen play out over and over everywhere I go...You may destroy the man, but the darkness remains."

• • •

They sat outside one of the adobes in the shade of a thatch awning. They drank iced tea. There was a cloth on the table and on the cloth a large clump of ice and an icepick which they used to chip handfuls to keep their drinks cold.

"I prefer my country greener," said the Doctor. "More lush."

"If you don't mind, sir? How the hell did it get to be called Grassland?"

"I believe in civilized quarters they call that false advertising."

The two men laughed and clinked glasses. John Lourdes could see at the ranchero that LaShelle was about done unloading the car. There'd be no killing him today. The dumb bastard had stumbled onto the path of good fortune, however temporary.

Sometimes good fortune comes humbly and in the guise of a gentleman. Lourdes sat listening to the Doctor and thinking—if anyone knew who the Whiteman was, might it not be the good Doctor? Could I lure it out of him under the guise of civil discourse? Trick him with good will and sincerity?

John Lourdes pointed to the book on the table that the Doctor had been carrying.

"What is it you're reading to your mother?"

He held up the thick volume. "*Around the World in Eighty Days.* Ever read it?"

John Lourdes told him he had. He didn't mention it was in Spanish.

"It gives my mother a chance to travel...in her imagination. It gives us time together. We get to be Phineas Fogg and Passepartout for an afternoon." He took a drink of his tea. He wiped the perspiration from his face with that trusty handkerchief he seemed to always be carrying. "I love my mother deeply. I would have been murdered if not for her. The disease has kept her from what she loves most."

"And what is that?"

"The world, John. The vast and beautiful world. Is your mother alive?"

"She died when I was twelve."

"And your father?"

"Gone to who knows where before she died."

"How did she support you?"

"She worked in a factory...as a seamstress."

"It wasn't Atlas who carried the celestial heavens on his shoulders. It was your common everyday mother."

A woman's sleepy voice called out.

"She's waking from her nap," said the Doctor. "Excuse me."

John Lourdes hacked away more ice and filled his glass. He cooled the back of his neck with it and watched LaShelle get in the car. It trundled up that road back to Laredo. The man was drinking from a bottle of beer. Enjoy it, you bastard.

"Mother...There's someone I'd like you to meet."

John Lourdes turned. The Doctor was guiding her through the open doorway. She was slim and straight backed like her son. But she was terribly frail and her face a map of lesions. She had no eyebrows. Her nose was disfigured. She had to be helped along because of some paralysis.

The Doctor made the introductions. Like a gentleman, John Lourdes stood.

"Missus English," he said. "It's my pleasure, ma'am."

He put out a hand for her to take. She just stared at it, as if it were a momentary grace from God himself.

Her own hands were trembling so, but she reached out struggling and finally managed with both her hands to clasp his. She was a physical tragedy, and this a trial to just hold on. But hold on she did. "It's good to meet you, John...And thank you."

The Doctor helped his mother back inside.

John Lourdes finished off his drink, gobbled up a mouthful of ice.

When the Doctor returned, he said, "No outsider has offered my mother their hand in years…Thank you. And God bless you. It meant a lot. And know, any time you're out this way, stop here and see us. You'll be well taken care of. At Big Medicine, too."

They shook hands. As the Doctor reached for the book on the table, John Lourdes said, "Sir."

"Yes?"

"Tell the Whiteman…to beware."

Doctor English slipped the book under an arm and leaned close to John Lourdes, and in almost a whisper, said, "How does anyone know there is a Whiteman…or not more than one, for that matter."

CHAPTER 40

WHEN JOHN LOURDES RETURNED TO THE HOTEL, Senor Aguirre was already on duty. The porter caught up with him crossing the lobby. He said he needed to talk privately. John Lourdes had the porter bring a bottle of whiskey and glasses. In his suite he told the porter to pour them each a glass. Senor Aguirre spoke with some urgency. He explained about the episode with "that scum down the hall" while he was bathing. The bloody clothes, and this spent cartridge that he seemed so enamored with.

The porter drank down his whiskey in one gulp. He was still agitated. John Lourdes poured him another drink. This one he took more slowly. John Lourdes waited.

"Mister Lourdes...I believe Mister Adams is quietly hunting you for some reason."

• • •

You'd never have suspected that from the way Cager flagged John Lourdes down from his seat at the hotel bar. Whistling classlessly to get his attention and join him as he passed by. John Lourdes swung down onto the barstool beside that reprobate. He called out to the bartender.

"I'll tell you the secrets of my life...if you tell me the secrets of yours."

"Have no secrets," said John Lourdes.

"Anyone says that is either a liar or a loser."

John Lourdes ordered a drink. "I plead guilty to at least one of your counts."

"You goin' to the vigil tonight?"

"I'm not interested in candlelight vigils...Or wakes or funerals...Or any place people go to commiserate." A whiskey was set down before him. John Lourdes toasted his bar mate. "May your most avaricious hopes come true."

"I don't know what avaricious means, but I'll drink to it."

And drink they did. They got those glasses good and empty and quick, then they ordered another round. John Lourdes took out a pack of cigarettes from his vest pocket.

"I got to head out with a security platoon working the border," said Cager. "Big Medicine got word from a Mex informant, 'cause a lot of our people will be at the vigil, it would be a good night for those greasers to sneak across and go Indian with some havoc. Won't they be surprised when we blow their brown asses back into tortilla land. You want to come along?"

"I've got some private hunting of my own to do."

Cager nudged John Lourdes and pointed at the open doorway to the lobby where stood a beautiful, well dressed woman talking with two gentlemen. And they weren't the only ones staring.

"Now, that should be the kind of woman that interests me," said Cager. "So how come I prefer young nasty hard cases with dirty drawers?"

John Lourdes, rather matter of factly, said, "Because you're a classless, uncouth bum."

Cager indulged in the description of himself. "That sounds about right."

The men drank. John Lourdes lit a cigarette.

"What kind of rifle you got, John L.?"

John Lourdes held the match for a long moment. He then blew it out and watched the smoke curl away. "Winchester. Semi-automatic."

"1910?"

"1907."

"Large cartridge…401?"

"The 1907 uses a 351…The 1910 uses a 401."

The spent cartridge that the porter had warned him about was set conveniently on the bar by Cager.

"What do you think?"

John Lourdes held it close to better see in the half light of the bar. "Looks like it's pretty damaged. That blood on it?"

"I think it's a 351."

"Good luck with that."

"I think I'm right."

"You think? What have you been doing…saving up all your genius? How do you know it's not a 401?" said John Lourdes. "And what kind of rifle you use?"

"Remington 1903…Rock Island Arsenal."

"Bolt action. 30-06. That could be a spent 30-06. And how many people are running around with that army rifle? And you know what else? That could be a spent 455. And you know what fires a 455? A Webley pistol. A Top Break. See for yourself. You know who carries one? LaShelle."

He then took the bloodstained lead curiosity and dropped it into Cager's glass of whiskey.

"By the way, I spent the afternoon with Doctor English and his mother. It was quite an experience. I'll have to tell you about it sometime."

John Lourdes got up to leave. Don't think that little fact didn't send a ripple through that poisoned well of a mind.

"Sharpen your wits, brother," he told Cager. "I may come to you sometime with an offer to make real money. And we wouldn't want your morals to get in the way."

He left Cager there looking at that chunk of lead sitting at the bottom of his glass. What the hell—he drank till the remains of that bullet was clacking against his teeth.

CHAPTER 41

JOHN LOURDES STOOD OUTSIDE ON THE SIDEWALK justifiably distraught. The footsteps of consequential facts were closing in.

The vigil that night was a thing to behold. The whole street in front of the Big Medicine headquarters was a sea of candles floating magically in the dark. And that Enunciator—it had been set up on the second story veranda where those metal voice boxes were hung by wires from the railing or out the upper floor windows. And when the Reverend opened the service, his full throated baritone could be heard from the Church Plaza all the way to City Hall.

As the crowd stood in awe of this technical wizardry, holding their candles and cupping them against the night winds, a shadow figure with a rifle tucked under its black cape was crossing through the sandy lots on Grant Street and behind the hotel that looked out upon the vigil.

You could hear the Reverend's mighty voice rising up across the night...*Our Father who art in heaven...hallowed be thy name...*

When John Lourdes reached the shed where the hotel kept the guests' horses, he scaled a rickety fence then hoisted himself up on the roof of that derelict structure. He kept to one knee, scanning the rooftops around him to make sure no one was there to see him.

The hotel was built around a courtyard entry for the animals and help, and you could walk the roofs from the shed to the kitchen then along a flat corrugated hood over a walkway to a dining room that fronted the street. A black image rose up from behind the brick ledge. From this point of vantage, John Lourdes could look straight down upon the crowd. ...*Thy kingdom come...Thy will be done...*

The street was awash with light from that sweep of candles, great blocks of it from the hotel windows, from the windows of the Big Medicine offices. Faces that seemed to be disconnected from their bodies, faces looking out from an enormous darkness and up toward that heavenly reverend in prayer. What were they thinking at this moment, he wondered, about the nature of God's plan for each and all?

There were Mexicans down there, and Tejanos. In a show of good faith, probably, or offering their respects. Trying to prove they were at one with the world that confronted them. He didn't know she was down there. She and her father both. To write about what they saw, what they felt. To try and put reason and meaning to what they knew—that this whole vigil was built on the construct of a lie. ...*Lead us not into temptation...But deliver us from evil...Amen...*

A silence ensued and the Reverend brought forth a woman and had her stand beside him. "This good Christian lady," he said, "will lead us in a hymn. The words are on the back of the fliers we passed out, so we encourage you to sing along and send Charles Bucky Warren on his way with the beauty of your voices."

He stood back and a woman stepped forward, her head bent toward the enunciator and she began to sing—*The Son of God goes forth to war...A kingly crown to gain...His blood red banner streams afar...Who follows in His train...*

Voice after voice after voice took part. A rough harmony. The woman, the words, her lilting vibrato echoing out over the streets of a dusty Texas night. This was the real gospel of life, he thought, holding his rifle, searching. The incomprehensible and the innocent together. A moment of pure humanity standing upon an ash heap of lies.

Then he saw a face he could place on the list, singing with the rest, illumed by a cathedrallike window of the Big Medicine offices. Easy to pick out because he was the tallest by far—Citizen Pettyjohn. One of the Captain's faithful legion. A man he knew nothing about, had never heard speak, had seen only twice, and all he could really be sure of was that Citizen Pettyjohn and his dreams were about to part ways.

He rested his rifle on the hotel roof ledge. He aimed and he waited. He wanted all these voices at the peak of their emotions, at their loudest and most impassioned to cover the crack of the gunshots and help gain his escape.

The martyr first, whose eagle eye...Could pierce beyond the grave...Who saw his Master in the sky...And called to Him to save...

He reeled off four fast rounds. At least one was unsparing. Citizen Pettyjohn was holding the flier high up to better see the words, he was singing full throated with the rest, his expression fighting the painful loss of a friend, when there came this explosion of blood and dusty cloth from the heart of his coat. John Lourdes was already up and on the move, when the dying man lay against the building wall gasping. He was wraithlike from roof to roof as Citizen Pettyjohn looked up to the crowding strangers around him and begged, "What's happened to me?"

John Lourdes was crossing the empty lots along Grant, slipping the rifle under his cape and looking back. There were people already on the hotel roof. Silhouettes backlit by the candles down in the street, searching in all directions, and one man shouting. "There," he said, "There!"

CHAPTER 42

MARISITA LOOKED UPON THIS SCENE OF BEDLAM. A world turned upside down in a sweep of seconds. Women and children being rushed to the safety of doorways and offices. People on the hotel roof pointing toward Convent Street where the contours of a man disappeared into the shadow world of sheds and alleys. Rangers were sprinting up Grant Street with their guns drawn. Cars sped onto West Iturbide to try and cut off any route of escape. A Big Medicine executive stood at the Enunciator… "If you can hear me on Convent Street…There has been a shooting on Flores…The gunman is escaping your way…If you see anyone suspicious hold them there until the Rangers arrive…If you can hear me on Convent Street—"

Everywhere fallen candles lay in the road, guttering away like small heartbeats of fire. Marisita tried to press through the confluence of the crowd around the dying youth. Blood near black leaking out his colorless lips.

She asked the person nearest her, "Do you know the young man's name?" She had to ask another person and then a woman turned and said, "Pettyjohn…His name is Pettyjohn. He works with my nephew at Big Medicine."

Pettyjohn—a name from the list. It had been him.

A man leaning over the dying body looked up and saw Marisita and with a lethal stare, demanded, "Get that Mexican away from here. Get her away now."

A man shoved her, another shoved even more violently to get her moving. She threw up her hands. "I'm going," she said.

A moment of anger passed through her with such purity, only to be matched by the pleasure that followed. A dark pleasure, indeed, but a pleasure nonetheless—the people around her had gotten a taste of the fear and outrage they had exacted upon others.

Suffer it, she thought. Live in that bitter and vile ground for a while. Darken your skin and treat your heart to a good beating. She filled with a moment of such power, until she saw to her own shock and dismay that this moment—was them. Their bigotry and intolerance was her comeuppance. She had drunk from their cup of racism and was ashamed.

Her father shouldered through the crowd and got hold of his child and stood between her and those hostile and violent threats. Now it was she who had to keep her father's outrage in check.

When they had gotten clear of the mob and were safely down the street, in an out of breath whisper, he said, "It was him, wasn't it?"

She was looking far up Grant to see if they had captured him.

"You know?" he said.

"I know."

"Why?"

"He was on the list. He might be the Whiteman."

"What has Lourdes done?"

"He's taken the fight to them."

• • •

The next morning, the Captain and two Rangers arrived unceremoniously at the *La Cronica* offices. They parked out front. The Captain noted Luis Perez sitting at a table by the entry beneath a foolish looking umbrella. He knew the man.

"Perez...you're still alive I see. You work here?"

Perez opened his coat to give witness to the shoulder holster he wore.

Inside, the print shop was going about the hard business of getting out a newspaper. Senor Barros saw the Captain enter and walked to his daughter's desk and tapped her on the shoulder.

The Captain did not wait on propriety. He walked right past the secretary and through the gate and down the two steps and moved among the workers, followed by his men.

"Senor Barros...Senorita...Is this your full staff?"

"Yes," said Eduardo.

By now everyone working there had taken note of the Captain. "I need your full attention..." he said. "Do you hear me?"

The shop quieted considerably, except for the machinery.

The Captain noticed a copy of the front page on Marisita's desk. He excused himself and reached past her. The headline read: RANGER SHOT AT VIGIL——HIS DEATH RAISES QUESTIONS.

The Captain held up the front page. He addressed the staff. "We believe the man who murdered Ranger Pettyjohn is also behind the three

Ranger disappearances a few weeks back. We have gotten word that he might have been in this barrio. We are investigating that possibility. We are going to break you into two groups for questioning. I am a dedicated Christian and a good citizen. I hope you will be the same. Answer honestly…or confront the consequences."

The two Rangers started to separate the staff. Captain Asa suggested to the Barros they go somewhere private to talk. It was no suggestion.

They politely led him to the kitchen. They offered him coffee, but he declined. While Captain Asa looked out the window and took in the garden and the gate, the father glanced at his daughter. Would they be able to lie their way along? She touched the small crucifix that she wore around her neck.

"Who is he?" said the Captain, turning.

"Who are you talking about?" said Eduardo.

"A man was in that garden," said the Captain. "At night. Coming to this house. To that door."

"People often come here at night," said Eduardo. "They ask for food. For work. The way the economy is now…and with the collapsing government in Mexico. The word gets out that we are Catholic and help the poor."

He studied the young lady. "I was told you were in your nightgown. With a man…In that garden. A gringo, they believe. Is that how you greet the poor?"

"The person who suggested this is wrong…or is lying."

"Could it be your father does not know? That this is a matter of infatuation? I understand that, being a father myself. I could forgive that. If you help us."

"You insult my daughter," said the elder Barros.

"Wolves are drawn to human fear. Did you know that?"

Captain Asa went and sat at the table. He had been holding the front page of the newspaper all the while. "Tell me about the Mexican who came to see you at your offices a week ago."

He was addressing Marisita.

"I don't know who you are referring to."

"A tall gentleman, Mexican. He wanted to speak with you alone. You went out from the print shop to the street. He had something for you… Yes?"

"People often come to the paper to see my father. Or with stories. Or news. Sometimes with messages from reporters who are out somewhere and cannot get back by deadline."

"He was elderly, grey haired. Distinguished is how he was described to me. I think you'd remember a distinguished looking Mexican.

"I don't recall," said Marisita.

"For newspaper people, you seem to have thin memories."

"That is why we take notes, sir."

"I must remember that, Senorita Barros." He had said that with some degree of cordiality. But woe to such cordiality.

"The other day," said the Captain, "you and members of La Liga Femenil were outside of the theatre on Flores when you suddenly disappeared. You had been talking with woman friends when a man bumped into you and you followed off in his direction directly after."

"A man jostled me. He apologized. I was late for a meeting with my father."

"You said nothing to your friends. You just…" He snapped his fingers.

"I told the woman inside I had to leave early. Ask Senora Rueda."

"The man was said to be a gringo…Nice looking…Young…Well dressed."

"I don't understand this," said Eduardo.

"I believe you do. I know your daughter does."

Captain Asa took to reading over the front page as if the father and daughter were no longer there.

Senor Barros glanced at his daughter and when he had her attention, he tapped the finger of one hand against the back of the other hand. She looked down to see her own hand trembling.

"I read all the papers this morning before I came here. Each headline had how we did not find the killer. They highlighted that fact. But for you, it was of much less importance. Or even interest. You centered on the question of why this Ranger was killed."

"We saw that as essential," said Eduardo.

"Maybe you are both glad the killer escaped."

"That is a terrible thing to say."

"Terrible because it is a lie, Senor Barros? Or because it is true? In your article, you suggest that Ranger must have been killed for a reason, but you offer no reason. I find that…suspicious."

"I'm sorry you did. I wrote that article myself," said Marisita. "But it was only a question, as you can see, if you read the whole article." She went to the table. She leaned over the newspaper and read what she had written. "People will ask why was this hard working and decent young man of the law murdered? Why not anyone else there? From the roof, the killer had his choice of victims. Easier targets to say the least. I'm sure it is a question our dedicated Texas Rangers are grappling with and will answer."

Now the Captain looked over this young woman. A woman who was so politely brash as to defy description.

"Do you think Mexican Americans can truly be considered as real Americans?"

Senor Barros went to speak.

"I will answer that, Father. The good Captain addressed it to me. Yes… We believe we are real Americans. As real and as dedicated and as patriotic as the most noble Texas Ranger."

Captain Asa stood. "I have something for your paper. For an article sometime. It goes like this…Some men dig holes, some men fill them."

CHAPTER 43

HE HAD TO CROSS THE BRIDGE OVER ZACATE CREEK at Electric Motor Street. That's where the road passed the Laredo Woolen Mills and then struck due east out of town. John Lourdes used as a marker the water tower that was on a confluence of hills known as The Heights. The reservoir was out there, and the water works. There were about a dozen homes spread out on those hills that he could barely make out but for their pitched second story roofs.

Leonard LaShelle lived in The Heights on what had been the family estate. His father had been a successful stock broker until he manipulated his way to suicide. The house had been torched after the bankruptcy. LaShelle now lived on the property in what was once the servant's quarters. LaShelle lived alone, and there wasn't a house within a mile.

LaShelle was finishing up hitching his saddle when he noticed a rider slowly approaching through the parched grass. His holster was still draped over the saddle pommel, but he didn't feel he needed it, even though he still was carrying last night around with him. John Lourdes doffed his hat when he got close enough and said, "Good morning, sir."

LaShelle leaned against his horse. "I know you...Big Medicine...with the Captain and that Adams fella."

"That's right...You're Leonard LaShelle, yeah?"

LaShelle nodded. John Lourdes looked over at the remains of the big house. A crumbly, charred frame and a chimney rising maybe three stories. "Home to birds and critters," he said now of that relic.

"You comin' from or goin' to Laredo?" said LaShelle.

"Comin' from."

"I'm headin' in. Did they catch that bastard yet?"

"If they had...I'd a known about it."

"You at the vigil?"

"Not exactly."

John Lourdes saw LaShelle's holster hanging there from the saddle. LaShelle was walking over to the corral fence to get his coat, which was draped over a railpost.

"We were all over Grant and Convent," he said. "Nothin.' It was like he just disappeared."

"No," said John Lourdes, "he didn't disappear. He was right there in plain sight all the time."

LaShelle was about to slip an arm into a coat sleeve. "What are you talking about?"

"By the time you all were running up Grant toward Convent, he had gotten off the cape he was wearing and the rifle he was totin' and dumped them both in a trash bin in an alley. Then he went and sat on a stoop on Grant Street next to a passed out drunk. He lit a cigarette and slumped there like some alkie vagabond. Rangers ran right by him, shouting all franticlike, 'You seen a fella carryin' a rifle run this way?' 'Noooo,' this fella said, shaking his head. Then he just got up and walked right through all that chaos on Flores like it was a morning at church.

LaShelle just couldn't come to grasp all this. "You makin' this up?"

"Not hardly."

"How is it you know such a thing?"

"I'm the one was acting the alkie vagabond on the stoop. I'm the one you're looking for." He set the semi-automatic pistol on his lap for LaShelle to see. "I'm the gent what killed those three Rangers...And shot K.J. Caparell...And sent Bucky Warren on his way...And Pettyjohn."

LaShelle looked as if he'd had a talk with God, and the news wasn't good. He was still holding his coat, it was dragging on the ground. He glanced at his horse.

"That brut of a Webley is too far. Step back and keep stepping."

LaShelle did as he was commanded until his back was against the corral railing. John Lourdes had dismounted. He walked over to where that Webley hung from the saddle.

"I want the Whiteman," said John Lourdes. "You want to live a long and happy life. How do we both get what we want?"

John Lourdes took the Webley and emptied it. "I left one shell," he said. Then he flung the weapon into the dirt about twenty feet away.

"I want the fuckin' Whiteman," shouted John Lourdes.

"K.J. is the Whiteman..." said LaShelle. "Bucky was the Whiteman... Pettyjohn was the Whiteman...I'm the fuckin' Whiteman... So get to it."

John Lourdes held up his weapon. "I'm gonna toss my gun right by yours. When I do...go to it."

"You might have a full clip in yours," said LaShelle.

"Then go for my gun."

He thought about this. "You wouldn't try and bait me, and your gun is empty?"

"Then go for your own gun."

LaShelle's nostrils flared. He wore a dark and burnt looking stare.

"It's not a good morning, is it?" said John Lourdes.

"I've had better."

He threw the gun and LaShelle charged. John Lourdes was right with him. He kept low to the ground and troweled up a handful of dirt. The two guns lay like bookends in the sand.

LaShelle flung his coat at John Lourdes. It turned in the sunlight and John Lourdes swiped it away. The two men hit into each other like a pair of bucks. Birds flew out of the blackened house timbers and streaked across the sky.

LaShelle tossed the youth aside. Before the man could reach his weapon, John Lourdes threw the handful of dirt in his face. The men locked together. The horses panicked. They bucked and reared. The dust rose around the struggle consuming the men. Their bodies contorted, fists whaling away. John Lourdes could feel a thick and sourish breath against his face. The men were stained with dust as they tumbled over one another. The world tilted and then turned and John Lourdes' cheeks ballooned as he struggled against the weight of the much larger man.

John Lourdes bit into LaShelle's neck. He tore at the flesh like a rabid dog. LaShelle screamed up the devil. John Lourdes was being pounded by an enormous fist that felt like a hot pipe to the top of his skull. The breath came out of him hard through bared teeth. Blood was streaming down LaShelle's neck and onto John Lourdes' face. He kicked at LaShelle violently. A piece of his boot heel caught the older man in the jaw and tore it wide open. LaShelle drove the top of his head right into John Lourdes face stunning him enough to get hold of his Webley and come up firing.

He got off round after round. The chamber clicking away. But the gun was empty. By the time he realized, there was a space in his throat where his voice had been. And smoke coming out an open hole in his neck. John Lourdes knelt there, holding himself up with one hand, and in the other, the semiautomatic he had just fired.

CHAPTER 44

WHEN THE CAPTAIN WAS DONE WITH HIS INTERROGATION, he walked out of the kitchen without a word more then back to the print shop. The Barros following at a polite distance. Captain Asa's men had finished their questioning of the *La Cronica* staff, and all three Rangers left together. Before returning to the shop, Marisita took her father's arm so they might talk a minute.

"What does it all mean, Father?"

"What does it mean? It means this newspaper is not long for the world. It means 'continue at your own peril.' Was it true?"

"What?"

"What that 'Rinche' said?"

"About?"

"About you and him. On the street. Don't banter with me, child. That you followed after him like some common peon."

"I am many things, Father. But I am not common."

"Was it him?"

"It was him."

"And you followed after him?"

"I went to catch up to him."

"And where did you meet him? At his hotel?"

"We are not going to relitigate this argument, are we?"

"Honest passions can be more dangerous than dishonest ones."

"It was honest passion that brought us to this place. It brought us to Father Pinto."

They could hear the Ranger's car pull away. The silence that followed carried danger with it all the way to their souls.

"He knows too much," said Marisita.

"Rueda and his wife have told him."

"They would betray us?"

"In this world, one's friends are closer to one's enemies. It is a bitter reality that confirms there are more converts to cowardice than there are to courage."

"I am to see the dear Senora later today at a meeting of La Liga," said Marisita.

"Say nothing to the women."

"I will spit in her face like a lady."

"Hear me, child. It will only inflame her and that husband of hers."

"Inflame them? We are being burned to the ground, Father. Do we not at least try to put out the fire?"

Senor Barros had the knuckles of a fist pressed against closed lips.

"Father?"

"The Mexican gentleman who came here—"

"He's the porter from the hotel. He is the one who had a business on Matamoros that was burned down. It is now the cafe where our people are not allowed to be served. I need to see him. To get word to John."

"They might be following us at all times now."

"We will have to contend with that."

He looked toward the door to the print shop. "Someone in there told them about the porter."

"One of our own?" she said. "But which one?"

"Does it matter? One is already too many."

• • •

The meeting of *La Liga Femenil* was to be at the Laredo Seminary which was on a clear stretch of bluff above the river. It was past the International Bridge and the tracks of the Mexican National Railway and the Great Northern. The Seminary offered its facilities, its conference rooms and grounds to social organizations of the city without favor to race or political viewpoint. For a small stipend, of course. This did not sit well in certain quarters, but it was hard to contend with the power of the church. Even Big Medicine and the Rangers tread with civic caution where the offices of Christianity were concerned.

When Marisita had arrived at the Seminary she had graced herself with a certain degree of self-control. Belen Rueda was in conversation with a few of the women when she saw the Barros girl had arrived. Marisita seemed untouched by what the Rueda woman knew had gone on that morning. She politely excused herself as she could not engage Marisita soon enough in conversation.

Marisita indulged in every topic except the one the sheriff's wife had an unhealthy curiosity about. Knowing this, Marisita lingered on every detail of every inconsequential matter that was on her mind. Sometimes to outwit someone, it is best just to play unaware. And so, Belen was forced to ask—as a concerned friend, of course. Liars and phonies are often disguised as concerned friends. Because they can look like themselves, dress like themselves, act like themselves, even be themselves.

She told Marisita that according to her husband, Captain Asa was in the barrio that day questioning certain parties about the murders of the three Rangers. And that *La Cronica* was on a list. By now, some of the women close to them began to involve themselves, because they too had heard such a thing.

Marisita was calm and measured. "The Rangers," she said, "seem to be chasing some kind of rumor of suspicious men at night at our house… Or at the newspaper office. It has something to do with the murder of the three Rangers, I believe."

One of the ladies suggested that she was taking this rather evenly, under the circumstances.

"I don't know if it's more infuriating or ridiculous." Then she looked at the Ladies of the League around her, her friends, some she knew only through the organization, and then Belen. With some degree of humor, she said, "Be careful… This could happen to any one of you. Especially if you have suspicious men around your house at night."

She suffered the meeting with Belen there next to her, taking possession of her hand from time to time. Someday, Marisita thought, there will be paintings of Judas as a woman.

Afterwards she asked for Father Demaris. He was a Seminary teacher who not only was the Barros family confessor but the one who had been in charge of the funeral that day on Flores. It was through his private intercession that the Barros' had been put in contact with the El Paso Jesuit, Father Pinto.

In the quiet of the chapel, she asked him to hear her confession. In that dark and shrouded world she spoke through a tiny wooden screen. "I am not only here to confess my sins, which are many. But to ask your help in an earthly matter."

GUILTY OF
BEING BORN

CHAPTER 45

THERE WAS A NOTE ON JOHN LOURDES' DRESSER beside his semi-automatic.

John L –
There's been a killing. Will pick you up
in an hour. Be ready.

It had been given to him by the desk clerk when he returned to the hotel. As he shaved, he looked over the nicks and bruises on his face. There was a knock. He called out from the bathroom. He could hear the suite door open and close.

"Give me a minute more, you bastard. Make yourself a drink and tell me who the fuck was killed."

"I'm not who you think it is."

John Lourdes did not recognize the voice. He leaned away from the sink and looked out the bathroom door. A priest stood there holding an envelope.

"I think you have the wrong room, Father."

"John Lourdes?"

"Yes."

"My name is Father Demaris."

He stared at this impassive little character in his black robe and his rosaries hanging from a black sash. Then the name—it all clicked. "You're the one…Father Pinto—"

The priest nodded. He looked to the open veranda door. "Are we alone?"

John Lourdes went over and swung the veranda door shut.

The priest held out the envelope. "It's from Marisita Barros."

"Is she all right?" he said, coming forward to take the letter.

"She'll explain herself."

As he took the note, he heard the harsh sound of a car horn. Once, then twice, then again. He excused himself and yanked open the veranda door and walked out and leaned over the railing. There was Cager behind the wheel of a sedan with the Big Medicine imprimatur splashed across the car doors.

"What are you fuckin' doin'?" said John Lourdes.

"We got to make time. Let's go."

John Lourdes waved and went back into his suite.

"I'm sorry, but—"

"I understand," said the priest.

The priest handed John Lourdes the letter. They walked together to the suite door.

"If you should need help of any kind…" said Father Demaris. "Or just someone to talk things out with. I am at the Seminary."

"When I need to get in touch with—"

"Yes, certainly."

They shook hands.

"The letter will explain why it would be best to no longer burden the porter here. For his own safety, let alone yours."

There was that car horn, that relentless horn.

"Be careful, John. There are many forces aligning against you."

• • •

John Lourdes swung the car door open, and before he'd gotten his ass down in the seat, Cager had taken off. He was working the horn and swerving his way through all that traffic of trucks and wagons with a vengeance.

It wasn't until John Lourdes said, "What happened?" that Cager turned and glanced at him and noticed that recently chinked up face. He grinned mischievously. "Was it your standard barroom fight, or something more personal and exciting I'd love to hear about?"

John Lourdes sat back and crossed his arms. "I have no fuckin' idea. I only showed up after it was over."

"One of *those*!" said Cager.

"You wanna tell me where we're going before you kill us getting there?"

"A Big Medicine employee. They say it's pretty gruesome."

He needn't ask more. When they crossed the bridge over Zacate Creek, Cager said, "You ever been out to The Heights?"

"You mean out by the reservoir? Once. But at night. I'd heard that's where the radicals go when they're plotting their political witchcraft."

They drove in silence after that. John Lourdes smoking. Cager mumbling to himself, when he wasn't singing in some miserable key. You'd have thought that son of a bitch was heading out for a holiday.

All John Lourdes kept thinking about was the letter in his pocket and that priest, Father Demaris, showing up like that. It was as if that night in El Paso was reprising itself. When the priest had appeared out of nowhere. And there he was, naked, with this outrageous young lady who always seemed to be one step ahead of an indictment, answering the door and returning with the letter from Father Pinto.

That world was gone. The last traces of it fading with each treacherous mile yet to come.

"Nothin' out of you at all," said Cager. "But the mind is working overtime."

John Lourdes blew smoke out his nostrils. Gave Cager a noncommittal stare. Cager nodded. "You got enough goin' on in that head of yours for half a dozen fellas like me. Most men would be talkin' it up about where we're going. But you…it's like you've been there already."

"A smart man doesn't talk about what he doesn't know about before he knows about it."

"And you're just too fuckin' rich."

It was a long road up to LaShelle's place. Endless burnt grass. The hills bare but for overgrown mesquite and ocotillo and their lonely shadows upon the earth.

Cager pulled up and parked by that shambly ruin of a big house. There were about a dozen men fanned out, searching the property. Captain Asa was on the porch of the servants' quarters, his hat off, cooling himself with it, giving orders.

John Lourdes noted two other Rangers on his list. Ahearn was looking over the ground where the fight had taken place. Hughes was pacing around LaShelle's corpse which had been stretched out and lain on its back in the sun. Hughes was a bellied man with a coarse, overgrown beard. He had a threadbare voice for a big man and was cursing heaven with it for what had befallen his friend. He kept pointing his hat at the body, demanding God get off whatever hell he was sitting on and come down there and give him a clue as to what the fuck had happened.

John Lourdes followed Cager. They stood over the body. It had been doused with some sort of flammable. LaShelle's face and arms and the whole front of his torso was burned beyond recognition.

"That's bloodthirsty," Cager said.

Blood thirsty, John Lourdes thought to answer him. Yes…but necessary.

CHAPTER 46

RANGER AHEARN CALLED OUT. He pointed to the signs of the fight. Boot tracks all scrambled together. Two people. And blood. Small coins of it that had dried blackish in the sand. The Ranger squatted there like some seer studying the runes.

Ahearn was nearer John Lourdes' age and he had a sweat stained and pitiless manner. A shadow born of the shadow of Captain Asa. A hardass Ranger in the making, with a damp shirt that clung to his muscular back.

Captain Asa stepped from the porch. He called his men to join him. He stood beside Ahearn.

"Wasn't killing him enough?" said Ranger Hughes.

"Mexicans," said one of the men. "It's the Indian blood."

Ahearn was moving his hat around in his hands. "It was a rough fight and not a short one."

John Lourdes could tell them how right he was in that. He listened to their rage and their rantings as they spun out questions and theories that were nothing more than a string of fits and starts that went nowhere.

No one could answer the one essential question—why this hardworking, goodblooded man was murdered. The only conjecture they could grasp was that it was because he worked for Big Medicine and violent radicals from across the river wanted the corporation taken down because it was a symbol of a corrupt America.

Of course, John Lourdes knew what Captain Asa and his two Rangers knew. The curdled truth was at a ranchero at the edge of the desert where a family had been left to lie and rot and had ended up as a few lines back among the advertisements in the *Laredo Times: Bandits Raid Home—Kill Mexican Family.*

"You better come to know why these patriotic men were killed," said John Lourdes. "That way you can know who's next on the list."

It came out as pure understatement. Him taking out a cigarette to light as he spoke. But it got their attention. And certainly the Captain's.

"You know," said Captain Asa, "when I was interrogating those people at the *La Cronica*, they had an article they'd written that pretty much said the same thing. And it aroused my suspicions."

"It's the one you've a reward out on," said Cager. "The one who says he's gonna hunt out the Whiteman. He's putting down a marker."

Ahearn asked how he could be gut sure of such a thing.

Cager glanced at John Lourdes who stood there quietly attentive and smoked. "I got a nose for such things," said Cager. He walked over to John Lourdes and reached out and took the cigarette from him. "You may want to convince Big Medicine to raise the reward on that bastard, Captain. That'll get people's blood up."

Ranger Ahearn spoke out as he suddenly stood. "Take a look there," he said, pointing with his hat. "We've got something."

Beyond the shimmery reservoir and the corrugated walls of the water-works and right into the eye of the sun, a flare left its burning trail across a cloudless Texas sky.

• • •

It was a hard ride for the twelve men on horseback and those in two sedans pushing it through the heat for the better part of an hour. They came upon the place where the tracers had been fired. It was there on a gentle slope that a young Mexican was kept kneeling in the sand, his back straight, hands clasped behind his head. Two men from Big Medicine stood watch over him. One sat atop his mount, the other on the ground under an umbrella.

John Lourdes could see the Mexican had started to weave side to side from the heat and the strain on his muscles. He looked to be in his early twenties, and it was doubtful he would get much older.

The Captain dismounted, as did a number of the others. "What do we have here?" he said.

The man under the umbrella stood. He held up a large burlap bag which clanged as he shook it. He emptied the contents on the ground. There were silver knives and forks and spoons. Expensive goblets and scribed plates and a silver tea set. One of the men lifted a tea cup and feigned drinking with a quaintly extended pinky. The men laughed. The laughter in that hot dry air deadening.

The Captain spoke pretty good Spanish. He and the youth conversed. The Mexican was educated and smart. He remained calm and polite, even though John Lourdes could see from his expression the man was petrified. He explained that the silver had belonged to his family. And that President Diaz had run them out. This was all he had left, and he was selling off pieces to survive until he could begin a new life. He even had paperwork in his saddlebags that would prove the silverware was his. John Lourdes thought—the youth might survive this yet.

The man atop the horse flung the Mexican's saddlebags. They landed at the Captain's feet. He squatted and emptied the contents into the sand.

There were pamphlets and books and fliers that were all to John Lourdes' eye political in nature. He had stepped from the sedan and gotten close enough to better read the bold print about how the Mexican government and the American government were partners in the exploitation of the Mexican people. How both governments needed to be stripped of their power. How Texas should be given back to its rightful heirs. There were copies of Mexican newspapers. He saw a few were of *La Cronica*. The Captain took one of those in hand and looked it over before tossing it aside. Something else caught his eye, and his mood darkened considerably.

The Captain held up an article torn from the *Laredo Times*. It was the story about the three dead Rangers, the rattlesnake, the badges, and the anonymous note about hunting out the Whiteman. The Captain was now in full ire.

"Are you him?" he said.

"Him?"

He shook the article in the youth's face. "The one who did this."

"I never did such a thing as that."

"Who then?"

"I don't know. Why would I know?"

Ahearn was leaning over the Captain's shoulder. "Let me warm up his feet some, Captain."

The Captain waved off that thought.

"I will ask you once more. I will ask you politely. And then I will hang you."

John Lourdes watched unfold what he could not stop, and that was moving now toward its inexorable end. It was everything before it and everything to come. The Mexican had no answer. How could he?

The Captain stood and scanned the countryside cupping a hand over his eyes. He pointed. About a quarter mile off. Through all that quivery heat, a dead manzanita rose up out of the earth like the ruined bones of a hand.

"If those branches will hold, do the deed right there."

The men organized. They got the Mexican up on his saddle. The Captain approached the sedan that Cager drove. "Adams...I want you and Lourdes to go to Big Medicine. Tell Evans what's happened. Tell him we need to drive up the amount of that reward.

As they drove away, Captain Asa and his little army of veniremen rode off, and Cager said, "Reminds me of that first night in the desert when we came upon them. And they were herding that Mexican along to be done away with."

"Yeah," said John Lourdes. "Seems there's a lot of nights just like that goin' around."

"I don't know why they just don't shoot that Mex bastard," said Cager. "Personally, I'm not for all that wasted drama of a hanging."

But John Lourdes understood why the youth was being hung and not shot. He knew it from that sacred place in his life that was Mexican. Where he had been born and nursed and raised.

The youth fit every sin. He fit every complaint. Every antagonism. Every resentment. Every hostility. Every revenge. Every painful loss or threat. Every need to better your own life at the expense of someone else's. He was being lynched because he was guilty of being born.

CHAPTER 47

IT WAS A LONG RIDE BACK TO BIG MEDICINE. The rattling motor, the chinky trundle of the frame. Long, hard, uncomfortable and solemn. They wouldn't arrive until nightfall at the earliest. They were carrying extra water and gas, and a damn good thing. They'd been driving for about half an hour when Cager said, "The Mexican is dead by now."

John Lourdes had been thinking about the youth. About the shifting scales of life and perspective, and the atrocious folly he had been witness to and part of. He wondered, with the way the world there was, could the Rangers ever be held accountable for their actions?

"I hope none of those jokesters leave a little air in the noose," said John Lourdes.

"That could get ugly," said Cager.

The earth behind them bled with sunset. There was dust from where the river stretched on miles away. Deep shadows began to fill the contours of the land ahead of them, closing it down, stripping it of detail.

"The kid was about our age," said Cager.

"Give or take."

"And he's gonna be about our age for eternity."

"If there is an eternity out there somewhere."

"At least he doesn't have to worry about selling off the family heirlooms," said Cager.

"No...I'm sure the boys back there are shooting dice for them."

"And he doesn't have to worry about getting his clothes cleaned or his shoes shined or what to have for dinner or going to the dentist for that matter."

"I feel like I'm missing out."

The two men looked at each other. Some hard seriousness had settled in.

"You think much about dying?" said Cager.

"The thought comes upon me from time to time."

"I had an uncle that used to say it's best to keep your head full of stars and stay clear of all the shit that goes on in the daylight."

"And what became of this wise uncle, if you don't mind my asking?"

Cager gave John Lourdes a kind of bleak grin that pretty much answered the question.

The headlights began to mark their way into the blue darkness. Crowns of earth rose up around them. The air chilled. John Lourdes offered to drive. Cager waved him off. John Lourdes slipped down in the seat. He pulled his hat low. He crossed his arms and closed his eyes.

"I'll leave the world to you," he told Cager.

"That's mighty white of you."

They drove on. A moody silence filled in the night. Until Cager finally came out with, "I believe I figured out why they couldn't catch the fella that killed Pettyjohn during the vigil."

John Lourdes didn't answer. Cager looked over at him. His body rocking slightly with the unsteadiness of the sedan.

"You hear me?"

"I heard you."

"It was simple…and slick in its own way."

"Yeah?"

"And it explains everything."

"Everything?"

They drove on. Cager's jaw flexed. "You're not gonna ask?"

"Consider yourself asked."

"John …you're rich. Most men would be crawling up my ass to get the answer."

"Yeah…How many are up there now?"

He was going to tell John Lourdes, "Fuck you," when a shot took apart the windshield. Glass shattered in Cager's face and he lost control of the wheel. The ground there rose and fell. It was arid and gullied and the wheels turned toward the edge of a decline. John Lourdes was up and grabbing for the wheel as the sedan sped down a long and sandy decline where it finally turned over.

The gas pedal had jammed, and the engine was running wild. There was the stench of burning rubber. Dust rose all the way up to the top of the hill. John Lourdes had been tossed clear. He was shaken, and on his hands and knees, from where he called out to Cager, "Are you all right?"

"I'll know in a fuckin' minute."

John Lourdes could hear Cager pounding at the car door. He crawled along and slipped around the back of the sedan where the tires spun uselessly and kicked out a choking smoke. Cager slithered out of the overturned Ford.

The men crabbed their way along the ravine. A thin border of dust obscured the road above them from where the shot had come.

"What do you think?" said Cager.

"Someone's out to draw blood against Big Medicine...Or this is about the car, and the car means we might have money. How far is Big Medicine?"

Cager had pulled a bandana from his trouser pocket. He had cuts on his face from the shattered glass which he wiped at.

"About five miles," he said.

They had gotten out their weapons.

"How many bullets do you have?" said John Lourdes.

"What's in my revolver. And about ten shells in my pocket."

"I have one extra clip."

"That's not much of a resistance between us."

"Are there flares in that sedan?"

"Most of the company cars have 'em in the back on the floor. I don't know about that one."

"If we shot up a flare—"

"Yeah. But one of us would have to—"

John Lourdes held out his semiautomatic and the extra clip.

Cager looked at the gun there. Then stared into a hard, straight expression staring back at him.

"Are you sure?"

John Lourdes clapped him on the shoulder. Cager took the gun and the clip. He whispered, "You son of a bitch." He put the clip between his teeth. Readied a gun in each hand.

John Lourdes slithered along on his belly most of the way back to the sedan. There were reefs of smoke from the burning engine drifting up toward the road. He wriggled behind the undercarriage, came up by the back door and when he turned the handle there was a metallic click.

A volley of riflefire ignited. Shots pinged down the length of the chassis. Cager opened fire with both handguns. Aiming into the smoke and haze along the lip of the ravine. The riflefire ceased as suddenly as it started. John Lourdes was scurrying back through the darkness and gasping heavily when he pulled up alongside Cager.

"Nothing," he said.

CHAPTER 48

Eduardo Barros was at his desk typing when he heard noises from the kitchen. Thinking it was his daughter, he went to see. She had not returned home from the Seminary and it was late. He was filled with worry and when he entered the kitchen his worry became well founded.

Captain Asa was sitting at the kitchen table. He had obviously hunted through the cabinets because he had out Senor Barros' bottle of whiskey and two glasses. It was as if he had been waiting for the editor, and so he had.

"I heard you typing away," he said. "So I thought it best not to disturb you."

"I thought it was my daughter."

"As you can see..."

"Where is she?"

"How would I know?"

"If you mean to use her in some fashion to—"

"I came here to have a private talk. So if you confided in me, no one need know." He ordered Barros to sit. He then poured the editor a drink. "You know who the man is," said Captain Asa. "You either met him directly, or from the Mexicans that speak their venom through your newspaper."

He slid the glass of whiskey across the table.

"We lost another man today," said the Captain. "A good man. A hard working Christian man. His name was Leonard LaShelle. He worked for Big Medicine. But you probably knew all that."

"I did not."

"A half dozen of your employees have given statements about this Mexican gentleman who came here. We will find him eventually. Someone will see him in the street and notify us. Friends of yours, honest citizens, people of law enforcement, have given statements that a man came here at night—"

Barros rose suddenly in anger. He went to the counter and returned with a notepad and paper. He sat back down.

"Here's what I will do," said the editor. "I will write an article that exactly details this conversation. I will make it clear I refused to admit what you ask. And that people who have given statements come forward to this newspaper and state them for the record. I will put in print the words to hang me with…if you can."

Through all this, the Captain listened politely. "Write what you wish, but first…" He stood. "Come with me."

He went to the door and opened it. Barros sat at the table, strained, uncertain.

"Where is the courage of the press?"

Captain Asa had his car outside. The street was silent. There were a few sleepy lights along the block. It felt of death in the air. Senor Barros had no idea where he was being taken until they crossed the tracks for the Mexican National Railroad. Then he knew.

Captain Asa pulled up to the stone pillars that marked the entrance to the cemetery. There, he parked. The Captain got out and Barros followed. Two men were sitting on a huge mound of dirt by a recently rendered grave. They were playing cards and drinking by boxlight. It was Rangers Ahearn and Hughes. The only sound the cranky turning of a windmill pumping water outside that still world of moontopped headstones.

There was an outcast loneliness to the place. The collar around Barros' neck was soaked. He did not feel like he would die a brave man's death, or the death of a man with a cause, a reason, some purpose, or even a child. He could hear the sound of the train coming. He could see the locomotive's headlight thundering toward them out of a pitched dark. That great heavy iron monster of freight cars carrying its weight in value to a despotic land.

Nothing was said. The Captain grabbed Barros by the shirt and slung him into the grave. The editor fell five feet on his back and there he was looking into a dusty light pouring down at him and the blinded shadows of three men with huge revolvers as they fired.

• • •

When Marisita heard the kitchen door open and then swing closed, she went hurriedly downstairs in her robe. It was not her father that she came upon.

"Where is my father?" she said.

Captain Asa stood at the door. He removed his hat in a gentlemanly fashion. "We had a very thoughtful conversation before I left him."

"Left him where?"

"To his own devices, I believe."

"What does that mean?"

He motioned for her to sit.

The bottle of whiskey and glasses were still on the table where the two men had left them.

"I knew he had been here drinking with someone," she said, "but—"

"Sit."

She tightened the robe around her.

"You have no right to come into our house at this hour without—"

"I am investigating a number of killings. Witnesses have placed a possible suspect at this house. Your own employees state there was a Mexican gentleman here that we also believe has information we might find helpful. So don't tell me where I have a right to go."

"You have never shown such dedication of purpose when it came to the murder of the funeral director."

He walked past her and that statement and poured himself a drink as if this were his house, and his whiskey. And he never raised his voice or flashed her a look of either intimidation or anger. He never showed that to ensnare someone was a pleasure.

"I've read your work. I am impressed. You are a very smart young lady."

"This is where you say, 'you are a smart young lady, but—'"

"No. I was just curious." He drank down the whiskey. "Why don't you use all that skill and talent to better your own country?"

"This is my country."

"It isn't. You are…a Mexican."

"I am a Mexican American."

"That is a term you have tried to connive into a reality. To make a home here. But it will never be so. A Mexican American is a dog with three legs."

"What do you want? Where is my father?"

She had almost shouted.

"Mexico is a failing dictatorship. Your people do not understand or

appreciate freedom and democracy. They are lazy, and they are back slid-
ers. Why not go there and use your talents to make them proud? To make
Mexico free and democratic and hard working. In that way you people can
live there instead of coming here to get what you can't there. I see that as
an act of cowardice.

"You are not going to turn Texas into 'Little Mexico' without a fight.
This is a European, Anglo Christian country. Look at yourself. Think about
what I'm saying. If you were proud to be a Mexican…Really proud of your
heritage…You wouldn't have stolen your way across the border to be here,
instead of there. You're here because you think as little of your own people,
as we do. It's the one thing we have in common."

He was done, except for one detail. "You're hardly over twenty. You
don't want to go to jail for the rest of your life. It ain't romantic."

• • •

Besides her father being missing, what that vile Ranger had said had her
crying. Because there was some truth even in the evil of it. The country
of Mexico, the country of her heritage and faith, needed so much. It was
a despotic failure with the ruined souls of its countrymen. It was becoming a ship with no one to command its legal will. It needed people like
her, people better than her, people more courageous about trying to better
their world, instead of escaping or abandoning it. She was guilty of these
thoughts the Captain had spoken of and she wondered, in her own way, if
those thoughts were racist. True thoughts, but racist in some regard none
the less. And was her being in the United States instead of Mexico an
indictment of how she truly felt about a place and its people, her people?

When she heard the door open and close, she was up like a cat from
the parlor sofa. Her father was crossing the kitchen when she entered. A
picture of solemn, exhausted and filthy. She threw her arms around him.

"You're all right."

"Not now."

He pushed her away and walked to the stairs and started up to his
room. With her in the hall, he slammed shut the door and stripped off his
clothes in disgust.

The Rangers had only meant to scare and humiliate and on both
accounts, most certainly had. They had fired at him there in the grave,

intentionally missing, but in so doing he had soiled himself. His trousers and undergarments were strewn with his bowels, and he'd been left to walk home bearing his shame.

He bundled his clothes in a sheet. He then went to the bathroom and cleansed himself—he slipped on a robe and took this bundle of personal humiliation and walked out.

She was at the bottom of the stairs when he descended, dire and black mooded. She saw the bundle and asked, "What is that? What are you doing?"

As he passed through the kitchen, he grabbed up a kerosene lamp and matches. He went out into the garden and tossed the bundle against the far wall. He covered the stenched clothing with kerosene and then lit a match and tossed it. A pyre of flame climbed the whitewashed wall. He stood there watching this deep yellow flame where his degradation went up in smoke.

CHAPTER 49

THE FORD ENGINE HAD ALL BUT BURNED ITSELF OUT. The drifting smoke along the road thinning considerably. The two men had moved farther up the ravine making their way close to the lip of the ridge as safely as they could and talked in suppressed whispers.

They had no idea who was out there or how many of them there were or what they wanted. It had been pretty much of a standoff of silence for over an hour. They also knew that come dawn, where they were was no better than an open grave.

"I don't think there's more than five of them out there," said Cager.

"Yeah…How'd you get to the number?"

"They know we were two. Over five, I think they'd just rush us and be done with it."

"If one of us can get to a horse of theirs, make for Big Medicine, brings back help."

"What does the other one do?"

"Stay alive," said John Lourdes.

"We can't be here come morning."

"No."

"Well…we better start planning."

John Lourdes pointed. "Still too much moon."

"Yeah."

Cager lay back, his gun across his chest. He was fingering the trigger, too much nervous energy. "How 'bout I tell you my reasoning on that shooting at the vigil."

"You're a conscientious bastard, you know that?"

He leaned in close beside John Lourdes, so he was practically whispering in his ear. "That fella didn't run at all after he killed Pettyjohn."

"No?"

"I say he just went down and joined the crowd. Got rid of the gun, of course, and walked right with them. Didn't run…no, no, no. Everybody be looking for a gent trying to escape."

John Lourdes had been half listening, because the other half had been focused on that wrecked sedan lying on its side in the sand.

"What do you think?" said Cager.

John Lourdes didn't answer.

"Well?"

John Lourdes eased himself up a bit. He ran the barrel of his gun across his chin.

"You're avoiding me, John L."

"You want to hear what I think? I think you're the second dumbest son of a bitch I know…"

"Yeah…The second, huh?"

"You want to know who the first is?"

"Why not? I hate not knowing my competition."

"I am, brother."

"What are you talking…"

"How fuckin' stupid are we?" said John Lourdes. "You want to know?" He pointed his gun at the car. Cager didn't understand.

"We got our own flare, Mister Adams. Courtesy of the Ford Motor Company."

A revelation went through Cager Adams like it was a holy friggin' thunderbolt. "The gas tank."

"And there's two extra cans in the backseat. How much does the gas tank of that sedan hold?"

"About ten gallons, I think. We were near half empty. And we got half as much again in the cans."

"We torch the car."

"That's a Roman fuckin' candle we're sittin' on," said Cager.

"You think they'll see it at Big Medicine?"

"The country is pretty flat. It's only five miles."

"And we're on a rise. We should be—"

A man in Spanish called out to them from the dark, "Anyone alive down there?"

It had happened so suddenly, it spooked both men. They had eased themselves up over the excitement about the gas tank, but now they thrust themselves back flat against the slope and lay there. They were both breathing heavily. They waited. They did not know from what direction the voice had come. Cager pointed where he had a suspicion, but John Lourdes could only shrug.

"Is anyone alive down there?"

John Lourdes put a finger to his lips. "Let them rot a while," he whispered. "Get their asses up."

Cager nodded. "When it's time to answer…you talk. Your Spanish is better than mine."

"Someone was alive down there," shouted a man. "Unless ghosts shoot back. Are you ghosts?"

A few rounds were fired off from up top. They pinged against the ravine walls kicking out chips of rock and dust.

Cager pointed to where he thought the shots were fired and John Lourdes nodded.

"We want the car…If it's still running. And money. We know you work for Big Medicine."

Cager whispered, "Sounds like they're ready to make a fight of it."

"They might be in the same fix we are. They're just shucking us."

"You down there…You're gonna have to talk to us."

Cager reached into his trouser pocket. Then there he was with an automatic knife in hand. He pressed the release button and the blade sprang forward. "Mail order," he said. "We got to gut the gas tank, and we need a rag for a fire."

John Lourdes reached his arm across Cager's chest. Pulled tight his shirt cuff with his loose hand. "Cut away."

"The company isn't worth dying for, is it?" the voice said.

Cager wound the cloth scrap around his fingers. He went to hand John Lourdes his revolver, but he made Cager keep it, on the chance they got separated. Before Cager started off, John Lourdes had one last thing to whisper.

Cager slid down the slope as softly as he could. He slithered across that rocky pit hardly breathing.

"They treat your people as near as bad as they do ours. They stole as much of your property."

Cager had to stop when his belt buckle got to scraping against the stony fastness of the ground he crawled over. He waited to make sure he had not been heard. And when he was sure, he shifted to his side and fished his way along after that.

"You're just niggers like we are…white niggers to our brown niggers."

When Cager got up against the undercarriage, he held up the hand with the knife and fanned the arm. John Lourdes saw something in all that night that approximated movement by the car and hoped to hell it was Cager.

Cager set the blade against the gas tank and waited. The tank would make a sharp sound when it got shivved, that's what John Lourdes had been whispering to him about.

"Hey...down there...you're not making this easy."

John Lourdes took a breath. Easy was about over. He fired three fast shots into the emptiness from where he'd thought that voice had come. The silence filled with the report of the gunfire, and Cager rammed in the blade. The tank began to bleed gasoline.

"I guess that's your answer down there...Not much of a negotiation."

Cager unspooled the cloth and pressed it against the hole until it was good and soaked. Then he wormed one end into the hole, first with a finger and then the knife blade. When he had about five inches left of shirt sleeve dangling there as a fuse, he pressed the blade and closed her up. He slipped the knife back into his trouser pocket. He took his revolver and a stick match and got himself good and ready.

He fanned his arm again a few times hoping John Lourdes would see and then whispered to the living and the dead everywhere, "Fuck you all," as he struck that wooden match upon the axle.

CHAPTER 50

CAGER SPRINTED FROM THE TOPPLED SEDAN and up that thin corridor of the gully. The gas soaked cloth sucked in the flames and the tank blew. Shorn metal raked the ravine walls around it. Cager was lifted into the air by the concussion. A shoot of flames rose straight up with such ferocity that when it got past the tip of the roadway it exploded outward, searing the air around it, and in that vast stage of desert, laying bare the naked outline of men running in confusion.

John Lourdes rose up and stood in the roadway where it was marked by the tracks of wolves. Two riderless horses went trampling past and leapt through a break in the fire, and there was Cager, diving for the reins that swung wildly in the air.

A man on horseback came charging out of the smoke and straight at John Lourdes, his coat fanning out like the wings of a vulture. Was he trying to escape or run John Lourdes down? It did not matter. John Lourdes shot the horse and its head reared back and its legs crumpled, and it hit the earth hard throwing the rider. And as the man tried to stand and run, John Lourdes shot him. He shot him and the man grabbed his chest and his teeth bared with pain and John Lourdes shot him again.

His clip was empty, and he held the gun out and he ejected the clip. He went to slam in the last clip he had when a man rushed toward him that he did not see.

The clip jammed and he stood there looking about him and trying to ram it in place with the open palm of his hand, but it would not go. Cager was now riding one of the runaway horses and he came wheeling around the edges of the fire shouting up the danger that was about to befall John Lourdes.

He turned to see a man rushing through the grey smoke that swept across the road. He kept jamming, trying to force that clip in place when Cager drove his mount right into the man and sent him tumbling.

"These aren't bandits," Cager shouted, "they're fuckin' hightoned Mex radicals. Look at them."

The man was still alive. He tried to stand and tottered with blood pouring out his broken nose and out his mouth and down his forehead where it had been sheared open.

"Fuckin' hightoned greaser bastard—"

Cager shot the man.

Wounded, the man tried to run. John Lourdes grabbed the reins of Cager's horse. Yelled to get out of there now. "Go. There might be others—"

Cager was still yelling, "Hightoned bastards—" and he shot the man yet again.

• • •

They rode back to Big Medicine, and not alone. A security team had seen the distant fire and raced to the scene. They escorted the two riders, having sent word on ahead. As they reached the great house, they were given what could only be described as a hero's welcome. The searchlight was put on them to illuminate their arrival. Men at the machine gun nests stood and raised their hats. From the crowded porch there was no end to the hurrah's. It was, to John Lourdes, a striking scene that powerfully confirmed the unfitness of things.

As for Cager, he leapt from his mount to the porch, jumped the railing, arms raised, and when handed a beer, he swilled her down like some mythic warrior drunkard, for whom killing snivelly political border crossers was a refuge from boredom.

Come dawn, Cager was lying passed out on a porch sofa. He drank to egomaniac exhaustion and was proud of it. His last words to those who'd witnessed his Homeric indulgence were, "I've fuckin' 'evaporated' myself."

John Lourdes and he were to catch a ride back to Laredo in a company gas tanker. Before they carried Cager aboard, Evans took John Lourdes aside. The Big Medicine executive had been up all night getting word out about the attack and having riders hookup with security teams along the border to warn them.

Evans was carrying a book, and he said to John Lourdes, "Things will get pretty intense in Laredo. The Captain is going to increase his interrogations. He might even begin to execute ways to shut down businesses he feels are working against the law. *La Cronica* is at the top of the list.

"That ought to introduce a little more ire in the situation," said John Lourdes.

He handed John Lourdes the book he'd been carrying. He noted the title: *Around the World in Eighty Days.*

"Doctor English is going on 'Society' business. He wondered if you could see his mother. Read to her for an hour. He will show his appreciation, I assure you."

He took the book.

"It doesn't spook you," said Evans. "Going near those—"

He resisted saying what he felt, knowing how rumors are spread.

"LaShelle was the only one of us that would bring food out to that place. The others left it at the main road. They'd shoot up a flare. And that was it."

"I'd like to tell you something," said John Lourdes, "that I told Captain Asa."

"And that was?"

"The Whiteman should always travel with bodyguards."

"Who said he isn't?"

"I mean...if you ever need someone...someone loyal to a fault."

• • •

On the drive back to Laredo in that gas tanker, Cager's head kept dipping onto John Lourdes' shoulder one minute, then onto the driver's the next. The driver was none too pleased about it. "We could always say he fell out and accidently went under the wheels."

John Lourdes smiled, but he wasn't really listening. He was taking in the first page of the book...

> **Mister Phileas Fogg lived, in 1872, at No. 7, Saville Row, Burlington Gardens, the house in which Sheridan died in 1814. He was one of the most noticeable men of the Reform Club, though he always seemed to avoid attracting attention, *an enigmatic person, about whom little was known...***

He thought of Doctor English's mother. Never underestimate the power of goodness to exploit the unaware—Burr had taught him this as part of his training to survive the world. For the world, Burr told him, was singularly vulnerable to such goodness.

He held the book against his chest and slept.

CHAPTER 51

JOHN LOURDES AND THE TRUCK DRIVER CARRIED THAT DRUNKEN LOUT out of the half dark street and into the hotel and up to his room. Senor Aguirre led the way with a pass key. Once they'd dumped him on the bed like so much weighted trash, John Lourdes said to the porter, "We need to talk."

Once in John Lourdes' room, he said to the porter, "I believe I have done you a great disservice."

"Disservices were done to me...but not by you."

"People at *La Cronica* have placed someone who looks like you there. The Captain is hunting you out for questioning. They were talking about it last night at Big Medicine. When that one next door gets his head screwed back on straight, he may look at you and think—"

The porter listened quietly. He walked over to the desk and sat. There was hotel stationery and a pencil. He began to write.

"This is a note to my nephew. He is what *La Cronica* calls a Mexican American. At present he lives across the river in Nuevo Leon. It is safer there, if not more fashionable. He works with people who mean to exact change here. If you understand my meaning."

John Lourdes took the note. He placed it in the same pocket as that in which he carried the letter saying he was with 'The Society.'

"I'm sorry," said John Lourdes.

"Sorry? There is so much better to be sorry about."

"It might be best if you quit your job here."

"What is best...is not always best."

"If Captain Asa questions you...you know where that can lead."

"Are you concerned that I cannot hold up?"

"I am concerned that you can hold up."

The porter grasped John Lourdes by the shoulders, he was moved so.

"I will show you something," said the porter.

He opened the coat of his porter uniform. A small revolver was tucked quaintly in the waistband. "As you can see, I come dressed for grander things."

• • •

Senor Barros gathered what was left of his staff together. He told them of his conversation the previous evening with Captain Asa who had illegally taken it upon himself to enter the Barros' home. And then he expressed to his employees how he believed the country was moving in a wild and head-long fashion toward a state of near absolute repression. That *La Cronica* did not have long to live, and that he intended to put it to the most dramatic use he could in the time left.

He worked on the article he had sworn to the Captain he would, making it clear he refused to admit what was demanded, and that the people the Ranger claimed had made statements should come forward as citizens to this newspaper and state them for the record. The article was to be titled, THE COWARDS AMONG US.

Marisita saw the article for what it was. A direct assault on the Rangers' power. And that since evening last when he returned, her father seemed to be in a state of volcanic animosity.

She asked if he would share with her what had happened, and he answered thus, "There are ways to humiliate and demean women that are particular and inflammatory to women. There are ways to humiliate and demean men that are particular and inflammatory to men. Last night I experienced one of those. Nothing more of it will I discuss with you."

"Is it because I am a woman?"

"It is because I am ashamed."

"Maybe we should take the newspaper to Nuevo Leon and tell the story from there."

"The only story will be the story of our paper's failure when we change the address at the top of the front page!"

"Maybe if we as Mexicans were stronger there, they would have less power over us as Mexican Americans here."

"And maybe," he said, "the Negro should go back to Africa to gain such power and return. And the Chinese go back to China. And the Jew back to wherever—"

He handed her his finished copy to set to type. "Today," he said, "they have the law…But we have the argument."

CHAPTER 52

WHEN THE JESUIT HAD BROUGHT JOHN LOURDES THE LETTER from Marisita, she had included the first notations of information she had gathered about the remaining men on the list. Some of which John Lourdes knew.

Captain Asa was never alone. He was a man who thrived on company or secrecy. He owned a house near Saint Peter's Catholic Church where he attended Mass every Sunday. He had also been in charge of raising money for the new bell tower after it had been damaged in the 1905 tornado. Ranger Ahearn was constantly at his side. They ate together, travelled together, lived together. *They would most likely have to be killed together*, thought John Lourdes.

Ranger Hughes, on the other hand, was a family man with a wife and three small boys. They lived in a small house owned by the Theilson Steam Brickyard. Agent Hughes' father-in-law was an executive at the brickyard and rented the house to his daughter. They had a Mexican maid who had passed all this along to Marisita, including the fact that the Ranger was a gambler and constantly in debt.

At least once a week, at night, Hughes rode off alone, taking the river road up past Fort McIntosh toward the mines. There was a rumor the maid had heard that he dealt in illegal contraband from across the border, and that contraband might include morphine and opium.

John Lourdes took to watching him through field glasses from a stand of trees that flanked a sump of runoff from the brickyard.

He seemed a good father, in the yard after work he played with his children. Red faced and fighting for his attention, memories by the minute. John Lourdes wondered if the wife and children had any idea he was a murderer. A swine who had killed women and children not much older than his own. And did Agent Hughes carry the truth of it around with him at Christmas and birthday parties?

He could imagine the children at dinner listening to their father's stories, stories that touched the imagination. When John Lourdes killed their father, what impact would it have on them? Would their lives be everything up to that day, and then everything thereafter? Would they, in time, become him?

He watched as the sun went down, and all that excited youth waving their father goodbye without a trace of the future on their mind.

Just as the maid had said, Hughes took the road past Fort McIntosh that followed the river north toward the mines. It was not quite dark, and he could still make out the coal barges coming south toward them. Huge and silent they were, the coal black and shining like the skin of some mythic sea beast.

About a mile upriver from Fort McIntosh was a roadside crib house and gambling parlor where the soldiers bet out their pay. There was a separate building for black soldiers with whores and dice.

The Ranger stopped there and went in. John Lourdes kept watch from over by the refuse pit. The garbage and the stink offered him a place to safely keep watch. He listened to the music and the loud voices and he smoked, and he waited, sipping from a flask against the night air. He meant to take Hughes as soon as he came out of there, but when he finally did, he was not alone. The man he was with looked to be a Ranger, and they rode off together away from the river.

As he began to follow, a feeling came over John Lourdes that made him uneasy. It grew more intense the farther along he got, and then the two riders turned off the main road and John Lourdes could see the lights of a hacienda and the vague detail of an azotea by the arched gateway. It was then it came to him—

The Cadillac on the banks of the Rio Grande being loaded with contraband... the black driver with a huge head of white hair... it was the same gated compound... the same Mexican on the same portico.

They were the two Rangers he could not quite make out that night he'd followed the Cadillac. The information Marisita had been given was good. The Cadillac had not arrived yet with the contraband—most likely opium or morphine—he could tell from the way the Mexican kept looking at his watch and making excuses.

• • •

About half a mile out, the lights from the hacienda looked like little more than smelterpots. The black behind the wheel of that Cadillac suddenly came upon stacked brush in the roadway that exploded into flames.

He didn't need a letter of introduction to know he was in dire straits. He was a big man but was gifted with quickness. He grabbed for a pistol he kept in his lap for just such occasions and spun the wheel to get clear around the flames when a man came sprinting out of the desert night and leapt onto the runner right behind him and before he could bend his arm around and get off a shot, a shotgun barrel was pressed against the back of his massive skull.

"I suggest coming to an easy stop...Don't you?" said John Lourdes.

"A fine suggestion, sir."

The car slowed, then rumbled to a stop. The black was ordered to toss his gun away then get out of the car but to keep looking straight ahead. He did both. He stood in the road, this huge man with a full head of curly white hair, with his hands up.

"You're as big as a fuckin' barroom," said John Lourdes.

"Yes, sir. I'm big...I'm upright...and I'm healthy...And I'd like to stay that way if it's all right with you."

"This is a Model Thirty Cadillac, isn't it?"

"Top of the line."

"Cost about fourteen hundred, new?"

"And worth every penny."

"That means you're doin' damn well for yourself."

"The American dream."

"What are you carrying back there? Morphine?"

"Yes, sir."

"What else?"

"Opium. Marijuana."

"You're quite the entrepreneur."

"We take opportunity where we can find it."

"Do as I ask, and you can keep on to your heart's content. Now step down and strip until you are indecent."

The man stepped from the car and began to undo his coarse woolen suit.

"I'll bet there's no way to track that car to you."

"It comes with the territory."

"How many people up in that house when you make your delivery?"

"There's three. Garcia...that's his place. And two Texas Rangers."

"You know their names?"

"I know them like I know the names of the devil…Hughes and Farnsworth."

"Muscled in on you, did they?"

"With all the trimmings."

"Does the Captain know? Captain Asa? About this little enterprise?"

"Fuck no."

"No one else up there. A wife…kids?"

"Garcia…I don't know…But he be lucky if he knew how to breed."

"What's your name?"

"They call me Sheephead…you can see why."

"Mister Sheephead. Without looking back, start down the road and be gone."

"Can I at least take my shoes?"

"Take your fuckin' shoes."

CHAPTER 53

THE CADILLAC CAME THROUGH THE OPEN GATE LIKE A HEADWIND. The headlights trained on the three men sitting at the table on the portico. The lights growing larger as they satellited across the courtyard. The men took to scattering in panic as John Lourdes stopped the vehicle just short of running them under.

The Mexican flung his chair and it bounced off the hood. "Sheephead, you dumbass nigger." The Rangers cursed him out worse yet.

A great wave of dust from the tires had to settle out before they realized it wasn't Sheephead stepping from the car, but a gringo carrying a shotgun. The men looked to each other, to try and settle their confusion.

"Where is Sheephead?" said the Mexican named Garcia. "And who the fuck are you?"

"I believe I know this man," said Hughes. "Lourdes...that you? This is a friend of Doctor English's."

"I don't care if he's fuckin' the Virgin Mother," said Garcia. "Where is Sheephead? What are you doing with that car?"

"Your stuff is in the back seat," said John Lourdes. "So just keep your asses still."

The other Ranger, who had not until this moment spoken, said, "If you're just here to deliver for Sheephead, you can put the shotgun down."

"That's not why I'm here."

Garcia began to curse, shaking his head, his eyes flashed. "He's going to kill us."

"Why you here, Lourdes?" said Ranger Hughes. "Money? You hustling us? Let's talk it out."

"You fuckin' 'Rinches,'" said Garcia. "Can't you see?"

"Answer me, man," said Hughes.

"I'm here to bring a little rebellion and intolerance into your lives."

"What did I tell you?" Garcia shouted.

John Lourdes took a step back to widen his field of fire. "I want to know the name of the Whiteman."

The Mexican croaked. "If this don't beat all. Fuck me."

He eased up that shotgun. "I want the name!"

"Tell him," shouted the other agent.

Garcia took off. Whether he was making for a weapon or trying to escape, it didn't matter. John Lourdes fired. The shot threaded the portico columns and lifted the Mexican into the air driving him back against the patio doors.

There was a scream after that. From somewhere in the hacienda, a woman's pitched cry in Spanish amidst the fierce volley of gunfire.

From all the way back in the lonely void of that desert you could see bursts of gunfire and the huge blue vapors from that trench gun. It was silent after that raw bloodletting, except for the Spanish woman pleading to God as if to rid herself of some ancient curse.

And John Lourdes, walking out of the compound under the vast arc of the sky, reloading as he went to retrieve his mount. And the woman? He had no business with her, but leaving her alive he knew might signal the beginning of his end.

• • •

Senor Aguirre was walking down the hotel corridor when someone whistled. He turned to find Cager Adams at his open door in his underwear, scratching the calf of one leg with the foot of his other. He waved the porter to his room.

"May I do something for you, sir?"

"You a betting man, Aguirre?"

The porter could feel the inherent sarcasm, as if Adams were his lawful master.

"Pardon me, sir?"

"A betting man. You a betting man? That sack you carry between your legs. Is it just for show or do you know how to use it?"

"Is there anything I can get you, sir?"

Cager reached into his pocket and took out his paper money. Peeled off bills, dropping them on his strewn about bed sheeting.

"A hundred dollars. I'll bet right now that you're carrying a weapon. Right now."

"How would you classify a weapon? A man's speech can be a weapon. His words, his tone."

"Why you slick old malabrista. Handgun. We'll leave it as a handgun. I say you're carrying a handgun."

"I don't bet, sir."

"That's what I thought. Where do you keep it? In your boot? Or tucked down in your drawers where you can keep each other nice and warm. You do wear drawers?"

"If there isn't anything I can get you, then—" He started for the door.

"John L...he around?"

"I haven't seen him, sir. He hasn't called for me yet."

"You and he are real partners, aren't you?"

"The hotel policy is to make the guests stay here as comfortable and pleasant as possible."

"It must gall you to have had your own business and now you're basically a boot shiner."

"If there isn't anything I can—"

"You keep yourself in check. You're all right. Did you read the *Laredo Times* this morning?"

"No, sir."

"I forgot. You're a *La Cronica* man." He had a copy of the paper on the bureau and he picked it up and carried it over to the porter reading from an article as he went.

"They say here the Rangers are looking to question a man who may have information about those three peace officers killed. They say he's a Mexican. Older. Grey hair. Distinguished. Do you consider yourself distinguished?"

"I consider myself a porter."

He walked out. Cager called to him, "Can you hear that, Senor Aguirre? That's the clock ticking."

Senor Aguirre walked down to the lobby. It was near the end of his shift. The lobby was quiet and empty except for the hum of a vacuum cleaner that a night custodian was running across a rug.

He finished his reports and handed in his passkeys as he had on the endless nights before it, but knowing this time was different as it was filled with finality.

At home he made coffee and watched the sun on the windowsill. He took a suitcase from under his bed. He filled it with a few necessaries and a photograph of his deceased wife and the boy they lost in childhood. He sat on the edge of his bed and wiped at tears from remembering. One of the neighbors saw him coming up the walkway with the suitcase and said, "Going to visit your nephew?"

He smiled, but really did not answer. He would never be seen or heard from again.

CHAPTER 54

THE SENIOR EDITOR AT *The Laredo Times* received an anonymous call about the murder of three men at the ranch of Manuel Garcia, north of the Thielson Brickyard. Two of the three dead were Texas Rangers, and there was illegal contraband still at the scene.

By the time Captain Asa appeared with a squad of deputies, reporters from the *Times* had searched the property, taken pictures of the bodies, of the Cadillac and the crates of narcotics. They had discovered a Mexican woman hiding in a root cellar who claimed to be a cousin of the deceased Garcia. During all this, a security team from Big Medicine arrived, among their number was Cager Adams.

The men were crowded in on the portico trying to eavesdrop as best they could through the windows as the Captain and Ahearn sat at a dining table in the cool stony darkness and privately interrogated the woman. The reporters pretty much had the whole story before the Captain arrived, and they were already hustling back to Laredo to meet the late edition.

The woman was uneducated and afraid and threatened over concealing anything. In tears she admitted her cousin and the two Rangers were involved in procuring and selling morphine and opium. That once every week a large Negro man in a Cadillac came from the river with contraband. Only this night was very different. Another man showed up that her cousin did not know. There were many questions. She was never allowed out when these men were there, so she saw little but heard much. The man sounded young and educated. He was, she felt, Anglo. He'd worn a black fedora, she knew that much from seeing him walk away after the killings. He'd walked very slowly, as if unconcerned. She told her interrogators that this young man kept asking the same thing over and over... "*Who is the Whiteman?*"

While all this went on, Cager walked the scene of the killings. The bodies still lay where they had fallen. They were now the domain of flies and the Texas sun. Cager stood by the Cadillac where signs told him that the shooter had stood. He knelt down and looked under the sedan. There he found the spent shell casing from a shotgun, which he secreted into his pocket.

When the interrogation was over, the Captain and Ahearn came out together. The Captain was in no mood for questions from his men or the Big Medicine people. He ordered the bodies tarped and saddled, the Cadillac driven back to town.

Cager watched the two men walk off alone toward the gate. Things were bad. The news of Rangers in the drug trade would damage the Captain's standing, that was for sure. But there was something more—

"That night…coming back from the Esteban ranchero…" The Captain was speaking very low to Ahearn. "…Bucky and Caparell…Then Pettyjohn at the vigil…LaShelle…And now Hughes…What does that tell you?"

Ahearn's mouth was very dry. He ran his tongue across his lips, "He's one of us."

The Captain nodded bitterly. "He's one of us."

• • •

When Cager returned to Laredo, he took a walk down into the Fourth Ward. That's where all the blacks lived in a barrio known as El Tonto. He was looking for a car repair shop across the tracks and within a chapel bell of Saint James.

The man who owned the shop was born Willie Aiken, but Anglos called him Coalblack Willie. Among his Negro peers, he was known as Sheephead or Sergeant Sheephead, being a former member of the 25th black infantry stationed at Fort McIntosh.

The repair shop was a brick shell with open barn doors and beside it, a lot with a graveyard of wagons and carriages and automobiles already unfit for anything but scrap parts.

When Cager walked in from all that daylight he had to squint to see. A Victrola was playing, and a fan whirred just near the door where a handful of Negro men were playing cards and carrying on. They quieted considerably when a white man entered.

"I'm looking for a Willie Aiken…Sergeant Sheephead."

There was a shirtless black leaning over the engine house of a Buick. And when he stood, Cager saw how he came by his name. He had this thick head of wooly white hair and a beard to match. So much hair, there was barely room for a forehead and narrow eyes.

"I'm Sheephead. What can I do for you?"

Cager had sets of eyes on him, so he waited.

"My office," said Sheephead. He jacked a thumb toward the back.

"Why don't we do that," said Cager.

Behind the shop was a shack that looked like it had been dropped there from on high and rattled loose. There were no windows, and the only air or light came in through the slatted walls and open doorway. Cager was invited to sit by the desk, but he had to maneuver through a maze of tires and engine parts.

"I hear you drive a Cadillac."

Cager left it like that. No follow up, no explanation. There was silence now but for the hard cases playing cards and some hightone woman crooning on that Victrola about the light of the silvery moon.

The black's eyes narrowed and took on a grave uneasiness.

"You don't know me, mister."

"I stop niggers on the street…I ask, 'you know one of your kind that drives a blue Cadillac?' …How many niggers you think are driving around Laredo, Texas, in a Model 30? And if I can find you, the fuckin' Rangers won't be far behind."

The Sergeant ran a hand through that mass of white hair. He could have passed for Moses sitting there, or even God himself in those church paintings. Of course, God and Moses were always white. At least that was the rumor.

The Sergeant rested an elbow on the arm of his desk chair. He raised his hand, perched his chin on the closed fist. He just sat there, and you could hear the chair creaking slightly as it rocked and that scratchy voice on the Victrola singing…*your silvery beams will bring love dreams, we'll be cuddling soon…*

"You puttin' the boot on me, or what?" said Sheephead.

"You shoulda stayed out of Whiteman business."

"Mister…You sit on this side of the desk sometime…It's all Whiteman business."

"Ain't that the fuckin' truth," said Cager, as if, for one minute, commiserating with this hustler.

"So…what is it?" said Sheephead. "You ain't the law."

"I ain't the law…but I want to know about the man."

SEVEN STICKS
OF DYNAMITE

CHAPTER 55

THERE WAS A STORM COMING. A darkness fell over the desert that told of it. John Lourdes stood on the hotel veranda and smoked. A misfit presence in a night of misfits. In the distance the low rumble of thunder and the tiny pulses of light so far out on the horizon as to seem otherworldly. The way the wind was blowing the trees in the street, he saw it would be a slashing rain. He glanced at his watch. It was time.

At the front desk, he asked about the night porter. It seemed Senor Aguirre had not shown up for work, nor had he left word. None of which was like him. A stableman was sent to his home out of concern, but no one answered.

As John Lourdes stepped out into the street, the first drops of rain stippled across the shoulders of his cape. By the time he reached the Seminary the buildings were lonely blocks of granite in a grey downpour. He knew how to keep watch and slip the noose of being followed, and when he thought it safe, he made his way to the chapel.

She was there in the smoky lamplight when he entered. A row of magenta candle holders with their yellow eyedrop flames framed her as she stood. He removed his hat and shook away the rain and then did the same with his cape and set them aside.

He and she kissed, and they sat together in the shadow of a wooden cross. She saw in his face the weight of the secrets he bore, and the burden of the violence born of it. He went to speak but she put a finger to his lips and whispered, "Not yet. Let's just rest here a while."

He put his head upon her shoulder which she cradled with her own. They stayed like that in this place where people came to shed their bitterest memories and make whole what has been relentlessly torn from them. And where they hope to at least meet God halfway.

"I wish," he said softly, "I had been born white."

She pulled her head back to see him better. His head rose. He looked to the altar where the wrongs of the world were to be washed away.

"It is so much a part of me, it would have been better. I understand them, because I am them. And then I hate myself because of it. Because it means I must deny my mother. And the goodness in me that came out of her. I'd have to turn away from all that and leave her to see my shame.

"But, if I were Mexican, how would I survive that? I experience what goes on around me, and I'm glad I'm not Mexican. And why…? It's too damn hard, too damn complicated. I like being white better. It is better because it has advantages. And that feeling I know is racist, because it whispers that John Lourdes believes it is better."

He rested his folded hands on the back of the pew before him. He shook his head. Over what, she did not know.

"At the rally," he said, "the people there. I watched them sing to the flag, and it touched my heart. I was at one with them. Why? Because I see they are mostly decent, hardworking people who have fought and bled, and seen those near to them die for this country. Who want to raise their children right and go to their graves justified. And I don't know what to do with all that.

"The man who stays down the hall from me. The one I told you about. He saved my life last night. He is a flat out racist, and I like him as a man. He is funny and charming and slick and smart and has more character and sand than most of the good men I've ever met. And I don't know what to do with all that."

There was thunder and a strip of lightning and the stained glass windows flashed with a vision of a benign Christ and his beatific saints. There one moment, stilled in darkness the next.

"Who I am?" he said. "I will tell you. I am one of those persons who lives between somewhere they don't belong and somewhere that doesn't want them."

He sat back quietly after that, and she reached out with the tips of her fingers under his chin and turned his head toward hers.

"Come with me," she said.

He followed her across the grounds, pressing against the rain. The buildings now bathed in such mist as to seem suspended in the clouds. The Seminary was there to teach children, mostly Mexican. Many lived there, many had no home but there. She led him behind one of the dormitories and down a flight of stairs and into a long drab hallway lit by a single bulb in the ceiling. There were storerooms and a boiler room and a singular door at the end of the hall which she opened with a key.

He followed her into the darkness and as she closed the door behind them, she said, "We are safe here…For a while anyway."

There was thunder and a small block of window by the ceiling crinkled with light. He saw they were in a tiny cell of an apartment with a bed in the far corner.

"A childhood friend teaches here. She is away."

He removed his hat and took off his cape and he set them on a bureau beside him. She was a faint silhouette sitting in a chair unlacing her boots and slipping them off one by one. He began to undo his vest. The room was warm, the boiler being just on the other side of the wall. He could hear it kicking over and the pipes rattling slightly. The rain slashed across that small window. The room had the deep and moody stillness of a lair. A place untouched and where anything possible was just a breath away.

He vaguely saw her stand and her skirt slip away. As he took off his vest, she came toward him.

"When we are done here," she said, "I will be moving on with my life. It is something I will have to tell my father."

As he undid the buttons of his shirt, she took hold of his arm.

"What is your intention?" he said.

"It seems I have become this person," she said, "or maybe I was that person all along, but did not realize it until now, who lives between somewhere they don't belong and some place that doesn't want them."

What could he say to what he lived but did not fully understand.

She leaned up and kissed him. She still had drops of rain in her hair. Her skin smelled of fresh soap and was warm to the touch. He kissed her and pulled her toward him, and it felt as if he had captured the world.

CHAPTER 56

IT WAS NO LONGER RAINING when Marisita returned home that night with a new life on her mind. Her block was partly flooded, it was dark, and there was a crowd around the front of the *La Cronica* offices when there should not have been.

She saw the front door had been torn from its bracings and Luis Perez was using a shotgun to keep those from the neighborhood back and away from the entrance. She rushed to him, and when he saw her, he made way for her through the crowd.

"My father…?"

"He's all right. Thank God."

A few of the lights that had not been shattered were on. The print shop was a ruination. Some of the employees who lived in the neighborhood walked the wreckage to see what could be salvaged. A few still had on their nightshirts.

"My father?" Marisita said to one of them.

"He's upstairs with the doctor."

"How bad is it down here?"

"You need a new press, or you're out of business."

Senor Barros was sitting at the kitchen table, his head back. A doctor who lived on that street stood over him stitching up a deep gash over one eye. Eduardo used a kitchen rag to wipe the blood that still ran down his face.

"Father," she said. She curled around him and held him about the shoulders.

He rolled back his eyes to stare at her as best he could. "As you can see," he said to the doctor, "my daughter lives a completely independent life."

"It was probably a good thing she was not here."

"Can I get you a drink, Father? Doctor?"

"What I need is for you to keep your head still," said the doctor. "I am not good at stitching a moving target."

"What happened tonight, Father?"

"What the hell do you think? They came. With their hoods and revolvers. Men were killed today, did you know that?"

"I learned that this evening."

"And I know where you got the information."

"I'm certain the doctor does not want to hear about our private concerns."

"I do not," said the doctor. "It is bad enough everyone on the street gossips about you both. And that I will be questioned all to hell about my time with you two here alone. So please…Be quiet."

• • •

Luis Perez had the door rebraced, at least well enough to keep out the curious. There was only he and the Barros' in the wreckage of that print shop.

"I'll be back in the morning," said Perez. "You're not alone in this. I promise. You will see."

When he left, Eduardo tried to run the press. The gears were scored horribly, and the roller drum was completely useless.

"They found out the name of the porter at the hotel," said Eduardo.

"How?"

He shrugged.

Marisita told her father, "John said the porter has disappeared."

"At least he knows. He better be out of there himself."

"If he does, he knows they will suspect him. Anyway, he's going away for a few days."

"And then?"

"He did not have an 'and then.'"

Senor Barros looked over his beloved print shop. The place he'd spent it all for.

He began to scream out wildly such vulgar laced hatreds like she had never heard from her father, or any living man for that matter. He was frightening in his rage, yet she was glad he had such furor still within him.

Once he had calmed down and gotten control of himself, he apologized to his daughter.

"I only hope, Father, that I have half as much fury as you do when the time comes."

"You did, child. That day of the funeral."

He put his arm out for her to walk with him. She was proud to be his daughter and told him so. In the kitchen he poured them both a drink. "To the Barros," he said. They clinked glasses and drank.

"They didn't kill me tonight," he said. "I wondered about that for a while."

"I was going to ask you, Father. When I thought the time right."

"I think that having two of their Rangers exposed for being in the illegal contraband business has shined a light on them. And they are on the defensive suddenly. And I think they're not sure how the newspapers will react if one of their own is murdered. And not just the Mexican press here and across the border. But the American political press. The New York press. Destroying a print shop under the guise of hooded outsiders is a lot different than 'evaporating' a newspaper owner.

"Remember Juan Sarabia, when he was kidnapped off the streets of Douglas, Arizona with the help of the Arizona Rangers four years ago? And the furor that caused. They had famous people travelling all over that state, including the labor leader, Mother Jones, calling out the suppression of real law."

He poured another drink.

"That doesn't mean they won't accidentally 'evaporate' us," he said.

He glanced at his daughter. She had been listening, but her eyes had drifted to the kitchen window and the garden, and the gate.

"I've lost you," he said. "Haven't I?"

She came over and bent down and put her arms around him. "You haven't lost me. You just have to share me with the world."

"But I don't trust the world."

"And that is what makes you such a great newspaper editor. But a very difficult father."

She kissed him on the top of the head. "I'm going to bed now before it's time to get up."

Before she reached the door, he said, "You're going to leave the paper, aren't you?"

She stopped and turned. She leaned against the door jamb. She was going to hurt him. And in a way that a person cannot be unhurt, because we are all the victims of our expectations. "Yes, Father," she said, "when this is done here. And I hope you will forgive me."

218

CHAPTER 57

THE NEXT MORNING WHEN MARISITA WENT DOWN TO THE KITCHEN for her morning coffee she saw, without warning, out the kitchen window an armed man coming quietly through the gate.

She ran back into the house calling to her father. She saw the door to the print shop open, and there she found him and a handful of employees doing what they could to make order of that disaster.

"Father," she shouted, "an armed man has—"

"Yes," he said, "go look outside."

He did not seem the least bit alarmed and she went to the front door that opened uneasily on its new bracings and stepped out into the sunlight. There was Luis Perez at his usual post relaxing beneath the umbrella. But he was not alone. A young man with a rifle across his lap sat with him. And there was another man at the corner.

Senor Perez offered her a good morning and looked over the night gown she was dressed in, and politely said, "If Sleeping Beauty comes out like this every morning, there is no telling how many young men I can get to offer up their time protecting this place."

By the time she had dressed and had her morning coffee, the world had come calling on *La Cronica*. Reporters from the other newspapers, even the Anglo papers, were there to interview her father. They would also want a statement from her. Politics and race aside, it was clear from the reporters' questions that a threat to one of their rank posed a threat to all.

Outside Luis Perez had set a huge basket on the table with a sign: DONATIONS FOR A FREE AND DECENT PRESS.

People from the neighborhood came by and offered what they could. The poor are always giving because they know best what it means to be without means. By the time the afternoon editions of the papers printed the story, a stream of people began to arrive, either walking or in cars, by carriage and wagon. They'd stop and offer a few words and throw in change or paper money, some even slipped in an envelope. Many said nothing, they just nodded.

And Luis Perez was always there, smiling, raising his hat, his shotgun on the table, the guards watching politely. Many were Anglo who came. Quiet, sympathetic citizens sensitive to the plight. Some were rough day workers or tradesmen. There were housewives, mothers. Some were old, survivors of harsh years.

This was that other America, the one that silently goes about God's day to day business of shared living. And that is not a tale of destruction or hell escaped, or the domain of dark souls and even darker blood. It is the America that lives out this undersong of wishing their fellow man well. Of seeing a plight and chipping in to cleanse it. That understands lost joys and missed opportunities, mistreatment and failure, but keeps going. That is part of the ship of state the poet Walt Whitman wrote about. The ship that carries us all, that may have patched sails from the endless trials it has borne, but sails none the less.

• • •

Captain Asa and a team of Rangers entered the Hamilton Hotel. They were agitated and all business. The Captain pointed to who should question the desk clerks, and who should interrogate the porters and kitchen help. No Mexican who worked in the hotel was to be overlooked, including the stable hands. Anyone not on shift—their names were to be collected, addresses, their homes visited. The Captain demanded access to John Lourdes' room. As a porter opened the door and the Captain stormed in with Ranger Ahearn behind him, who should he find there—

Cager Adams was sitting at a desk reading through crumpled bits of paper left in the trash.

"What are you doing here?" said the Captain.

"The same as you, Captain." He held up some of the scraps he had flattened out and read through. "Nothing here." He pointed to the bed where some of John Lourdes' clothes lay in a heap. "Nothing there, either. Seems John L has quietly made his escape."

Ahearn ordered the porter out and slammed the door shut behind him.

"You talked to the nigger," said the Captain.

"We talked. He had enough of a description that—"

"You must have had suspicions," said Ahearn.

"After I talked to that Sheephead fool, I came here. This answered it."

"With all that time you and him spent cradling up to each other?" said Ahearn.

"Unlike some...I save my cradling for women."

"You're lying," said Ahearn.

"I was born lying," said Cager, "and it comes as naturally to me as pissing. So what of it? Big Medicine didn't hire me because I'm a righteous and upstanding character or because I've got polished grace and good manners. I'm a snake. I'm a shitbag hustler. Didn't you notice?"

He'd had his time with them. He got up and retrieved his hat from the bed. He'd lied well enough, he thought.

"Do you have any idea where he might be now?" said the Captain.

Cager grinned and pointed with his hat toward the open veranda door. "He's after the Whiteman, and I believe he thinks it's one of you two boys. So I feel he's coming to a rooftop near you. So when you are around your little domicile, I'd be watching rooftops, so I don't get picked off like a dinner chicken."

CHAPTER 58

A DUSKY HAWK SAT ATOP A DESICCATED WOOD SIGN whose chipped lettering read: GRASSLANDS SANITARIUM.

As John Lourdes turned his mount down the road to the Leper Colony, that hunter's brown rusty head and yellow cere followed the rider's passing with hard still eyes. John Lourdes doffed his hat to the bird and rode on.

He thought he had a few days anyway before facts would inevitably verge against him. But he was wrong. By nightfall, the Department of Public Safety would issue a warrant for his arrest in connection with the disappearance and death of a number of Texas Rangers and employees of the Big Medicine Corporation. The newspapers would publish the release of that information the following day. Rewards would be posted.

As he rode down into the colony, he became the subject of intense interest. Stares you feel from the most sidelong glance. A few of the lepers were in the courtyard of the main house talking with the colony doctor who, it turned out, was black. The attendants he saw going about their daily rituals were Mexican and straight from the depths of poverty. The lepers were all white. Every world has its own reason.

He tipped his hat and the doctor nodded. He said good morning to them all and mentioned he was there to see Missus English.

The lepers watched askance as he passed along and when he got close enough, they looked away. Shame, he thought, for what the disease had done to them. And that seeing him, only made it worse.

A dog came rushing out of the shade, snapping at the horse's legs then backing away. A man whistled and the dog sprinted down to the pond where a leper sat beneath a tarp canopy and fished. John Lourdes wondered what the hell kind of fish were in that stinking, lifeless pond.

It was a lonely and spare place, even more so the second time around.

Missus English was sitting outside her small adobe under that thatched awning. She was being served lunch when she saw John Lourdes ride up. She put her hands over her heart. "John...what brings you here?"

He dismounted and held up the book.

"Ohhh," she said. "Are you hungry? I'm having pancita. Do you like pancita? Do you know what it is?"

"Yes, my"—he almost said mother—"It's tripe. Cow belly. I like it very much. I know it as menudo."

The attendant set an extra bowl and spoon at the table.

Missus English's hands were badly deformed from the disease and cracked open with sores. She was missing parts of fingers. A special spoon had been made for her. It had a wide handle and a trench cut down the length of it, wide enough to loop her fingers through so she could grasp it like a knife. Eating was hard and graceless.

She asked him question after question, as if the world had come visiting. There was such kindness in the woman. He could hear it in her voice like some honey colored goodness. It made him think of his own mother. What a moment like this with her would be now. He remembered how she'd kissed his neck. The full measure of her love still lived there to be felt.

He hated himself at that moment. Knowing he'd come there to bait this old woman into answering questions about the Captain and who was the Whiteman?

After lunch he took up that volume of *Around the World in Eighty Days*. "Where did you and the good doctor leave off?" he said. "London... Suez...Bombay...Hong Kong...New York?"

"It doesn't matter," she said. "The sun never sets on the British Empire. Did you know that when you read the book?"

"No, ma'am. I did not."

"That's what the book is about. How the sun never sets on the British Empire. That will be America in time," she said. "Our America. Thanks to men like my son and yourself...and 'The Society,' of course. Let's go inside where it's cooler."

He helped her up and took her by the arm. Within those mud brick walls was quite another world. A beautiful rug and elegantly clothed sofa graced the room. A rocking chair was set by a latticed window. And the walls and a breakfront—my God, they were lined with photographs and tintypes.

"They're wonderful," he said.

"It's my son. He took all those."

"No...," said John Lourdes.

"That's one of his cameras."

She pointed to the breakfront to what looked to John Lourdes like nothing more than a box of wood with a metal cap sticking out of it.

But the photographs—some were light drenched images of exotic places or beautiful silky portraits of people. Picnickers along the Rio Grande, strapping youths stepping soaked from the water, a wedding party in the desert, an old man smiling in the shadow of a huge cross.

She sat in her rocker and he on the sofa and he read to her. Her chair creaking, her eyes closed, her hands folded across her lap, listening. But as he read, unimportant details began to seize his thoughts and take on this incredible weight.

Who took the picture? ... The picture, fool... Who took it? ... The picture of the dead funeral director with the snake in his lap... Who took it? Someone took it...

The photographs now had a chilling presence. Had he been wrong about the Captain and Ahearn and the rest? Was Doctor English the Whiteman? When the old woman got to napping, he rose and, once outside, lit a cigarette.

The leper was still at the pond fishing. John Lourdes went down there. The dog came out from beneath the tarp and charged John Lourdes. The man whistled and the dog spun about and a moment later was lying at the man's side.

"You catch anything in that pond?"

"Yeah."

"What?"

"Memories."

That diseased soul grinned and John Lourdes nodded, as he understood.

"There's a man out there," said the leper.

"Where?"

He looked across the pond.

"About a mile out. Every half hour or so I see something shimmer. I believe he's moving in an arc to keep at an angle to the sun so he can watch better."

"You sound like someone who has experience in these matters."

"Army," he said.

"Cuba...Philippines?"

"Gettysburg," he said. "Marksman. I signed up when I was fifteen."

He had to be sixty practically. The disease had him, but not as badly as it did Missus English. He sat there the whole while holding the fishing pole like he was a stone carving. The dog at his side sleeping. He could have been the picture of any old man with his fishing pole and dog in any old town across this country.

"What in creation do you think he could be doing out there?" said the leper.

It was a hard desert John Lourdes was looking out upon with hills like burnt chaff.

"He's deciding, sir."

"Deciding…deciding what?"

"Can he pull off a killing."

CHAPTER 59

THE WOMAN'S COMMITTEE OF LA LIGA had arrived at the *La Cronica* offices with word that all proceeds from the play *The Wizard of Oz* were to be donated to the newspaper. The play was to be performed at the Seminary auditorium for a number of weeks. The Barros were moved, but just as deeply concerned on the chance this could incite an act of violence and there would be so many children attending.

The women of La Liga had been promised by Captain Asa's superiors at the Department of Public Safety this would not be the case. There would be serious warnings posted in the newspapers and sufficient security. Whether their concern was genuine, or they were just looking for good publicity in the wake of two of their Rangers being involved in illicit contraband, no one could be sure. It might well be both. But reputations needed shining. And suddenly *La Cronica* was a cause and means. It was the kind of irony, the father whispered to his daughter, that the world can do without.

Throughout this shared good news, Marisita allowed herself to only stare at Missus Rueda, believing she, along with her husband, more responsible than any others for feeding suspicions that supported the powerful and suppressed the weak. The woman felt the stare and the silence and when Marisita finally spoke to her in private, it was to say just this. "I'll write about you one day, Belen…If I am not murdered because of you." And it was enough to strip the woman of her pallor.

Luis Perez stepped into the print shop and called out for Senor Barros and his daughter to come and be quick. The atmosphere outside *La Cronica* had settled down. Guards protected the building and a street corner. The curious had thinned out. Occasionally people went past shouting obscenities or spewing out their bias. Some went by waving Mexican flags. At the very least, there was a tenuous state of normalcy.

A wagon had pulled up and strapped down in the flatbed was a well worn iron Colombian printing press. The driver handed Senor Barros a note that read:

—Get back to work—

It was unsigned.

Astounded to the point of tears, the stocky man scaled the backboards like a youth. He ran his hands over that aged printing press. He called out to his daughter, "Before your time…but it can do two hundred broad sheets an hour."

Marisita watched her father with pure joy, how he handled that cast iron press, moving the levers to check their smoothness with the eye of a seasoned veteran on Christmas morning. The Colombian was famous for having a large gold painted cast iron bald eagle sitting on the top lever. It was not only a decorative emblem as tribute to American Freedom of the Press, it was an important counterweight when rolling out pages over ink.

• • •

Missus English awoke to the amber light of late afternoon through the latticed shutters. It took her a while to gather herself. She stirred slightly, then noticed John Lourdes there on the sofa sitting quietly.

Her mouth was so dry the words came out ratchety, "How long… have…I been asleep?"

"Not long, ma'am."

"I'm sorry."

"It's all right. It gave me time to admire the Doctor's photos."

"Yes. He's quite the artist."

"Where is he now?"

"He went to San Antonio on business for 'The Society.' Then he was to go on a retreat."

"A retreat?"

"A sabbatical. He goes to be alone. To meditate…pray…think out future plans."

She took a deep breath. "You know, when I first wake up, I forget that I have this disease."

"I had no idea. It must be hard."

"How we react to what's hard is how we attain our rightful place in heaven."

"Yes, ma'am."

She rocked a bit.

"Your parents must love you very much."

"I couldn't express to you how much, ma'am."

"I hope you will come here often. I feel very close to you."

"Thank you, ma'am."

He took a breath.

"By the way, ma'am. The Doctor confided in me."

The chair stopped creaking. "He did?"

"Yes, ma'am."

He could feel the silence that followed.

"It doesn't surprise me," she said.

"I will guard his secret with my life, ma'am."

"I know you will…To whom much is given, much is expected…He and I have talked many times. He says that if something should happen to him, someone would have to take his place. The Captain is not cut out for it, though he believes he is. The Whiteman has to have something here." She placed a hand to her heart. "He must be able to command the souls of people. To inspire them. They must see reason and goodness in his actions. Men like yourself."

They talked until dinner. The attendant served them inside her adobe. They ate by the gentle light of dusk. She confided to him her dreams for her son, her country, and the hope she would live long enough to see the change. John Lourdes listened silently, knowing she had sealed her son's fate.

After dinner, he told her, "I'll be leaving tonight." He stood and came around the table and he leaned down and kissed her on the cheek. She grasped his hand and could not help but cry.

"I'm sorry," he said.

"For what, son?"

How could he tell her. "I'm just sorry."

He went outside. His horse had been unsaddled and left to graze. The saddle was set over a hitching post, his shoulder holster draped from the pommel. He slipped his arm through the harness, made sure he had extra clips.

The old man was coming up from the pond. His fishing pole balanced in one hand, the dog at his side. They passed each other on the road.

"He's still out there," said the old man.

He pointed.

Far out on that darkened plain, the slightest yaw of a fire. Like a calling card.

The old man took note of John Lourdes' shoulder holster.

"Should I say anything to the Doctor?"

"Yeah…tell him not to stray too far."

CHAPTER 60

JOHN LOURDES WALKED AROUND THE POND. The moon on that lifeless slick of water from where he started his march out into the desert. It took some time before he came upon the camp. But there it was. A fire burned and there was plenty of dried tree root and brush to keep it going all night. Cager's horse was staked, his rifle in the scabbard. Everything right and proper, except there was no Cager Adams.

John Lourdes had not drawn his weapon. In fact, he stood there in the glow of the flames with his hands on his hips and called out, "Where are you, you fuckin' ghoul?"

Cager came stomping out of the darkness, but not right away. And he was in possession of a scatter gun.

"I watched you sauntering down from that pesthole," said Cager, "just as easy as Sunday afternoon. You must have been pretty confident I wouldn't shoot you on sight."

"Does that give you cause for concern?"

"There's cause for concern, and then there's cause for concern."

"I knew you'd want to make sure there wasn't a reason not to put me down. After all, you could have shot me in the back up there at the sanitarium any time."

"Sanitarium? You mean leper colony."

"It's a good thing you didn't kill me."

"It's a good thing so far, but so far isn't much."

"You're in trouble," said John Lourdes. "And by the end of this conversation you may come to see you're at death's door."

"And it would serve me right. You learn anything from that old lady about who the Whiteman is? That's why you're here."

"Nope."

"You're a liar."

"Well, I'm in good company then."

"That's rich. That's what you came here for. To try and hustle the information out of that old monster. I got close enough with field glasses to see you reading to her. Having tea. A real mama's boy. The whole thing makes me want to wretch. Did you wipe her fanny while you were conning her? Did you promise to bang her if she gave up the goods? It wouldn't shock me. You were there to find out who it is."

"That's right."

"Did you find out?"

"No."

"You're a fuckin' liar."

"Absolutely…and a pretty good one. Present company included."

"I knew practically from the beginning. And when you came riding in that night not long after those boys were shot up…Yeah. And the bullets I dug out of those—"

"There's no depth you won't sink to, is there?"

"You show me the depth I need to sink to, and I will go there with good cheer. Now…it was LaShelle that really sold it. He must have been pretty bruised up like you. That's why you torched his face and hands so they wouldn't look from him to you and get—"

"And it was meant to shock the hell out of those scrappers."

"Put the fear of God in them, right?"

"God has nothing to do with it."

"The innocent bystander. That it? Is the Whiteman Ahearn? I always felt it would be him. Not the Captain. I think he does the deed, but not the thinking. Why do you want him down? I mean, why bother? You being paid by—"

"The answer will put the noose around your neck."

Cager paused for a minute. He moved around the fire some. "I don't know how you could go into that pesthole. With those disgusting creatures. They could be contagious. You have no idea—"

"You're worried about a sanitarium?"

"Leper colony."

"Sanitarium…leper colony. What do you think hell is gonna be like?"

"I don't know, write me," he said, grinning.

"You're in trouble, gent."

"Prove it."

"I'm with the Bureau of Investigation. I have been sent here to capture and or kill the Whiteman. I send in reports. I sent one about you right after you shot that boy on the train in Ulvalde. I could have a lapse of memory. A mistake of identity. But if I die…See where I'm going with this?"

Cager let the gun drop.

"You think fast," said John Lourdes.

"Self preservation. You know…I've been goin' around thinking. This guy is scamming the operation. And if we could partner up—"

He set the scatter gun on his saddle which was by the fire. From a saddle wallet he took out a pint of drinking whiskey.

"I'm thoroughly disappointed, John L…I had illusions, I won't deny it."

He took a drink and then he passed the pint bottle to John Lourdes.

"You saved my life once," said John Lourdes. "Let me do the same for you."

"I had no intention of letting some greaser riff raff cut a white brother down. What do you think I am?"

John Lourdes shook his head. There was no accounting for taste or friendship. The son of a bitch was a walking textbook of every flaw of character in man. But there was an animal grace and charm about him and a one hundred proof sense of humor that John Lourdes had an affection for. Or maybe it was because John Lourdes' own father might have been Cager Adams once upon a time. He didn't know. And he didn't rightfully care. He just liked the bastard.

"Let me help you," said John Lourdes. "But in order for me to have a lapse of ethical memory, I need to enlist your services. Which means I have to put my trust in you. And you're not exactly a beacon of light in that department."

Cager threw up a hand. "Sssshhh," he said. "Did you hear that?"

John Lourdes instantly was on guard, standing back, panning the desert with his eyes. Listening. "What did you hear?" he whispered.

"I thought it was the sound of a cash register cachinging."

CHAPTER 61

THE SANITARIUM DOCTOR STOOD IN AN OPEN DOORWAY smoking a pipe. He was an overworked and tired looking soul there in the lamplight. "There was no trouble, I see," he said.

"You don't see," said John Lourdes, "and there is trouble. Did you know Doctor English is the man wanted in the Santo Thomas murders, among others, and the one they call the Whiteman?"

The doctor removed the pipe from his mouth. He stared into the face of this strange man touched by a rosette of light. The doctor was suddenly a prisoner of the fact that he was a black man in a white country. "Even if I did know. Who would I tell?"

• • •

A SIXTEEN YEAR OLD BOY CARRYING A CARPETBAG got onto a downtown trolley. He sat alone, as usual. His intention was to go to the Seminary for opening night of *The Wizard of Oz* and blow up one of the buildings.

The only friend he'd ever had, true friend, friend you could live up to and emulate was Jon Pettyjohn, and he had been shot down on the streets of Laredo like some itinerant piece of trash. And here the good citizenry was raising money for a Mexican newspaper, and what had anyone done for Jon? No one offered to raise money for his funeral, for a fine casket, not even flowers. Jon was sent to his rest fast and forgotten. But not by him.

He had been raised at the Laredo Home for Boys. Left there by a bindlestiff father. Dropped off in the very same carpet bag. That's how young he'd been. In that same carpetbag now were seven sticks of dynamite. One for each of the five missing or dead Rangers, and one each for the two men who worked for Big Medicine.

The Seminary grounds were a hive of people and lights. The buildings around the quadrangle glowed where stands had been set up to sell food and spirits. There were booths with games of chance and dexterity or strength, and barkers shouting out their prizes. The auditorium was packed to overflowing, its doors to the lawn thrown open and there, too, people pressed in, fathers hoisting children up on their shoulders awaiting Dorothy and a cast of oddities to come singing their way to Oz.

Amid all the lively madness, Cager Adams stopped every black robe he could and asked, "Where the hell can I find this Father Demaris?"

The father was finally pointed out by the ticket stand at the auditorium entrance, and right in the middle of a conversation Cager grasped the priest's arm and pulled him away. Before the priest could get a question out, Cager whispered, "John Lourdes said I was to find your ass and talk to you. But to make sure I did it in confession. So where the fuck can we go?"

The priest looked over this ill mannered and stony faced reprobate and said, "Follow me."

He led Cager into the chapel and opened the small door to the confessional and pointed for him to go in.

"It looks like a damn mop closet." Before he entered, he said, "Whatever I tell you in there, you can never speak of. You can't use against me, right?"

"That's right."

"Let's get to it."

The priest entered the confessional. The lattice screen between the rooms lifted. "Go on," said the father.

"John Lourdes wanted you to know that Doctor English is the Whiteman. He is in a town called Los Ojuelos. John is on his way there now. You're to tell the priest in El Paso on the chance John Lourdes is fuckin' killed. He doesn't know how he'll return. Either by way of Laredo or San Antonio. To watch the railroads."

"Is that all?" said the priest.

"Isn't that enough?"

"How are you involved in all this, if I may ask?"

"Killing people. How do you think? I killed whites and I killed Mexicans. And I hate Mexicans. And I'm here as part of a bribe to keep from being indicted. And you got to forgive me all of it. How does that fuckin' strike you?"

• • •

You could hear the actors on stage all the way out on the quadrangle where Marisita was. She had immersed herself in the book as a girl and seen the play when it first came to Laredo.

And here it was again. How timely she thought. The search to find home. The eternal journey people take to find family and peace and where the future will reside.

Was Dorothy's quest much different than that of Ulysses after the Trojan War? Or Huckleberry Finn rafting down the Mississippi? Or Don Quixote and his steadfast Rocinante as they fought windmills? Not hardly.

It is always there. The timeless need at the margins of all our thoughts. She would have to write about this. Because it spoke to the truth inside her. She was Dorothy. And her journey companions the likes of John Lourdes and Father Pinto and Father Demaris. And home was now a little farther and a little different than what she had first assumed.

She looked about her. There were Anglos and Mexican Americans, and there were Rangers everywhere keeping the peace, at the very least that. But this was no longer home. This was partway home and would have to be let go of before she could return. She was thinking on all this, wondering how she could shape what was on her mind into an editorial, what she could use as a framework, when the quadrangle was shaken by an explosion.

The side wall of a dormitory that rose three stories was blown apart. Fire gashed the sky. A tree alongside the building was consumed with flame. A hail of detritus rained down strips of wood and glass shards, chips of brick wall and roof tile and burning white bits of metal. It was an otherworldly scene of people scattering into a black smoke.

EL HOMBRE BLANCO

CHAPTER 62

Los Ojuelos was east of Torcillas Towers down in the corner of Webb County. It was practically a ghost town the day John Lourdes rode in. When the Texas Mexican Railway put its main line north of town, it pretty much ended Los Ojuelos being the trade road between Laredo and Corpus Christi.

This was harsh brush country and deeply overgrown. The main street of town was little more than the El Puerto Grocery and a dust ridden hovel that passed itself off as a post office for its one hundred inhabitants. The buildings were all made of stone, but most had no roofs and empty windows.

There was a deer tied off to a hitching post by the grocery. A couple of drunks were sitting on the back of a wrecked flatbed and flicking stones at it. It was panicked and suffering.

John Lourdes dismounted and walked to the post office, but it was locked. A sign said the Postmaster could be found at the grocery. As he crossed the road, the Mexicans torturing that poor animal eyed John Lourdes with that kind of gloomy curiosity strangers in these one spit towns have to bear.

The grocery smelled of boiling meat from a kitchen in the back. A bell above the door tinkled as John Lourdes entered. A man with a bad hitch came out from the kitchen, pushing aside the tarp that covered the doorway. He was wiping his thick hands on a bloodstained rag.

John Lourdes spoke to him in Spanish. "Are you the Postmaster?"

"Yes."

"I'm looking for a man who is supposed to be here in Los Ojuelos. He is a Gringo. His name is English. He is a doctor."

"A man about your height? Deserty hair? Very quiet?"

"That's him."

"And he's a doctor. He calls himself a doctor anyway."

"Yes."

"He has a house." The grocer walked over to the window and pointed. "Down that road. At the very end."

"Thank you. Have you seen him today?"

"No."

"Have any men come through here today looking for him?"

The grocer now stopped wiping his hands.

"No."

"No one?"

"No one comes through here anymore."

John Lourdes turned to leave. He could see through the window that poor beast practically choking to death to escape his plight.

"What are they doing?" said John Lourdes.

"What they always do. Get drunk. Look for mischief. Where they even get the little they have to drink is a mystery to me."

"Not so much a mystery. What are they gonna do with that deer?"

"Abuse him. Then they will kill him. And then they will try to trade him to me for liquor. And this is the future." He spit on the floor.

John Lourdes walked out of the grocery and down the steps and crossed the road, the whole while the Mexicans eyeing him, wondering about him. Making cracks, whispering vulgarities John Lourdes could just pick up.

He opened a saddlewallet and took out a Bowie knife. He unloosed his trench gun and started back across the street. This got the Mexicans' attention all right, and caused a sudden case of the quiets. He walked up to the hitching post. The deer railed and struggled, but what could it do but choke itself to death?

When those Mexicans saw him start to cut that rope, up they came, cursing, threatening. But drunk as they were, they knew better than to face a trench gun, which had now decidedly swung in their direction.

When he got the rope cut, it took a few moments for that animal to realize it was free. It shot across the road and straight for the brush. It leapt a fallen tree and was gone now to a new fate.

John Lourdes turned his attention to the three drunks. "Your own people are trying to make it right here in this country...And for trash like you—"

He fired off a worry shot at the wreckage of that truck. This sent the three to scattering. John Lourdes walked back to his mount, put away the knife and the shotgun. He climbed into the saddle and started away.

He had wanted to make sure his presence was known, and so he had.

CHAPTER 63

THE ROAD WAS A QUARTER MILE LONG and overgrown at that. There were a few abandoned homes along the way. The roadside was dense with mesquite and knotty oaks higher than a man on horseback.

The last house back of that cartpath could only be seen because it was two stories. When he got closer, he saw a tent had been put up alongside it and a horse was staked out so it might graze on whatever meager tuffs of grass there were around it. John Lourdes dismounted.

The house was roofless like the rest, and Doctor English was inside the two story shell, tearing away vines that had grown up through the foundations and trellised in the empty windows. He wore a white workshirt that was filthy and sweatstained. He heard someone approaching through the undergrowth, and looking out from beneath the wide brim of a straw hat, it came as quite a shock when John Lourdes stepped into the doorway.

"John?"

"Yes, sir."

"What are you doing here?" A notion struck him. "It's not my mother, is it?"

"No."

"Has anything happened to her? Be honest, now—"

"Not at all. I saw her yesterday, as a matter of fact I read to her and we had supper."

The Doctor breathed a deep sigh. He went over to a water bag hung from a spike hammered into the stone wall.

"You scared me, son. I thought—"

He drank and then he offered the water bag to John Lourdes who declined. He was watching the Doctor to see how he reacted to his just showing up. Would he expose himself? Would he make for a weapon? John Lourdes didn't see one handy.

"My home," said the Doctor. "Meaning, of course, this ruin. My church. I come here when I need to be alone and clear my thoughts of all the failures of society we have to amend. We need to repaint the world, John. Come here a minute. I want to show you something."

He'd walked right up to the wall, and John Lourdes kept a hand where he could reach his weapon and joined the good Doctor.

"All the buildings in this town are constructed from a type of volcanic rock known as rhyolite. This particular rhyolite is known as 'sillar.' It comes from erupted volcanoes, and it is a white rock…A white rock, John. And the people who cut the stone and set the walls did so at an angle, so if something should befall them, like an earthquake, the walls will come down but fall away so the inhabitants will be protected. This is us, John," he said, sweeping an arm about. "These set walls…We are the white rock. The I – You – We – walls that 'The Society' is raising."

The Doctor threw his head back and drank more from the water bag until it ran down the sides of his neck. He took out his trusty handkerchief and wiped his face.

"How did you know where to find me? The doctor at the sanitarium, I bet."

"The Rangers know who the man is. The one hunting the Whiteman."

The Doctor seemed little concerned. "You can't hunt a fable. Don't they know that?"

He set the water bag back on the spike where it hung. He then went to gather up more brush when a pair of handcuffs landed in the dust before him. He looked at them there, and then he stood and studied John Lourdes.

"If I seem confused, it is because I am," the Doctor said.

"Clarity will come."

A moment later, John Lourdes pulled his gun and fired. Not ten feet behind the Doctor, a squirrel had been sitting on the stones that had been the windowsill, sniffing at the air. He was now a hemorrhaging carcass.

The Doctor saw what John Lourdes had done, and as he walked past, the Doctor said, "What did you do that for?"

"I need the blood."

CHAPTER 64

A WOMAN CAME RUNNING INTO THE GROCERY STORE out of breath, panicked, her slender arms pressed against her breasts. "Outside," she said. "A man. Badly wounded. Wants tequila and turpentine. He has a gun."

The grocer had no intention of going out until he knew more. From the window, he squinted out into the sunlight. There were two riders in the dusty street waiting. The gringo doctor sat atop one horse. He was handcuffed. A chain went around his waist locking his arms at his side and he was gagged. On the other horse was the man who he had spoken with not an hour ago. He held a rag to his side where his white shirt was smeared with blood.

John Lourdes shouted toward the store. He threw money on the ground. The grocery doors opened in time and the grocer came down the steps, watching, carrying the requested items.

"Put them in the saddlebags," said John Lourdes.

The man did as ordered. He got a close look at the rider's side. Beneath the rag held there, it was a bloody mess.

"I've been shot," said John Lourdes.

"You will not get far, it looks like."

"I only have to get as far as the train."

He started away, leading the Doctor's horse. The Mexicans he'd had trouble with were by the side of the post office, down on their haunches in the shade, filling the world with their particular brand of brutish presence. They saw everything play out in front of the grocery store and that John Lourdes had a handgun in one hand resting on the pommel, so they pleasured themselves with unholy remarks. And then in a moment of incredible bravery, one of them flicked a cigarette in his direction.

About a mile up the road, John Lourdes stopped. He flung the bloody rag into the brush. He grabbed hold of the chain and reeled in the Doctor's horse. He ripped the bandana down from his mouth. He took off the shirt he'd stained with blood and stuffed it into a saddlebag. He took out another and slipped it on. Neither he nor the Doctor had spoken. He rode ahead of the Doctor and pulled his mount along. Instead of taking the road north toward the rail line as he'd said, he swung west and struck off into wilds that were not on the older maps.

"You can't buy time," said the Doctor.

"Neither can you," said John Lourdes.

• • •

Within two hours the Captain and a platoon of fifteen Rangers had taken over Los Ojuelos. They knew bible and verse of what had happened that morning. The Captain ordered Ranger Ahearn to commandeer every reliable mount in the town. He issued individual commands. Which man was to ride to the nearest telephone line and which the closest telegraph offices so to extend the warrant, stating that John Lourdes was badly wounded and possibly more desperate? Rangers in San Antonio were to begin watching the stations between there and Laredo.

Captain Asa wanted Evans at Big Medicine notified that he was to send out security teams searching every road that went east. While he himself would lead a squad of five men tracking John Lourdes from the town. He meant for men to pursue this with apocalyptic fury. That they were to ride the extra mount till its heart burst. And that there would be no satisfactory resolution, except one.

• • •

John Lourdes had been veering toward Torrecillas Towers. He did not try to disguise his trail. He kept pressing on through a terrible heat with the Doctor in tow behind him. The horses were suffering. The country they rode through looked blistered. The grass beneath the horses' hooves crackled like sparks of fire as they passed along. People had wandered through this county only to become lost in death. On a slight rise there was a windmill and a cistern where a few leathery cattle drank. He stopped there so the horses might rest and take water.

"You should have shot me," said the Doctor. "It would have made it easier."

"I'm with the Bureau of Investigation."

"I thought it would be something like that."

"I have been tasked with bringing you to justice."

"That task will outlive us both."

John Lourdes scooped up a hatful of water and poured it across his face now streaked with dust.

"Do you think you can trick them? And make it seem that you're heading to the rail line at the Towers...or Aguilares?"

He had a plan. He had conceived the plan. He had executed the plan. He also knew every plan had one flaw in it. The flaw being life.

"It's going to be a hard day," the Doctor said.

He then bent over and dunked his face in the cistern. He came up soaked and coolly unmoved.

"Take a look," he said.

John Lourdes followed the Doctor's eyes. He grabbed his field glasses from the saddle and scanned a brutish landscape. The Doctor had damn good eyes, for sure. There were small spectres of dust spread far apart and coming on quick. They'd had to have left a lot of dying horses in their wake to be on him so fast. Exhausted and gutted out creatures now in the desert somewhere gasping out their last, and all for the cause.

He went and pulled his rifle from its scabbard. He stood away from the horses on the chance of return fire. When he felt a rider was within range, he took aim. He could not make out who the man was. He was just a Stetson and a billowing shirt leaning in against the withers of a thick and sturdy mount.

He fired. There was a crackle from the rifle barrel in the dry air that seemed to carry and carry. The horse dropped instantly. It went to the ground crushing in on itself. The rider was thrown. Shot or not, it didn't matter. A man on foot in this country was a worthless man, or a dead man.

CHAPTER 65

THE DESERT AIR FILLED WITH CALAMITY. He watched to see if runners of dust would converge upon a fallen comrade, but they did not. These were men stripped of any meaning but the task at hand. The one who had his horse shot out from under him rose up. He waved his hat to let the others know he was alive.

John Lourdes didn't bother with him. The riders spread out even more. They were a shimmering relentless crew beneath a desert sky stripped of color. He aimed at another. He emptied a clip. The man grabbed for his leg and his horse wheeled about. John Lourdes chambered another clip and then he shot the damn horse.

The air stung with the brackish smell of cordite. He chambered another clip. He slung his arm through the shoulder strap. He forced the Doctor back up on his horse and he remounted and grabbed both sets of reins and struck off to the northwest.

The country ahead of them was broken up. There were declines and strips of hill with a scattering of trees. His pursuers would have to show more caution, and less bravado. He had to reach sundown because once it shored across that plain, his chances of escape and survival were not so imperiled as now.

He stopped and looked back, resting one hand on the cantle to steady himself. His face and body were beaded with sweat. The salt of it from his forehead burned his eyes. He drank from the water bag taken from the Doctor's house. His hands shook he was so spent. The Doctor, too, was covered in sweat. He looked exhausted. He held the water bag so the Doctor could drink. And it was not out of pity. He could not have either of them collapsing in the saddle.

"You're Mexican…part Mexican anyway."

John Lourdes did not answer.

"I thought that was it."

He leaned out and grabbed the Doctor's reins.

"They couldn't trust sending an Anglo…Just a slave that looked like one."

The two men exchanged looks. Each wrestling with the future.

"I wonder," said the good Doctor, "which one of us will people see as Lincoln...And which one as John Wilkes Booth?"

• • •

As they approached the desolate tracks of the Texas Mexico Railroad the earth before them looked like a burning lake that receded with their forward march. Man and mount were spent. The swales they descended were already cooling with the dusk and from where startled birds struck toward the sky. Each time this happened, John Lourdes looked back knowing this was a sign his pursuers would be searching out to know where was their prey.

When they reached the tracks, John Lourdes halted. The railroad ties left a long straight dark scar upon that desert plain.

"Follow the tracks and we'll be back in Laredo in a couple of hours," said the good Doctor.

What the Doctor knew, he knew, and they too knew. And knowing, they would have men far down the line. He looked into a fiery sunset that the darkness was closing around. That was his destination. He felt this sudden and slight tremor coming up from the ground and through the horse's legs and into his own. He took out his field glasses.

Along the edges of that barren light he could just make out a long black snake of freight cars where the tracks arced. He crossed both horses over, their hooves clopping on the wooden ties. He started west toward Laredo just veering away from the tracks enough not to be seen if men were on board hunting him.

They hadn't gone but a few hundred yards when small explosions of sand blew up around him. He heard the report of rifle fire a moment later. He wheeled his horse about. Two riders were bearing down on him from the north. He looked back. There was nothing in the direction he'd come. One of the riders fired off a flare. It rocketed up into a dusky heaven. He was marked now. He wasn't going to be able to outrun them for long. It was only a matter of choosing where the fight was to be had.

He started back toward the tracks keeping to his flank. The headlights of that engine gathering immensity. The long reach of its beam boring in on the desert, flaring it up from nothingness. The riders closing in, the gunfire more intense, another flare. John Lourdes reined the two horses and swept up and over the tracks in front of that locomotive.

The engineer must have seen him because he grabbed the horn cable and a great steam shrill cut across the silence like some unbroken death cry.

John Lourdes pulled up and dismounted. He staked the horses. He yanked the Doctor from the saddle. He grabbed his rifle and extra clips. Stood over the Doctor. "Move and I will kill you…Warn them and I will kill you."

He stood there with those cars shuttling past waiting in the shore of their immense shadows. It was so dark as to make it impossible to see through the cars to the far side of the tracks. So there he was, waiting, moving slowly along the right of way, watching, rifle at the ready, the endless train of coal and cargo, the freight of the nation thundering along, and then in one last great whoooooosh of stifling air, the cars had passed.

The two men he was to face had dismounted. All were little more than shadows that slipped through the night seamlessly. A ferocious volley of gunfire erupted. Tracers streaking aimlessly in every direction.

A horse cried out. Another sprinted across the tracks. Its stirrups flopping wildly, its mane a battle flag. John Lourdes was almost trampled.

He went down on his belly and fought from there. He emptied a clip and then another, as he reloaded, he realized the desert was silent. No one was returning fire.

CHAPTER 66

Cager Adams had one larceny to perform before he disappeared from the world of Big Medicine with his life.

He had been one of the security teams put on the road. Each man was supplied with flares, each was to cover a swath of country. If John Lourdes were discovered or confronted, a flare was to be fired off to mark the location and bring the manhunt to him. When a flare was spotted through a telescope from the roof of the main house, far, far to the east, men flooded in that direction.

That is when Cager veered away from the direction of the pursuit. He rode a half dozen miles and from a low rise in the deep reaches of the desert he fired off a flare.

He watched it climb, and he watched it burn and he watched it rain down a fireworks of phosphor.

It was a beautiful looking lie, and thinking of how much each of those flares was earning had him deeply satisfied.

He rode a few more miles and fired off another flare. He knew it wouldn't pull all the men away. Many were too far to see. But it would thin the ranks of those chasing John Lourdes considerably.

• • •

John Lourdes walked across the tracks, all the while watching behind him to be sure he was not suddenly waylaid. One horse lay near death trying to rise up, as if that might end its agony. John Lourdes put a bullet in its brain. One of the dead he came upon he did not recognize, except for the star within the circular badge pinned to a bloody shirt. The other dead lay near the tracks. John Lourdes walked over and used his foot to roll the body. When the head lolled to one side like something loosely hinged, he saw it was Ranger Ahearn. He had, it appeared, a bullet hole through his cheek.

John Lourdes knelt down. He wanted one close, private moment with the recently dead Ranger. He just looked at the man and what he remembered. There was some poisoned beauty to that moment. He leaned in close and said, "Ranger Ahearn…Can you hear that?" John Lourdes bent his head as if listening. "Can you hear that? That's forever talking."

The Doctor heard and called out, "Forever comes in many guises."

John Lourdes stopped and looked across the tracks. The Doctor was up on his knees. He was slightly hunched over. John Lourdes said nothing. He crossed the tracks and went and unstaked the horses and led them over to the good Doctor. As he did, he noticed to the northwest, far out upon that silent loom of desert, a flare shot skyward. A tiny eyelet of burning white that rained down fiery stars.

The son of a bitch, he thought. His word was good.

"I see you have an ally out there somewhere."

He helped the Doctor to his feet. The chains that bound him rattling.

"You know who you are?" said the Doctor.

John Lourdes secured him to the saddle. The Doctor's head was bowed slightly, his voice weary.

"You are one of those men the system drugs with promises of being at one with them, until you are addicted to the idea and will do their bidding. But it will never be. Look back a thousand years and see for yourself. Better you cross the river and go home."

John Lourdes said nothing, he offered nothing, defended nothing.

Ride through the witching hours and you reach Laredo. Its streets that close. He kept looking from where they'd come. The desert was lampblack, the sky moonless and clouded. Where was the Captain? Could his skills have set him on a course, once he saw that first flare, to strike west toward Laredo and cut off John Lourdes' escape? Could he be ahead of them somewhere? He wouldn't abandon Ranger Ahearn without knowing.

While he thought all this out, there was the Doctor, his voice tired, talking to him from the dark. "If I am the Whiteman…as you say…who are you? If I am some purported evil…what are you? Look at yourself, John. Look at the cup you've poured of blood. You are generous to a fault in your violence. And I pale in comparison."

I am with the devil, thought John Lourdes. I am an unwanted stranger in a place I do not fully comprehend and whose only course is to continue on in the face of what one can scarcely believe.

CHAPTER 67

JOHN LOURDES COULD BEGIN TO MAKE OUT THE EDGES of a ground mist seeping through stands of cottonwood and live oak. The air was getting cooler, sharper. He could smell it. If they were approaching San Juanito Creek as he suspected, then they were just a few miles from the outskirts of Laredo.

When they reached the timber, it was overgrown with honey mesquite and fallen branches. The going was slow. John Lourdes had to dismount and lead the horses. He would stop and listen and then move on. He could hear the creek well before he could see it. A sleepy fog coursed over that waterway and he found a ford that he could walk. There was a grotto of stones just back from the shore that offered cover. He got the Doctor down from his saddle and pointed where he should sit. The Doctor eased himself down, resting his back against the stones. While John Lourdes watered the horses and took in the darkness around him, the Doctor sat looking up at the sky.

"There's a book," said the Doctor, "about a whaling ship captain that loses part of a leg to a white whale that he hunts around the world for revenge."

"I can't have you talking out here," said John Lourdes.

"The ship's captain, you see, believed the whale was evil."

"I said I can't have you—"

"But it was the ship captain that was evil."

"I'll gag you if you—"

"Listen," said the Doctor. "Did you hear that?"

John Lourdes was caught off guard. He listened for a moment, until the Doctor said, "You know what that is? That's forever."

The Doctor had played him, he thought. He strode over and knelt down.

"Enough," he said.

He went to reach for the Doctor's trusty bandana around his neck and so gag him, when his hand snapped back.

The Doctor was sitting there with his eyes open and looking up at the sky. Motionless in that most telling of ways.

"Doctor?"

John Lourdes reached out and touched the man's shoulders and the body slipped over. John Lourdes had to grab him to keep the Doctor from dipping to the ground.

John Lourdes made this slight gasp. He lifted him back up so he sat there like he had been.

How was he dead?

He took hold of the man's face. He searched it. He ran his hands over the man's face. He ran his hands over the man's neck, the man's chest, his arms. That's when he saw what he felt. The coat under the right armpit was sopped through with blood. He unbuttoned the coat and pulled it open. The shirt down the right side of his chest was covered with thickening glops of blood.

He lifted the arm. There was a bullet hole right up near the armpit. He must have been shot back at the tracks, that's all John Lourdes could think. He was shot and killed by one of his own.

John Lourdes pulled back. He went and sat across from the Doctor, with his own back against a stone. He studied the man in death.

He had not said a word. He had not cried out, he had not called out. He had not asked for help, or pity, or mercy. He had ridden all those miles bleeding to death while maintaining his manhood. He was, to John Lourdes way of thinking, making a point. Proving something to the world.

He saw a man who'd believed in his own legacy. And men like that are born to be reckoned with.

He could leave him here for the wolves and just go. But he was not in the business of half measures. They would come upon him, or they would not. But at sunup, he would ride into that town with the one they called the Whiteman. And then be done with it.

He sat with that dead body in silence, the mist creeping along the creek bottom making everything seem to be growing out of a grey cauldron.

He pressed his cheek against the shotgun barrel hearing everything the Doctor had said to and about him, and then he heard something else.

His flesh crawled with the ghostly sound of harness metal somewhere downstream. He listened through the water training over planed down stones and the croak of toads and the night breeze across the treetops that whispered of terrible things to come.

He rose up quietly, his eyes peering over the rocks and there they were. Shapeless figures draped in the mist. The Captain he recognized from his countenance. The other two he knew not at all. They were coming on blindly. At a slow, methodical hunter's pace. He could hide here and take his chances, or he could spring upon them like something straight out of a fever.

It would soon be light, and there was no sense in wasting the darkness or that runny fog. He could mostly shoot them down before they knew better.

He glanced at Doctor English. Why? He would never know. The Doctor looked as if he were watching him. He made sure a shell was chambered. He took a breath.

The Captain was midstream. Each shore bracketed by one of his men. John Lourdes came straight out from the trees where he had forded the creek and set himself and opened fire. White blasts from that shotgun slashed across their paths.

The fighting was brutal and swift. The Captain charged John Lourdes with the soul of the hard bitten bastard that he was. The men's eyes narrowed, weapons were drawn and fired. Being on horseback in that contained causeway was a decided disadvantage. The creek filled with the signs and smells of gunfire and death. They shouted to each other, but who could hear over the escopeta that John Lourdes fired into them?

The Captain and his horse were hit with the same shot. They crashed into the stream kicking up huge sprays of water. One of the riders looped down from the saddle and tried to shoot John Lourdes from beneath the mount's neck. The horse lost its footing on the river stones and listed to one side and the rider was caught up in the branches of a fallen tree along the shore and skewered. He was pulled from the saddle and hung from that desiccated tree like a ragged strip of beef. The horse had gathered itself and sped on into the world of underbrush and deep shadows.

And then the firing ceased. John Lourdes kept low to the water, and barely visible above the mist, reloading that trench gun as he moved forward, looking to his left...to his right. There was a third man. Where was he? He spotted a horse wandering aimless upstream. And then he saw him. The fog was drifting up over his dead body.

John Lourdes stood all the way up. He could see the Captain pinned down under his dead mount there in the creek. He could just lift himself enough to keep from drowning. There was blood running down his open mouth. He was struggling. The water rushing over his face, and him gagging. He was breathing heavily as he fought to loose himself. But there was no loosing himself.

He and John Lourdes were now just feet apart. He slung the escopeta up over his shoulder. The Captain kept struggling against the weight that would doom him. John Lourdes could kill the Ranger or let him drown.

CHAPTER 68

THE FIRST TRACES OF DAWN TO THE EAST. The spare outline of buildings began to materialize out of the dark on the far outskirts of town. Marisita stood on the flat roof of the warehouse behind the garden of her home. There were half a dozen anxious women from La Liga with her, and at least that many down in the garden. They drank coffee and tea and kept their shawls wrapped tightly around them against the brisk air. They were waiting, as Marisita was waiting.

A reporter from the *Laredo Times* came upon the scene. He tried to make his way up the outside stairwell to the roof. He was berated and scolded and forced back by the women there. He was not equipped for their early morning virulence. Marisita recognized him by sight and from his high pitched insecty voice. She asked the women to let him through, knowing he would just haunt the street anyway, picking up what information or rumor that he could.

"Miss Barros," the reporter said, "my name is Cole and—"

"The *Laredo Times*. I know your work."

"What's going on here?"

"It is an informal meeting of La Liga Femenil."

"Really? You all seem to be waiting for something. Are you waiting for something?"

She was going to say, 'I'm waiting for a miracle,' but she knew he might steal that quote and use it as a banner for a story. And she had no intention of that happening.

She smiled innocently. She also knew that his presence might prove an asset in keeping a man from being killed.

"A contact at Big Medicine," said the reporter, "tells me their people are out in the desert along with the Rangers hunting a man. Does this have anything to do with—"

A woman on the roof shouted, "There…Look…There it is."

And there it was, to be sure. A lone flare you could just make out against the first of daylight. Singular and white burning starlets falling from the sky. For a moment it felt like she herself had taken flight.

"Shall I go to the church?" one of the women shouted from the garden.

Marisita leaned over the ledge. There was such excitement in her voice, such fearful anticipation. "Not yet. See how far out that flare is. He could be another half hour. We wait until he is here. Then all together, we go."

Cole grabbed her by the arm. "It is him you're waiting for."

"Wait and see."

The street took on the trappings of early morning. Pale walls brightened. Cooking fires salted the air. Wagons went on their trundling way. Then she saw what had to be him, and he was not alone. A few boys darted around his horse and the one he led like small dogs ensnared by what they were staring at.

It would be no different for her or the others as she ran down the stairs, the women behind her, the reporter futilely trying to shoulder past them all. Women came from the garden and they were confronted by a sight they could not have imagined.

Before them was a dusty, filthy and wasted John Lourdes, and in the saddle of the horse he led was the man known as Doctor English. He was sitting and chained, and his eyes were open but, to a fault, the women there in the street could see what the children had—he was dead.

"Holy Christ," said the reporter.

John Lourdes had cut a tree branch in the shape of a wye. He had slid the singular end up under the Doctor's coat and used the wye as a brace to keep him upright. To have him so the world could see who the Whiteman was, and to judge with their souls.

"Shall I go to the church now?" the woman from before called out.

"Yes," said Marisita with urgency. "Yes…Go…And hurry."

She took off up the street, running, leaving little puffs of dust in her wake. The women reeled back and out of John Lourdes' path and began to flank him.

Marisita came up next to John Lourdes and just barely touched his leg. "Are you all right?"

He had no earthly way yet to know.

Senor Barros had been in the print shop preparing two versions of the story for press depending on which came to pass.

He had been called to come out in the street. He and Luis Perez and a number of Mexican sheriffs walked out of the *La Cronica* offices, and when they saw what they saw, it was like the bones of their dead had risen up out of the ground to shake their hands.

Bearing weapons, they joined the ranks of the women, and this small procession surrounding John Lourdes started for Flores Street and the journey up to City Hall and jail.

A church bell began to chime at a time that it should not have. And soon after, across town, another church bell began its tolling at a time it should not have. But chime they did, and they did not stop. They kept on with their earnest cadence. And then a third church bell joined them. And all across Laredo the citizenry became aware that something was happening here, but what it was ain't exactly clear.

Word had been passed the night before through the secret ranks of housekeepers and janitors, warehouse hands and porters and cooks and stable men. Who would pass it to nuns and shopkeepers and parish priests and members of Mexican Benevolent Societies and Lodges and Cultural Associations. The signals were the church bells calling out to come to Flores Street.

The caravan with John Lourdes grew by ones and twos. It grew as people stepped from shops and restaurants and places of home and saw what they saw. It grew with people who were tired of mistreatment or who wanted to have their voices heard. It grew with people who wanted their ruin confronted. Who wanted a moment of social justice. Who had something to say about subjects such as lynchings and the Bill of Rights and brave Uncle Sam and legalized brutality and political suppression and the power of Big Business to hammer a simple man into the earth as easy as they would a fuckin' nail. The procession's shadow lengthened with the light because people wanted to see how change was born.

And this was not all, not by any damn state of affairs. They followed that exhausted soul on horseback, who had surrendered himself to the world, to be his voice, to be his eyes, to insure his protection. So that he did not wake up in jail one morning to find that his throat had been mysteriously cut, or that he had managed to walk off the roof of City Hall and commit suicide. And surely so that after all he had been through, he would not be politely 'evaporated' by a dozen armed Rangers in a futile attempt at escape.

For the first time in his life John Lourdes was witness to a collective sense of purpose, and amidst the church bells and the streaming line of humanity, beyond all personal suffering and failings, he was riding in communion with the world.

The journey was not without vitriol and danger, especially when they reached the headquarters of Big Medicine and 'The Society.' To see the Doctor dead incited threats and thrown horse dung and stones. Toughs wailed into the crowd. Only this crowd had its own armed guards and Rangers who had been brought in from San Antonio, since the wrecking of the *La Cronica* offices and the bombing of the Seminary dormitory.

The Department of Public Safety had been put on warning. Outside agitators, like the New York press, were in Laredo to drum up negative stories about the racial bias and hatreds of Texans, who were nothing more than white redneck trash. There were assaults and random gunshots, but the guilty were quickly subdued and arrested.

John Lourdes took all of this in silence. He felt the weight of it, but refused it power over him. It had been his birth and it had marked his manhood with its violence and where it would take him on the road was anyone's guess. It had been witness to his birth, but would he live long enough to witness its death, was the question.

At City Hall he halted and the people there with him did the same. He looked back and resting a hand on the cantle, whispered to himself, "We've come to our end, Doctor. And in less than eighty days. I will see you at our reckoning."

He dismounted.

A blue eyed son of America he was not, but he was a son of America none the less, who had walked the deepest dark forest where the wrongs of the world await us.

Word had come to City Hall about what was going on, and the officers of the court pressed their way through a surging crowd to where John Lourdes put out his hands and offered himself up for arrest. He tried for one private moment with Marisita, but the sheriffs stepped between them and he was handcuffed and taken away.

A PRESENT FROM 'THE SOCIETY'

CHAPTER 69

WHEN THE DEPARTMENT OF PUBLIC SAFETY was notified of John Lourdes' position with the Bureau of Investigation and what he had been tasked with, the agent was quietly released and the charges against him left as 'pending.' Wadsworth Burr hired four bodyguards—former members of law enforcement with checkered backgrounds he had worked with—to insure the youth was brought safely home.

At the El Paso train station the young Chinese girl who took care of Burr was overjoyed and wept. She kissed John Lourdes about the face endless times, and to his embarrassment, she opened his shirt to see that he was still wearing the Taoist charm she had given him. She had not forgotten Burr's nasty comment and glared at him.

John Lourdes and the lawyer sat on the upper veranda of Burr's home just as they had that last night before he left for Laredo. Burr made him tell of all that had happened and along the way John Lourdes confided how he still felt the shadow of her across his heart. And how does one rid himself of these unspent dreams, he'd wondered aloud.

"You'll be fine," Burr said. "And how can someone of my character be sure? Because the future doesn't take no for an answer."

John Lourdes would receive a letter from her early the next year. He would learn she was living in Guadalupe and engaged to a fine Mexican who was editor of a newspaper that was a leading voice in the revolution against the government. She would never write again.

As he and Burr talked, a motorcycle could be heard suddenly roaring up Yandell. Both men grew silent momentarily at the memory of the attack farther up in the Addition.

But on this night, the motorcycle came to a skidding halt in front of Burr's home. And there in the throw of a streetlamp, as if it were a spotlight on a stage, a rider wearing a white bandana to hide his face sat revving the engine.

"Hey, you...up there...I'm looking for John Lourdes."

Burr went to get up and go inside and get a gun, but John Lourdes waved that off and said to just sit still. Then he stood and walked to the veranda railing.

"You're him," said the rider.

John Lourdes could see and hear enough to know it was a boy down there.

"*We* want you to know…Doctor English is still alive…And I've got something for you from 'The Society.'"

A match lit. He'd put the flame to a wet cloth tailing out of a small bottle of kerosene. He flung it up at the veranda and sped off back down Yandell. The bottle shattered against the balcony railing into a sheet of tiny sparks. John Lourdes had stepped back and grabbed a pitcher of water off the table and tried to douse the flames. Both men stomped out the rest until there was nothing but small pots of smoke.

John Lourdes leaned over the railing and looked down Yandell. He remembered something the Doctor had said… "You may destroy the man, but the darkness remains."

He thought suddenly of his father and the man he himself had become, as he kept watching the motorcycle until it slipped in with the lights of El Paso and was gone.